Albert Ross

**Love at Seventy**

Albert Ross

**Love at Seventy**

ISBN/EAN: 9783337418786

Printed in Europe, USA, Canada, Australia, Japan

Cover: Foto ©Andreas Hilbeck / pixelio.de

More available books at **www.hansebooks.com**

# THE
# ALBATROSS NOVELS

## By ALBERT ROSS

### 23 Volumes

May be had wherever books are sold at the price you
paid for this volume

Black Adonis, A
Garston Bigamy, The
Her Husband's Friend
His Foster Sister
His Private Character
In Stella's Shadow
Love at Seventy
Love Gone Astray
Moulding a Maiden
Naked Truth, The
New Sensation, A
Original Sinner, An
Out of Wedlock
Speaking of Ellen
Stranger Than Fiction
Sugar Princess, A
That Gay Deceiver
Their Marriage Bond
Thou Shalt Not
Thy Neighbor's Wife
Why I'm Single
Young Fawcett's Mabel
Young Miss Giddy

## G. W. DILLINGHAM CO.

Publishers     ::     ::     New York

# LOVE AT SEVENTY.

## BY ALBERT ROSS.

AUTHOR OF

"YOUNG MISS GIDDY," "IN STELLA'S SHADOW,"
"THOU SHALT NOT," "WHY I'M SINGLE,"
"AN ORIGINAL SINNER," ETC.

*"Ah, Tom!" he cried, "the coming on of years does not deaden the heart in a healthy man, nor does the springing up of love in his bosom indicate decay of the mental faculties."*—Page 286.

NEW YORK:



G. W. Dillingham Co., Publishers.

# CONTENTS.

# CONTENTS.

# TO MY READERS.

————

After giving you stories in which the scenes are located largely in Germany, France, Italy, Spain and Mexico, it seems only right to return to the United States and write one in which nearly every incident takes place on American soil. It is true that Roland Linnette tells of some of his experiences abroad, in one or two chapters; but both he, and his dear old uncle, who furnishes my title, his friend Dalton, Eva Warren, Maud Arline and Tom Hobbs are essentially home products.

It is sometimes gravely disputed that my characters are "types." Sometimes, I must explain, they are not intended to be. Willard Linnette is a type, Eva Warren is not; that is to say, Eva's character is too peculiar to find many duplicates in real life. In the same way, going back to "Young Miss Giddy," Senator Scarlett is as true a type as can be found—in some respects almost a copy—while Flora may well be called an exception to most rules. In "Thou Shalt not," Greyburn, Walter Campbell, Jacob Mendall, Gabrielle—I think every character of importance—is a type. The type of Madame

Biron in " Why I'm Single" has been used by Ibsen in his play of " Ghosts " so closely as to suggest plagiarism.

After much criticism on moral grounds, in past days, it gives me pleasure to feel that this story cannot injure the fabric of the most delicate mind. It can safely be left in unlocked rooms where elderly maiden ladies are accustomed to prowl. I hope you will find it interesting, for it cost me some months of labor and the valued services of a typewriter, though it is written in a minor key that will not disturb the sleepers in the rear pews.

Unless all signs fail there will be a round million of novels credited to my account, before I make my bow to you again in January. That means at least five million readers. It should certainly inspire an author to do his best when he has to reckon with such a magnificent constituency.

ALBERT ROSS.

Cambridge, Mass.
*May,* 1894.

# LOVE AT SEVENTY.

## CHAPTER I.

### PICTURESQUE AND POOR.

In the little room known to the employés of the Montvale Optical Company as "the counting room," two persons were sitting one cold March morning. One of them was Rufus Hobbs, the book-keeper, who was engaged in an apparently interminable effort to add some columns of figures. The other was Mr. (nobody would have thought of calling Rufus "*Mister*") Roland Linnette, nephew and presumptive heir of Willard Linnette, owner not only of the Optical Works, but of about everything else in Montvale.

Mr. Roland was not engaged in adding figures. Indeed, he had spent much more of his life in studying the science of subtraction than that of addition. He was a confirmed idler and a very comfortable sort of fellow. At the moment when he is introduced to the reader, he was gazing aimlessly into a heap of coals which burned brightly in the grate before him.

Both the book-keeper and his companion suddenly became aware that there was a knock at the outer door of the counting room. At least, they knew that either this had happened, or that the wind, which was very boisterous, had blown so severely against the building as to convey the impression that some one wished to enter. The book-keeper looked inquiringly at Mr. Roland, who in return looked inquiringly at the book-keeper. And the upshot was that Rufus called "Come in !" in an elevated tone of voice.

The door opened slowly and closed behind a young man, or it might be more correct to say, lad, for he did not look more than seventeen or eighteen years of age. He was thinly dressed, notwithstanding the extreme coldness of the day, and his features wore a pinched look, such as is usually taken for a sign of physical suffering.

"Have you any work that I could do, sir ?" inquired the newcomer, directing his question to the book-keeper, as Mr. Roland was partly concealed from view by one of the large chairs in the room.

The book-keeper was plainly annoyed. He had been interrupted at the very worst time. Before he could find words, the intruder knew by the unpleasant expression of his face what to expect.

"No, no !" replied Rufus, gruffly. "We've got nothing for you. Come, be off !"

The last exclamation was caused by the hesitation of the inquirer and his evident desire to prolong the conversation.  Mr. Roland, glancing obliquely from his seat by the fire, saw the disappointed expression —one that was not far from indicating genuine pain. He moved his chair slightly and surveyed the new-comer with interest.

"Well, are you going?" repeated Rufus, seeing that the applicant still remained.  "We have nothing for you in any shape.  The works are all full and there is no prospect of a vacancy.  Be sure and shut the door, as you have already let in a good deal of cold."

The attitude of the young fellow changed with marvellous rapidity under the words and manner with which he had been received.  He raised his head and threw at the book-keeper a glance of defiance.

"I am poor, and I am cold, and I am hungry," he said, in a firm voice, "but that is no reason why you should speak to me like a dog.  I asked you for work, not for charity, and you might have replied in decent language."

This conversation occupied but a few seconds, but it gave Mr. Roland time to take a minute survey of the boy.  He saw at once that he had a fine face, most intelligent eyes, and an air that does not usually accompany such poor garments as he wore. He noticed also that the lad's hands, which were entirely bare, were well shaped and very delicate. Although the thermometer outside the window registered far below the freezing point, he had no overcoat.

The extreme paleness of his countenance was like

that of one recently recovered from a severe illness, and this environment gave his eyes an unusually large appearance. The angry look which flashed into them when he replied to the book-keeper's brusque words caused them to light up in a way quite attractive to any one but the object of their wrath.

"He is very picturesque!" muttered Mr. Roland, beneath his breath.

Feeling the necessity of doing something to preserve his dignity from the onslaught of the youth, Rufus Hobbs left his stool and figures and approached him threateningly.

"Get out of here," he said, sharply, "or I'll put you out! I'll teach you manners, beggar!"

For answer the young fellow, who was much slenderer and shorter than his prospective assailant, clenched his thin hands, but did not move an inch. He evidently had no intention of being bullied without a protest. His eyes, which had been dark before, seemed to flash fire from out their depths. His teeth, marvellously white and even, showed set and determined beneath the pale lips. There could be but one issue to a contest so unequal, but if Hobbs imagined that he was to have his own way in the scrimmage he had evidently made a miscalculation.

"How *very* picturesque he is!" murmured the young gentleman by the fire again. Then, in a louder voice, he addressed himself to the book-keeper: "Let him alone, Rufus. I want to talk to him."

The tone in which this was said was the most ordinary one in the world, but there are two classes of beings who know and obey their masters without hesitation. Rufus Hobbs was a member of one of these classes; and though Mr. Roland was in one sense no master of his, he knew that the time might come when he would be, and had a due regard for the bread and butter question on that future day.

At this moment the piercing whistle of the works blew, indicating the hour of noon. The book-keeper recognized the welcome sound, and a sense of pleasure at his approaching dinner overpowered every other feeling. He took down a heavy overcoat from an adjacent closet, turning up the ample collar above his neck; put on his fur gloves and hat, eyeing the scantily clad visitor with that contempt which well-dressed people very properly have for their inferiors in this regard; and finally, stalking by him as if he were some specimen of reptile, made his exit from the building.

Not until the door had closed behind the form of Rufus Hobbs did any change whatever come into the pale face of the young fellow. But the next moment he turned with quite a different expression to Mr. Roland.

"Did I understand that you wished to see me?" he asked.

"Y-e-s," replied the other, slowly.

That was exactly what the young gentleman wished to do with the boy—to *see* him. He pleased intensely his sense of sight. He would have enjoyed nothing better than merely to look at him for the rest of the afternoon. Having taken a very late breakfast he was not troubled by those thrills which made Rufus glad to hear the noon signal.

"Sit down," he added, presently. "It is surely more comfortable here than out of doors."

As the lad feebly took a chair Roland whispered to himself for the third time, "I think he is the most picturesque boy I ever saw !"

The air of the counting room was undoubtedly preferable to that of the street, but the youth had something to think of beside his temporary comfort.

"You are very kind," said he, "but I cannot remain long. I must find work to-day somewhere."

Roland looked at the slight figure. There was much determination in its bearing, an appearance entirely at variance with its slight bulk. He had found Montvale very dull for the past month, and this was the first thing that had in the least entertained him. He wanted to retain the pleasurable sensation. What a godsend a creature like this would be in that desolate region !

"Let me make a suggestion," he said, after a slight pause. "I am obliged to stay in this village, and I am simply dying of *ennui*. In saying this I am making a confession to you with which I would not honor anyone else for the world. You might suppose, to look at me, that I was the most contented chap on earth, but the fact is I am just the opposite. Now, I live at the hotel and have no one to talk to in the whole place, unless it be some idiot like Hobbs, the book-keeper, with whom you have just had a bit of experience. I want you to come up to the house with me, and remain there awhile as my guest. I will not insult you by offering a salary, for I want to treat you as one gentleman treats another. What do you say?"

A notion that this well-dressed man was making fun of him came into the lad's head, but he could see nothing to endorse the idea in the straightforward glance that met his inquiring gaze.

"I cannot accept your offer," said he, "though I thank you for it. It is absolutely necessary that I lose no time in getting employment."

Roland was evidently disappointed.

"And so you prefer work to taking your ease! Excuse me for saying that such a choice is quite incomprehensible. I cannot see why anybody should want to work. I have always thought it one of the dullest ways of passing one's time—duller even than sitting by this beastly grate and watching the gases release themselves from that anthracite."

The lad stared at the speaker in great astonishment.

"I have no friends, no home, no money," he replied, and his voice faltered. "What *can* I do but work?"

The young gentleman could not take his eyes from the handsome fellow. It was an outrage that such a picturesque specimen should be condemned to a life of drudgery.

"What can you do?" he echoed. "Why, I have just told you. Have you never read that brilliant saying of Theophile Gautier's? He says 'The only fitting occupation for a civilized man is to do nothing.'"

He stopped short in the snow, in a miniature rage.

"Where have they kept you?" he cried, impetuously.

A turn in the road hid them from sight. Forgeting everything, Roland caught both the hands of the girl in his own.

"It is a shame!" he said, speaking rapidly. "It is an outrage, when they compel me to spend week after week in this dull town, to keep from my sight the only interesting thing the village can boast. I shall speak to Hanson—I shall tell him my opinion of his conduct—I shall—"

She struggled gently to free her hands, and her breath came rapidly.

"Your uncle, sir! You forget. He will think it my fault. You have no time!"

He looked into the eyes which she raised to his, and his pulses were on fire.

"Time!" he cried. "What is time, or eternity, to me? I shall leave you, but remember, this is not the last time we shall see each other. Tell me one thing only—your name."

"Maud Arline," she whispered.

He waited still another moment.

"With such a face and such a name," he murmured, "what cursed fate placed you in such a position? Maud," he added, "you won't forget me?"

"No, sir; but, please, will you not hasten?"

Turning abruptly, he walked as fast as long strides could carry him in the direction of the Montvale House.

# CHAPTER II.

## A BIT OF HISTORY.

And now, with the reader's permission, the author proposes to take him back a good many years and to give him as much as is wise at this time of the history of the Linnettes' family.

In the ordinary sense of the term this family had its beginning with the uncle of young Mr. Roland, who made his appearance in the last chapter.

Willard Linnette and his brother Payson were common workmen up to the day when the former made his great discovery, now so well known to everybody interested in searching the heavens. His fortune came to him, as it were, at one bound. Within five years from the time he established his small shop at Ashfield he purchased the entire site of the coming village of Montvale, and began preparations for the future manufactories, the busy streets, and the elegant estate upon which he was to rear his own palatial residence.

"I am going to be a very rich man," he said to his architect when he first took him to Montvale, "and I want all my preparations made on a large scale. On this side, we must lay out the site for a village. Over here will be the factories. Here we shall have cottages for the workmen, and beyond them a hotel. In this direction I have reserved fifty had no intention of sharing them with any other person, merely for the pleasure of possessing such an elegant establishment. Still, it was largely on account of his brother's infant that he set up house-keeping on such an immense scale.

After the death of Roland's mother, Willard Linnette, on his occasional visits to Payson, found him so engrossed in his books that he hardly seemed to know there was a baby to bear his name. The child was left entirely to the care of servants, and though this may have been quite as well for its health at that period of his life, it distressed the kind heart of the uncle, who soon conceived for the half-orphaned boy a very warm affection. Having no closer ties he early formed a resolution to make this little fellow his heir; and the real father, who might not have been able to recognize his child out of a dozen, on a wager, was quite content so long as he was not to be troubled in any way about him.

Mrs. Martin, who presided over the household affairs of the elder brother, and ruled them, it must be said, with a rod of iron, welcomed the young stranger doubtfully. But she soon found that she was to have very little to do with him. A suitable retinue of special attendants was engaged, and Roland was to all intents and purposes as much at home as if he had been the real son of the owner of Montvale.

This condition of things, if it did nothing else, relieved the optician of one cause for worry. Since his fortune had been accumulating so fast he had speculated a great deal as to what ought to be done with it, in the event of his death. He felt that it would be useless to leave to his brother a larger income than he now enjoyed, which he had reason to know was much bigger than he found use for. His lawyers had made various wills for him, having reference mainly to the spiritual needs of sundry natives of the Guinea coast and Kamschatka. He now had them draw up another leaving the bulk of his property to Roland, without restrictions.

The elder Dombey, in Dickens' delightful story, never felt more certain that little Paul would become a famous figure in his house than did Willard Linnette that Roland would be his partner in the Montvale Optical Works when he became of age. As soon as the boy was old enough to understand, the uncle liked nothing better than taking him through the manufactories, and impressing upon him the various processes required to make the telescopes which brought him his fortune and reputation. He fondly dreamed of a time when Roland would build the name of Linnette still higher among astronomers.

It was well that he enjoyed these reflections while he was able to do so, for as the lad grew older it became apparent that he had none of those instincts which the future owner of such an establishment ought to possess. The boy liked a gun, and a horse, and a story book, especially if the book dealt in tales of travel and adventure ; but he turned wearily from his arithmetic and physics, and could not conceal how thoroughly he was bored when the conversation turned upon the newest comet or the discovery of a star of the seventeenth magnitude by some searcher in Madagascar.

The uncle hid his disappointment as best he could, saying to himself at first that the boy was young, and that it was too soon to expect his mind to develop in these directions. He sent him away to school, impressing upon the principal the necessity of paying particular attention to such studies as would assist the lad in managing his future trusts.

Roland stayed through the time allotted him, but his professors failed entirely to alter his natural bent, in spite of their most vigorous efforts. They were obliged to admit, when they had done all they could, that while he was most proficient in history, he made a very poor showing in algebra and geometry. He had no difficulty in getting a hundred per cent. in geography, and he was the best pupil they had in modern languages ; but a logarithm was entirely beyond his comprehension, and all attempts to interest him in astronomy were dismal failures.

When Willard Linnette found himself face to face with these facts he did just the opposite to what many men in his position would have done. He put all his hopes aside, and began to realize that he had no reason to expect any other result. The boy's father was a dreamer and a poet, and his mother had come of a race of clergymen. What was there in this lineage to warrant an expectation that he would have an adaptability to things scientific ? Linnette loved his nephew, and as·he could not make him what he had wished, he resolved to let him pursue his own way, with every advantage that money could give.

When the young man came home from school the uncle sat down and had a long talk with him. He told him frankly that he had expected to teach him his own business, but being convinced that it was not to his liking he should say no more about it. He then urged the lad to open his heart, and to say for what profession he believed himself best fitted.

Roland, till then unspoiled as any youth imaginable, felt the blood rush to his brain at the tenderness thus exhibited. He had come to regard this man as a father, much more than that other relation to whom he was in the habit of paying a brief visit about once a year. He expressed his regret that his uncle should find him lacking in the qualities he desired, but admitted that there was nothing attractive to him about a business or scientific career. As to what he would eventually prefer for an occupation he could hardly say as yet, but for the present he would like to travel in some of the foreign countries whose history interested him so much and whose tongues he had acquired.

"I am quite pleased that this is your desire," said Mr. Linnette, kindly. "There is nothing like travel to develop the mind. I shall miss you very much, but if you make good use of your opportunities I shall be willing, for your sake, to endure the separation."

Roland replied, with real feeling, and asked how soon he might start.

"Whenever you are ready," was the answer.

"That is, if your father has no objections. Of course he must be consulted."

"Certainly," said Roland, with constraint. "I will write to him at once."

This fiction of consulting Mr. Payson Linnette had been followed from the first, though both Roland and his uncle understood perfectly that it was a merely perfunctory affair.

"I shall not limit you in the matter of expense," said Mr. Linnette, when the time of parting came. "Make your journey as long or as short as it suits you. I should be sorry to have you travel in anything but the best manner, and I wish to leave you the sole judge in everything. Only—wherever you go—*remember that you are a gentleman.*"

# CHAPTER III.

## "YOU DO NOT KNOW JULIE."

Thus it happened that, when he had barely reached his nineteenth birthday, Roland Linnette found himself on English soil, with no commission except to do as he liked, and with unlimited means to draw upon. He was in good health and of a pleasing face and figure. A young fellow to be *envied*, will say, I am very sure, the majority of my readers. A young fellow to be *pitied* will be the verdict of a minority, and perhaps they are the nearer right of the two.

Roland saw considerable of Europe—much more, in fact, than he described in the letters which he wrote home. His uncle's life was too busy, and his father's too poetic, to give them much apprehension in relation to him. But it is as well established as any fact in chemistry that most young men need some object in life, some kind of useful employment, to keep them out of mischief. Give them plenty of money and abundant leisure, and in nine cases out of ten they will find use for both in ways which the judicious might not wholly approve.

Many young men would have been irretrievably ruined by the course which young Linnette passed through during his stay abroad, but there was one thing which saved him from sinking below a certain point. He retained, through everything, an inborn love for the beautiful. Though he had developed no particular talent as an artist, he had an intense appreciation of form and color, a love of beauty for beauty's sake.

If idleness led him to degrade his ideals he never wholly forgot them.

Like the statues of the old masters, which the excavator finds buried deep in the clay of centuries, the original loveliness was still there in the caverns of his mind, and at the slightest appeal to his senses it came newly-born to the surface.

Had he remained in England his morals might easily have survived all the onslaughts made upon them. As he strolled through the unfamiliar streets of Liverpool, on the night following his arrival, he was horrified by the women who accosted him, leering with reddened eyes into his face, and breathing brown stout and gin into his nostrils. The highways seemed to be full of them. He could easily believe it when he afterwards read in some book of statistics that there were more of this class in proportion to the population in that great maritime city than in any other spot in Christendom. He was glad when he reached his hotel, for he felt like one who had passed through a territory infested with poisonous and ugly reptiles. He wondered if any man could be found so low as to accept the fearful invitations with which his ears had been dinned.

From Liverpool he went to Chester, and walked upon the Roman walls; then through the pastoral country, rich in historic interest, lying between it and London, stopping at Stratford-on-Avon, Warwick Castle, and other well-known resorts, where almost as many Americans as Englishmen are encountered. In these places nothing meretricious disturbed him. If there be women of easy virtue in that region they are not foisted upon the notice of unwilling travellers, as they are at the seaboard. Then he reached London, where he found a condition of things second only to that of Liverpool, and which shocks and astounds every man who comes from this side of the ocean, and has occasion to walk out after ten o'clock at night, in the metropolis of the world.

Roland stayed in London a fortnight and would have stayed longer but for the unbearable annoyance of the crowd of women who seemed to think him their natural and legitimate prey, and who pursued him with a persistency equalled by nothing on earth, unless it be the beggars at Naples or Cairo. He anticipated great enjoyment in strolling at night through the half-deserted streets, examining the exteriors with which his reading made him familiar. But everywhere, to his consternation, he found a legion of scarlet women on his track.

He took lodgings in Russell Square, and if there is a respectable square in London it is this one, and found the streets leading from it infested with them. He followed the advice of his guidebook and rode into the suburbs on omnibuses, walking back so as to inspect the various localities more at his leisure. Wherever he went, they were before him. At Piccadilly Circus they were more plenty than the legitimate patrons of the conveyances which start from there to every corner of London. They were almost as numerous in the streets of South Kensington as in Commercial Road, Whitechapel, or Petticoat Lane.

One evening, when he had to walk at a late hour through Oxford Street, it seemed to him that their pickets were placed as regularly as those of an army. They would accept neither his indignant negatives nor his sullen silence. Sometimes they followed him for blocks, recounting the advantages of their propositions, making a price and then lowering it like a Dutch auctioneer, and finally dismissing him with a curse.

Long after, he learned the reason why none of the members of the immense police force of London make any interference with these people. One of them happened to arrest a respectable lady, by mistake, several years ago, and naturally a great fuss was made about it. In order to be perfectly sure not to repeat this error, no similar arrests have been made in London from that day to this.

Crossing the Channel at Dover, Roland stopped at but one or two places of historic interest before he reached Paris. Strolling with a new sense of delight along the Grand Boulevards, upon the quays and through the numerous parks, he found women there, too ; not as plenty as they had been in London, but numerous enough. And what an astounding difference! Soft-voiced demoiselles, tastily clad, shot glances at him with their *" bon jours,"* from which it was not easy to turn away. When he invited one of them—as he did, why should I falsify for him?—to sit at a little table in front of a restaurant, she sipped light wine from a *petit verre* and replied to his interrogations in modest monosyllables that won his Anglo-Saxon heart and turned his Anglo-Saxon brain.

As they sat there he mentally appraised the garments she wore, marvelling at the taste displayed in making very ordinary materials so attractive. From the bits of straw and lace which formed her hat to the exquisite bottines which clad her dainty feet, everything excited his admiration. He compared her eloquent silence to the noisy chatter of women of her class that he had seen elsewhere, and knew that it would embarrass him even to say goodnight.

The American had no idea of completing this acquaintance at the first interview, and began to wonder how he should manage to continue it. He began by inventing tales of an engagement for this particular evening, and instantly realized from her unmoved countenance that she did not believe a word of his explanation.

" I shall have to leave you," he said, diffidently, trying to stare his watch out of countenance. " Could you—could you come here to-morrow, at six? I should like to have you take dinner with me. But—" he had read many French novels— " I suppose you have a lover—"

" No," she replied, looking him in the eye in a way that made it impossible to doubt her.

" May I—you won't be offended—"

She bowed absently, in a way that made him feel

that she was conferring a favor rather than receiving one.

He slipped two louis into her hand.

The next day was the longest one of his life. At six she met him, as agreed, and they dined at one of the great restaurants on the Boulevard des Italiens. When he asked her to show him where she lived, she demurred, saying that her apartment was in an unfashionable quarter and very plainly furnished. When he had overcome her scruples, they took a carriage and rode quite a long distance. Passing through a courtyard they climbed many stairs to her room at the top of the house. Roland looked out of the window upon a wilderness of roofs, and bits of the Seine, and little vistas of streets and parks in the distance, and a stretch of railroad.

Plainly furnished it certainly was, but everything was of the most scrupulous neatness. The counterpane of the bed was as white as snow. The window curtains were tastily tied with bright ribbons. From a bracket a pair of canaries hung in a brass cage. And what riveted the stranger's attention most was the fact that nearly every inch of the wall was covered with pictures arranged with great care ; pictures which had cost almost nothing, being made up of supplements to the cheaper newspapers, but which gave a cheerful air to the apartment, and made him feel for the first time since he had left America that he was in a real home.

Willard Linnette's money came freely and Julie shared it with Roland. In the first flush of what he imagined was his love for the girl, he promised her

something like eternal fidelity and she gave him
evidence of an intention to take him at his word.
But at the end of six months in Paris the American
began to think it high time to take his departure
for other parts of Europe. Letters from his uncle
contained mild hints that he was making too long
a stay in one city, and the approach of winter began
to remind him of Italy.

Now, mademoiselle was all very well in her own
sphere, but he could not see how he was going to
travel with her. He confided to one of his masculine
French acquaintances that he feared a scene when
he had to tell Julie he must leave.

His friend stared at him with unconcealed
wonder.

"You surely do not intend to *tell* her?" he
exclaimed.

"How can I help it?"

The Parisian smiled softly.

"When there is an easy way to do anything, and
a difficult way, why should you choose the hard
one?"

"An easy way?" repeated the American.

"To be sure. If you tell her you are going, she
*may* only have a crying spell; but it is much more
likely she will tear your eyes out!"

It was now Roland's turn to smile.

"You do not know Julie," he said. "She never
shows the least symptom of temper."

"Naturally," responded the other. "There has
been nothing to cause it. You have given her everything she has wanted, and she believes herself settled

for years in her present comfortable position.  Tell
her to-morrow that you intend to give her the
go-by, and my word for it, you will have a different
entertainment.  These girls are precisely like cats.
Stroke their fur the *right* way and you will never see
the steel that lies hidden beneath their velvet claws.
Stroke it just once the *wrong* way, and—presto !—
out will fly the sharp briers and your skin will be
lacerated.  Oh, you are not obliged to believe me !
You can try it yourself if you prefer."

But Roland did not fancy trying it himself.

" How can I get away ?" he asked, helplessly.

" Easily enough.  She goes every morning to her
mother's, does she not, to take her *déjeuner-à-la-
fourchette ?*  When she departs she inquires at what
hour you wish her to return.  You respond that you
will expect her at six o'clock for dinner.  That gives
you seven hours in which to leave the city.  You
will pack your things, call a cab and skip to the
station, leaving a little note to say that a telegram
has been received informing you of the dangerous
illness of a kinsman in England."

" You mean America," interpolated Roland, more
for the sake of saying something than because he
considered the difference important.

" America or England, it is all the same.  Julie
thinks them one country, I'll wager fifty francs.
These Parisian girls have no more idea of geography
than an oyster.  They always divide the world into
two parts—Paris and the rest—and believe Paris by
far the larger.  Leave her the note, saying that your
relation in England is dying, and that you were

summoned in such haste that you could not wait to kiss her good-by.  Put a nice little sum of money in the envelope, to soften her regrets.  Pay the concierge three months in advance for her lodgings, and —there you are !"

The author of this ingenious plan spread open the palms of his hands and shrugged his shoulders, after the manner of his countrymen.

But Roland's face was very grave.

"It seems contemptible," he said.  "Julie cares a great deal for me."

"So she will for your successor," laughed the Frenchman.  "Bah !"

"She really is a very nice girl," mused Roland, regretfully.

"I am sure you have found her so," replied the other.  "And that is a strong reason why you should take nothing away but pleasant memories.  It is a good rule never to look into a coffin."

In a dolorous voice Roland stammered that this would be his last adventure of this kind.

"*C'la va sans dire*," laughed the other.  "Well, which will you do, follow my suggestion or your own fancy ?  Because, if you are determined to say good-by to her in person, I shall think it necessary to send up a surgeon on the morning of your departure."

The affair of Julie, Roland Linnette used to think in after years, when he looked back upon it, was only a slight incident in his life.  There soon came a time when he regarded the delicate scruples he exhibited as the most senseless things in the world. But the sentiments of which he grew ashamed did him more credit than those which supplanted them. Those feelings of compassion with which the French girl inspired him marked a mile-post on the road he was to travel, separating widely the two extremes of his life.

The first place he went to after leaving Paris was Switzerland, where he soon forgot his resolutions in the smiles of a fair daughter of Geneva. He then toured the principal cities of Italy, finding a new divinity in each. He crossed to Africa and basked consecutively in the sunlight of a Tunisian, an Algerian and an Egyptian. After that he passed through Asia. And everywhere he saw more of the women of the land than of the topographical beauties, or the handiwork of ancient or modern men.

In Rome he visited the Colisseum, the Vatican, the Forums and the great churches; but when he recalled that city the clearest thing in his memory was a dark-eyed girl, who babbled to him in the soft accents of her native tongue, as they wandered about under the moonlight, one of his arms around her slender waist. He admired the bay of Naples, which he thought inferior only to that of Genoa, explored the depths of Herculaneum, walked through the ashen streets of Pompeii and climbed the steep sides of Vesuvius; but he remembered better than any of these the oval beauty of a Neapolitaine, with whom he drove back to the city late at night, eating grapes they had stolen from a vineyard. He rode in gondolas over the watery streets of Venice, the nearest like dreamland that any mortal city could be; but always in the foreground of his vision, when he recalled the place, was the drooping head of a young girl, sitting by his side in a boat on the Grand Canal, her dark hair falling over a low forehead, her white hand making ripples in the wave.

In Berlin and Stockholm he saw the tragedy of Faust and Margherita re-enacted, a flaxen-locked young woman, with braided hair and tinted bodice, taking the now familiar role of the beguiled one. Even in Japan and China, on the plains of Tartary and in the City of Mosques he always found his stay made more agreeable by some sweet creature with the charm of femininity and the bloom of youth.

Years later, when asked the exact appearance of a certain historical part of Jerusalem, he was forced to admit his forgetfulness; but he could have recognized without question the photograph of a certain Zerlina whom he knew there. And when, after belting the globe, he landed from the Oriental steamer at San Francisco, he confessed that his greatest anxiety after years of absence was to know how well the women of his own country compared with those of foreign lands.

He would have been surprised, had anyone intimated such a thought, that he had been faithless to his uncle's advice when he left home, to be "a gentleman" wherever he went. But then, "being a gentleman" means many things to different people.

# CHAPTER IV.

### THE HOUSEKEEPER'S DAUGHTER.

At the risk of leaving Master Guy Dalton still wandering through the snowdrifts in the neighborhood of Montvale, in search of employment, it is necessary to relate at this time something more of the experiences of the Linnette family. For some time after the departure of Roland for Europe the affairs of his uncle's household continued to be presided over by Mrs. Martin. She had become a genuine fixture upon the place, and the idea that she could leave it had never entered the head of its proprietor. Her health began to fail, however, and one day she announced that she was about to take up her residence with a son who lived in Michigan.

Though not without her faults, Mrs. Martin was a pattern of neatness and order. The architect who drew the plans of the buildings had sent her on from Philadelphia, apparently to match the rest of the trimmings, which were grand, solemn and impressive. When Mr. Linnette received news of her intention to leave him he was in a state of consternation and did his best to dissuade her. But the housekeeper, having made up her mind, was not to be turned from it, and when the next month expired she went her way.

Mr. Linnette had lived so long with everything arranged for him by one set of careful hands that ıor the next few weeks he endured real torture. The house was all at sixes and sevens. His meals were execrably served. His bed was not made right, though the same chambermaid attended to it as formerly. He could not find anything he wanted. Still he dreaded the advent of a new housekeeper quite as much as the inconveniences he was endur· ing; and he had just reached a point where he thought seriously of closing up the house and board- ing at the hotel, when he was informed one evening that a lady awaited him in his parlor.

It was the first time a lady had ever asked to see him in his parlor that he could remember. The vil- lage people were not of such a social grade as to presume upon calling in that manner, and his clergy- man's wife was about the only female person he knew who would have felt justified, under any cir- cumstances, in ringing his front door-bell. As he sent his check quarterly to that lady's husband, and limited his acquaintance with the ministerial family to that extent, he did not suppose for an instant that his present caller was the one in question. He there- fore went down with some curiosity.

"I heard, sir, that you were in want of a house- keeper."

It was a lady in mourning garments who spoke. So that was all, eh? He confessed to a feeling of disappointment. It was a mere applicant for work.

"I am in need of a person in the capacity which you mention," he replied, "but as I have said noth- ing about it in this village, I am at a loss to under- stand—"

Mr. Linnette stopped short in his speech, and a gleam of recognition came into his face.

"Why," he exclaimed, "it is Miss Moulton !"

"No, it is Mrs. Warren now," she answered, quietly. "I do not wonder you did not recognize me. It has been a long time since we met."

"And so you—you have been married ?" he responded, now speaking with complete cordiality. "And, excuse me, you are—a widow ?"

She bowed pensively.

"It has become necessary for me to earn my living, Mr. Linnette, and I think I could suit you. I should certainly try very hard."

He looked at her in some doubt.

"I do not like changes," he said. "I want a person who will be permanent. I want one who will remain as long as I live. Now, you are young, and the probability is, will marry again."

A shadow crossed the lady's features.

"Oh, no, I never shall, I assure you," she replied, gently.

"And you have no attachments, no encumbrances ?"

She hesitated a moment, fearful lest what she had to say would prejudice him against her cause.

"Only a child—a daughter. I know what you will think, but she is not the least bit of trouble. She is fifteen years of age, a very good girl, too. Let me show you her picture."

Upon which she handed him the photograph of a little sprite, with the sweetest expression, and with hair hanging in a wavy mass about her shoulders.

"My husband did not leave us much," continued the mother, "but with economy we have kept along until now. It is evident that I must soon get employment, and as I knew you—"

The old man was holding the child's picture in his hand and gazing abstractedly upon it. The little one had pleaded her mother's cause successfully. His heart went out to her at once.

"When can you come?" he asked.

The mother drew a deep breath of relief.

"Then I am really engaged! But you won't refuse me leave to bring Eva, will you? I want very little wages. Of course," she added, doubtfully, "if you insist, I shall have to board her somewhere in the village."

He put the photograph on the table, as if he accepted it as his own.

"Eva—is that her name?—is part of the contract," said he. "Where are you staying at present?"

"We arrived at the hotel an hour ago."

"Then I suppose you can come in the morning?"

Mrs. Warren smiled an affirmative.

"Your salary will be fifty dollars a month, the same that I paid Mrs. Martin. I will send a carriage for you at nine o'clock."

He rose and accompanied her to the door.

"Are you alone?" he asked, seeing that no one was in waiting. "I think I will walk back with you. It is late."

This is how Eva and her mother—for it was always in this order that they appeared to him—became residents of the mansion of Willard Linnette.

For some weeks after Roland's departure his uncle had missed him acutely. Nothing but shame kept him from writing to request his return. Even when at school the boy had come home at least once a fortnight, and nearly the whole of his vacations had been passed there. At no time was he so far away that a few hours' ride would not have sufficed to reach him in an emergency. Now, with thousands of miles of land and water between them, a feeling of intense loneliness would often oppress the foster-father. But for the coming of the Warrens he surely would never have consented to the long tour that his nephew made.

Little Eva galloped into the affections of the old man with as much facility as she galloped about the roads in the neighborhood on a pony that he very soon bought for her. She even filled a vacancy in his heart which the boy had never quite succeeded in doing. He found the greatest delight in her society, and thought nothing finer than to take her little hand in his and stroll through the grounds, or down to the village, or over to the works.

Gossip, that plant which flourishes in all seasons and at all times, took up the subject, and many were the observations and surmises regarding the strange fancy of the taciturn man for the child of his housekeeper. As he never heard any of these things, however, they did not trouble him. His servants repelled with indignation the insinuations which came to their ears, declaring that the master's life raised him above criticism. Having nothing to feed on, the rumors soon subsided.

Mr. Linnette met his nephew at New York and welcomed him cordially, though with rather less effusiveness than the latter expected. When they spoke of Montvale, Mr. Linnette, Sr., suggested guardedly that the young man would probably find much better accommodations at the hotel than at the family mansion.

"I live like a sort of hermit," he explained, "taking my meals at random, and I'm afraid it would be dull for you. When you get ready to come up I will arrange with Mr. Hanson to give you the best rooms he has, and I can meet you every day, at the counting room."

So far from being disagreeable to Roland, this plan entirely met his views. He felt that it would be necessary to pass considerable time at Montvale, for the looks of the thing, and he regarded the whole affair as a species of penance from which there was no feasible means of escape. He had grown a great deal older in the past three years. He dreaded the sepulchral air of his uncle's house, and chafed at the prospect of bed at nine and breakfast at six, which he recalled as the rule of former days. Life at the hotel, though it must be dreary enough, would not involve these restrictions. He could come and go when he pleased, with no one to interfere. He felt certain that Mr. Hanson would not spend much time in attending to things which were none of his business.

He accordingly responded, to his uncle's evident satisfaction, that he would be content with **any arrangements that were made for him.**

"You have your letter of credit on Baring's still, of course," remarked the elder gentleman.

"Oh, yes."

"I believe it is not limited in amount ?"

"No, sir. I hope I have not drawn more than you thought proper."

"By no means," was the reply. "I left it altogether with Rufus. I wanted you to have enough. How long do you mean to stay in Montvale ?"

Roland was surprised at the question, and wished he knew how best to answer it. He stole a sidelong glance at his uncle, in hopes to find some guide in his expression, but that gentleman was looking vacantly at the carpet.

"I do not know, exactly," he replied, at last. "Have you any suggestions ?" he asked, desperately.

"N-o," said Mr. Linnette. And here the conversation changed to other subjects and the matter was not taken up again.

Willard Linnette had never mentioned, in any of his letters to Roland, that he had changed housekeepers. The young man knew nothing of the child who had gone so far toward taking his place in his uncle's house and heart. He must know it at some time, but the one most interested wanted to postpone the day as late as possible.

Why should not everything have been revealed at once ? What reason was there for this secrecy, so foreign to everything else in the old man's character ?

Roland was now an experienced man. Eva was seventeen ; quite a woman. Perhaps that had something to do with it.

# CHAPTER V.

## MISS GIDDINGS IS SHOCKED.

Roland's recollections of the character of Mr. Hanson, who "ran" the hotel at Montvale were entirely correct. The house over which he presided, like almost everything else in Montvale, was owned by Willard Linnette. As Roland was the favorite relation and probable heir of his uncle, Hanson was glad to see him, and had no idea of letting anything interfere with his contentment. The day before his arrival the landlord spoke to each of the employés in turn, bidding them make every effort to please the young gentleman who was to come.

"He has travelled a great deal," he said, oracularly, "and may appear unreasonable in some things ; but there is to be just one rule for him. Whatever he asks for he must have."

To this Mr. Hanson added a mild hint that it would be very disastrous for any particular servant with whom Mr. Roland came in collision ; and an air of trepidation, not to say awe, permeated the entire household as the critical day drew near.

The number of domestics was naturally small, as the establishment seldom had a dozen transient guests at one time. There was a female cook, who never came into any portion of the house where the guests would be likely to encounter her, but who played a most important part, for all that, in the economy of the concern. There was a middle-aged woman who officiated in the double capacity of chief chambermaid and head table waitress ; a scullery maid ; a boy who did odd jobs ; and one or two men whose duties were mainly at the stable.

To this retinue had recently been added the pretty girl whom Roland met on his way from the counting room, on the morning when he first saw young Dalton. Shè was under general instructions to be ready for any emergency, and, never having had the least experience in a hotel, was considerably exercised over the prospect. The chief chambermaid and head waitress, whose name was Giddings, partly quieted the fears of this young damsel in relation to Mr. Roland, by saying that she (the Giddings) would answer all of *his* bells in person, and that it was doubtful if she (the pretty girl) would even so much as get a glimpse of him.

Roland made up his mind, as he was to be forced to remain for some time in Montvale, that he would get all the fun possible out of his residence at the hotel. Before he had been in the house an hour he had the cordial ill-will of every person with whom he came in contact, except the landlord, who could not afford to harbor such a feeling against a guest of his description.

Nothing done in anticipation of his arrival suited him in the least.

"These are your rooms, sir," said the smiling Miss Giddings, when she had piloted him up the stairs.

I say the "smiling" Miss Giddings, but it was the last smile that fair creature wore for many days.

"Rooms!" echoed the heir of Montvale. "*Rooms!* These are not *rooms!* they are *ovens!* No human being could exist for five minutes in this atmosphere. Throw open those windows, every one of them—or knock them out, or something!"

"We thought—" began the chambermaid.

"That I was a salamander? Very likely; but I am not! Unhappily I have lungs, which are set in motion by supplies of oxygen." He walked to the window as soon as it was opened, and took in a deep breath of the frosty air. "What in Heaven's name are these things?" he continued, in allusion to the lace curtains that had been arranged with great care across the upper panes. "Pull them down—quick! I want to look out without sitting on a stool." Then he glanced around the walls, and uttered an exclamation of horror. "What are those dreadful things in frames! Not pictures! Don't tell me *that!* Whatever they are, have them removed immediately. I would not sleep in the same room with them for a fortune!"

Miss Giddings, much agitated by this avalanche, gladly seized the opportunity to escape to the lower floor and inform the landlord of the strange requests which his new guest had made. Mr. Hanson promptly called William and Patsey, two of his male retainers, and ordered them to go to Roland's room and execute as rapidly as possible every order that he gave.

"Here! Take these off first,' called Roland to the

advance guard, as the reinforced detachment appeared in sight.  He tossed toward them several bed coverings known in the vernacular as "comfortables."  "What under the blessed sun do you call those?  They would asphyxiate a man in about thirty seconds."

Miss Giddings thought it time to make a stand.

"Why, sir, they are the very best we have in the house.  They were bought on purpose for your room."

"They might do for mats," retorted Mr. Roland, "but they are totally unfit for any other purpose.  Have you no woolen blankets?"

"Yes, sir, but—"

"Then get them.  Lug out that trash!" he added, to the man, alluding to the pictures.  "And what is this?  A *stove*, as I'm alive!  A *stove*, with a red hot fire in it, and an unused fire-place!  Drop those chromos and take this stove out first.  No wonder I was suffocating!"

William, the hostler, who had taken up several articles in succession and let them fall again, started for the stove, as if with the intention of removing it forthwith.  But Miss Giddings sprang toward him with a scream, declaring that the fire must be extinguished.

"Go down and get some kindlings, Patsey," she said to the boy, "and start a blaze in the fireplace.  We shall have to wait till the stove is cooler, before removing it," she remarked to Roland, in a shaking voice.

The traveller felt a keen delight in the commotion he was causing.

"There is kindling enough here," he said, pointing to the pictures that lay in a heap on the floor. "Those frames would burn, I should think."

The woman felt compelled to enter a feeble protest to this proposition.

"Patsey will be here soon with plenty of better stuff," she ventured.

"But they *must* be burned—*some time !*" replied Roland.

"The last gentleman who had these rooms," retorted Miss Giddings, rallying under the impression that the entire house was being assailed, "never said a word against them. He was a sick man, too, and had to lie here all day, with nothing else to look at."

Roland stared at her with counterfeited alarm.

"Where am I ?" he demanded. "Is this a hospital ? I thought it was a hotel. He was sick, was he ? He died, I'll bet a guinea. And he lay there—in that bed—day after day—looking at those pictures ! And they called doctors, and prescribed for him, no one suspecting the dreadful cause that was gradually sapping the foundations of his existence !" His voice began to tremble. "Did he have this stove, too ?"

The woman's teeth chattered.

"Yes, sir—in the fall. We put it up when it began to grow cold."

Roland turned away and buried his face in his handkerchief.

"Poor fellow! Poor fellow!" he murmureu, wiping his eyes.

Patsey came up with the kindling. The fire in the stove was subdued sufficiently to admit of the removal of that obnoxious piece of furniture. Blankets were substituted for the heavy "comfortables." The lambrequins that had been carefully arranged to hide the magnificent view were taken down. And then Miss Giddings ventured to inquire humbly if that was all he wanted.

"*All!*" echoed Roland, looking at the woman as if about to break into another rage. It seemed as if he could never reply to one of her questions without repeating something she had said. "No, it is not *all!!* It is not *half!* Doesn't it occur to you that a man who had his dinner two hundred miles from here may want something in the way of food?"

"I meant all in the room," faltered the chambermaid, her heart ready to burst. She had never imagined that anyone would address her in this manner before William and Patsey, who had hitherto regarded her as a person of superior position.

"Then you should have said so. What have you in the house that is fit for a Christian to eat?"

"Anything you like to order, sir."

"But I shall not 'order, sir!' I am not going to spend my time attending to your business. You can bring me what you think best. Only," he paused and looked more darkly than ever at his attendant, "if it should happen to be a *beefsteak*, and it was cooked more than one minute on each side, on a broiler, over coals, I would not touch it! If it

was fried in a spider, as I have known your countrymen to cook it, I would sue the landlord of this
house for assault and battery, and I would get judgment, too! If there is *coffee*—and I don't say there
*will* be—it must come up here half cream, and very
hot, or it will go down again! If there are *fried
potatoes*, they will have to be brown, but not burned,
mind you! And if anyone should offer me *pie*—not
merely to-night, but at any time during my stay—
there would be blood spilled! You may go."

Miss Giddings delivered this message, shorn of its
verbiage, to the cook, and then went to the rear
door of the kitchen for air. She was actually dizzy
from the shock to her feelings at her strange reception. As soon as she was out of the room young
Linnette threw himself into one of the easy chairs,
the only articles of furniture present of which he
fully approved, and laughed consumedly.

"Idiots!" he muttered. "Talk about your cool-
ies, your Bengalese! It takes a free-born American
to bow before the power of gold. As long as I
have plenty of money to salve over the wounds to
their sentiments I can wipe my feet on any of them.
There is not a *femme de chambre* in Europe who
would endure half the insolence I gave that woman.
I shall be ashamed of my country, if Hanson does
not come up here and toss me out of the window."

The cook, who had heard all that William and
Patsey could tell her of what had passed upstairs,
was in a nervous state lest the viands she was preparing should be returned as unsatisfactory ; but
Roland had exhausted, for the moment, his love of

fun, and ate his supper, which was really very good, without comment. When it was finished he walked the piazza, to watch the stars which shone brightly over the still mountain and valley, and in the pleasure of the contemplation forgot his loneliness for the time.

His uncle was away on business when he arrived at Montvale, but returned within a day or two and came promptly to the hotel. Roland noticed, as he had in the interview at New York, that there was something for which he could not account in the manner of this relation. He felt that he had in some unknown way displeased him, and expected, every time Mr. Linnette opened his mouth, to learn the cause of his changed attitude. He feared that he had delayed too long to suit his uncle's ideas in deciding what to adopt as a profession ; but he had become so used to doing nothing that he did not like the thought of giving it up.

Though the conversation lasted for more than an hour, however, it bore no reference to this subject. It ran backward and forward at random among things native and foreign, and not a word was spoken conveying the least hint that anything disagreeable was in mind.

Roland could not help wondering whether he had alarmed himself unnecessarily. Could it be that his busy uncle was willing he should lead a life of entire idleness ?

"I hope they make things agreeable for you here," said Mr. Linnette, after one of his long pauses.

"Quite so," responded Roland. "Having lived

in countries where the manners are so entirely different, things seem a little odd at first, but Hanson is doing the best he can."

The elder man seemed relieved at the answer.

"I live so plainly myself," said he, "that I fear you would not be comfortable at my house. However, some day before you go, if you would like to come for a dinner, I—I could arrange it. That is, of course, with time for preparation."

Roland laughed lightly.

"That sounds awfully formal," said he. "I would be glad to take pot-luck with you, but the hotel is just as well. When you get a chance you might come in and dine with me, and save all the trouble."

"I will do that, then," responded the other, drawing a long breath. "On the whole, it would be better. Yes," he added, musingly, "it would be much better."

Although Mr. Linnette had dined twice with his nephew after this, he had said nothing in relation to the dreaded subject up to the time when he sent the pretty waitress to call him, as detailed in the first chapter of this story.

## CHÁPTER VI.

### "I'M SURE I CAN TRUST YOU."

Mr. Linnette had nothing of special moment to communicate to his nephew beyond the message presaged in the words of Miss Arline. A matter connected with his business had suddenly occurred which made it necessary for him to take a journey that might occupy a fortnight or more. He only wished to say good-by to Roland and to inquire whether he would probably find him at Montvale on his return.

Had this question been asked an hour sooner—at any time, in fact, before he met the charming girl— the young man would have answered without hesitation that he would spend the time of his uncle's absence by taking a trip to New York. He cordially disliked Montvale, and remained merely from motives of policy. Nothing but his interest in the face he had just seen would have kept him there over night. But, to such a man, this reason was amply sufficient. He had no idea of leaving a village containing such a worthy object of attention, and he told Mr. Linnette he thought he would stay where he was for the present.

"You are still satisfied with the hotel ?" asked the uncle,

"Quite," replied Roland, with the pretty girl in his mind.

"There would be nothing for you to do at the house," continued Mr. Linnette, reflectively. "It is a dull place. I have locked up most of the rooms and taken the keys." He exhibited a bunch as he spoke. Then he noticed Mr. Hanson crossing the yard, and tapped on the window, signalling him to enter. "Do your best to entertain my nephew," he said to the landlord, when he appeared. "He has travelled in lands where every comfort is given to the stranger, almost as a matter of religion. He must not find his native country less hospitable."

Hanson responded that he hoped he had already done what was required of him, to which Roland answered that he had no fault to find. Mr. Linnette then shook his nephew's hand cordially—not as warmly as he had done when the boy started on his foreign journey, but still kindly enough. And getting into the sleigh which his man had in waiting he was driven towards the railway station.

No sooner was the vehicle out of sight than Roland turned upon Mr. Hanson with a savage air.

"May Allah forgive me the lie I told to that good man !" he cried. "I would not for the world let him know the outrageous way that you have treated me. You know what I mean, you rascal ! Why have you allowed me to be slowly tortured to death by that Giddings, when you had all the time under your roof the charmingest girl in the country, carefully kept out of my sight and hearing ?"

The landlord began to expostulate.

"I did not know—"

"Don't prevaricate! You can't do it well enough."

"But, really, Mr. Roland," stammered Hanson, "I am quite innocent of any wrong intention. Miss Giddings is experienced in waiting upon people, while the other has never before worked in a hotel. I certainly meant to give you the best one."

The young gentleman gazed at his companion with a comic look of contempt.

"The *best* one!" he repeated, as was his wont. "Experienced! I should say so! She must have had half a century, at least. Don't let her answer my bell again, if you want me to stay another day under your roof. Either expect me to take the evening train, or give orders that no one but Miss Maud is to respond to calls from Nos. 9 and 10."

The landlord replied that he would certainly do so, if that was the wish of his guest.

"Miss Arline is a nice girl, I have no doubt," he added. "Her parents died some years ago, and Maud was left to the care of a guardian, who seems to have turned her out as soon as her money was gone. I agreed to let her board here this winter, though I really did not need her, and—"

But his guest had left him abruptly. Roland lost all patience at the story. He went to his rooms and for the next hour mused upon the fate that had thrown such a lovely creature upon the awfully cold mercies of the world.

His breakfast was invariably brought to his chamber. The other meals he usually took in the public dining-room.  To-day he decided to have his dinner brought up, and rang the bell for that purpose.  As he stood with his hand on the rope visions of the sweet face which would respond to his "Come in," filled his mind.  He heard in imagination the little feet of his divinity ascending the stairs, and the dulcet voice inquiring, "What did you wish, sir?"  But the knock revealed quite a different order of person; none other, in fact, than Miss Sarah Giddings.

Roland's surprise and disappointment were sufficient to cause him to utter a vigorous exclamation, not indicative of the utmost serenity of mind.

"Who sent for *you?*" he cried, somewhat testily

"I thought you rang, sir."

"Did you?  Well, for once you were right.  I did ring.  I rang for Miss Arline.  And remember, hereafter, whenever I ring, it is for the same person, and never, under any circumstances, for *you!*"

Miss Giddings did not intend to abandon the field so easily.

"She is busy just now, sir, in another part of the house.  Won't I do just as well?"

The young man turned from the window, to which he had gone, and surveyed the questioner discriminatingly.

"Won't—*you*—do—just—as—well?" he repeated.  "I should say not!  Let me ask you candidly if you call that a sensible inquiry?"

The woman evinced signs of a lachrymose disposition.

"I'm sure I don't see what you've got against me, sir. I've tried in every way to suit you."

"Well, don't try any more," he answered, sharply. Then, as she showed no intention of leaving, he added, "The doctor has positively forbidden me to get excited, and you must not irritate me. It can't possibly do you any good to sweep my room and make my bed. I shall give you the same amount— in fact, much more—if you will kindly keep away. Here," he handed her a bank bill as he spoke, "is something on account. I will send you the same sum each week if you will never present yourself before my vision."

Miss Giddings took the money, but it did not make her happy. She still lingered.

"Will you find Miss Arline and request her to come here," demanded Roland, "or will you not? I had an appetite and it is disappearing. Shall I have to go down and see the proprietor?"

"I will go at once," replied the woman, sniffing. "Only—if she does not suit you—she is so inexperi‹ enced—you can let me know."

He opened the door and held it in the attitude of one who wishes to facilitate the departure of his guest.

"Yes, I *can*," he repeated. "But that is quite different from saying that I *shall*. Now, good-morning, Miss Giddings. Perhaps I ought to say 'good-by,' as we may never meet again. If you consult my wishes—and your own interest—it will be a permanent farewell. Miss Arline, if you please, without unnecessary delay."

He had time to throw himself into a chair and

laugh heartily at what he considered his excellent joke before a second knock sounded.

"Come in !" he called, somewhat roughly.

He did not intend to make love to Maud and frighten her again that day. He had gone farther in that direction when they met in the road than he thought wise, on mature reflection.

He inquired what there was for dinner and gave his order, without raising his eyes from a newspaper which he had hastily caught up.

"You may spread the table here, if you please," he added, as he heard her leaving the chamber.

Roland lay back in his chair by the window, and placed his feet cosily on an ottoman. He was content to inhale the fragrance of the air her presence had perfumed. His appetite had vanished. Except as an excuse to bring her to him he would have eaten nothing. He gave himself up to dreaming.

Presently the girl returned with a table-cloth, napkins and dishes. She rapped again at the door, and he responded that she might enter, but still he did not turn his eyes toward her. She set the tray on the table and drew that article of furniture into the centre of the apartment. Then she hesitated a moment, undecided what to do next. She was, in truth, wholly unused to making preparations of this kind without assistance, and not a little confused at being alone with a young gentleman of the disposition which she had found in this one.

She shot a mute glance of appeal for information in his direction, but he was silent as a stone, apparently wholly engrossed with his newspaper. It was clear that she must remove the tray from the table before she could lay the cloth, and there was no stand in the room upon which she could place it. Recollecting at last that such an article was sure to be found in the bedroom adjoining, she went thither to get it, deeming this preferable to asking any questions of the sphinx into which Mr. Roland had suddenly changed.

Maud brought out the stand, first removing from it various articles of gentlemen's attire, which she put, for want of a better place, upon the bed. Then she carried the tray to it and proceeded to set the table.

Although the young man did not look up once he felt every thrill of nervousness which his waitress experienced. His highly sensitive organization responded to hers, like the strings of a harp to the touch of a performer. When she left the room to go for the viands he inspected her preparations. A smile stole over his countenance as he saw that the cloth was uneven, the dishes laid irregularly and the table quite out of the place where the careful Miss Giddings had always put it. Fastidious to a degree, he had insisted upon the utmost particularity in these things, and had given his former attendant many a pang by the sarcastic remarks with which he punctuated his directions.

Now all was quite different; but had the meal been spread on the carpet he would hardly have cared. The food and the manner in which it was served were secondary considerations. It was the nymph who brought it that absorbed his attention.

Miss Arline and the dinner soon made their appearance. When all was ready and the girl mustered courage to inform him of that fact he rose slowly and took his seat at the table. He was obliged to make a feint of eating, because she was watching him. After sipping his soup he drew the cork of a bottle of claret and filled a glass absently. But his appetite for food would not come, and presently he pushed the dishes away.

"You may take them," he said. "I am not hungry."

"Is there anything else that I can get you, sir?"

"Nothing, thank you."

As he did not rise she asked him presently if she should clear the table; and he responded in the affirmative, taking up the newspaper he had laid down, and pretending again to become deeply interested in it. She gathered up the dishes, passing around him, as her duties made it necessary. He was oppressed by her presence, and felt that he could not bear it much longer. One may admire the perfume of roses, and yet feel a sense of suffocation when shut up in a room that is full of them.

Roland Linnette had learned to hate the world that had used him so well, long before this day. But at this moment he hated it worse than ever. Why, he demanded of himself, should so many ugly-featured and ugly-formed women ride in their carriages, while an houri like this served, a common waitress, in a common hotel. He remembered the white-capped maids of England, rosy with health, bright of eye and round of limb, putting to shame their fat and pudgy mistresses. He could recall a hundred houses of wealth in which he had been made welcome on the Continent, where the last vision of beauty disappeared with the hall-maid. He had seen the bonnes at Paris and at Vienna, grouped prettily in the parks with their infantile charges, and thought how a better civilization would have made them the mothers of the little creatures, who could never know such grace of face and figure as their temporary slaves possessed.

Then his thoughts shifted again, and took in the workmen at his uncle's, every one of them better men than he, idling away his existence while they supplied him with the abundance of which they robbed themselves.

Practically Roland was an aristocrat, theoretically he was an anarchist.

"I do a thousand things which I never will argue are right," was one of his favorite sayings.

Maud cleared away the dishes, put the table and stand where she had found them, and quietly left the room. He said no more to her, and she began to think he would prove a less disagreeable person to wait on than she had feared. If she had known all that passed in his mind she might have had less cause for congratulation.

An hour later Roland sauntered into the hotel office, and found the proprietor at his accounts.

"Everything is satisfactory, now, I hope?" remarked Mr. Hanson, with the brand of smile which we give to those from whom we earn our livelihood.

"It has improved, at least," was the response.

"What do you think of the price you get for my board? Is it large enough?"

The landlord, who had charged this guest his very highest rate, was somewhat disturbed at the question.

"I do not think it is," continued the young man, before the other could frame a reply. "I want a good many extras, and I expect to see them in the bill. For one thing, I want Miss Arline to wait upon no one else while I am here. When I ring for her I do not wish to hear that she is engaged in other duties. Her time must be mine exclusively. Do you understand?"

Mr. Hanson bowed a slow assent.

"It shall be as you desire. But you will not forget, I hope, that I am careful of the reputation of the house, and—"

Roland broke in upon him savagely, in the midst of his sentence.

"What do you mean by that?" he demanded. "Your statement is a reflection upon the character of that young woman, which I do not believe you have the slightest cause to make!"

"I surely did not so intend it," stammered the landlord, in great confusion, terrified lest he had angered his guest beyond repair. "On the contrary, I am positive she is innocent, and I should not like—"

He paused of his own accord this time, uncertain how to end the sentence he had begun.

"Oh, go on! go on!" cried Roland. "Finish!"

"I meant nothing," Mr. Hanson hastened to say. "I'm sure I can trust you."

"*You* can 'trust' *me!*" echoed Roland. "Who the devil are you, to trust anyone? I shall leave the house to-night!"

"Don't do that, sir," expostulated the landlord, greatly distressed at the prospect. "You can do . what you like, sir; I am sure it's no business of mine."

Roland had not the slightest intention of leaving the Montvale House, but he wanted to give Hanson a fright. How much further he might have gone in this direction can only be surmised, for at this moment a man entered the office hastily and inquired for young Mr. Linnette. On being told that the individual he sought stood before him, he handed Roland one of the latter's address cards.

"A young fellow was found in the snow, by the side of the road, several miles east of here, an hour ago," said the man, "with this card in his pocket. Some of us thought you might know him, and I drove over to tell you."

Mechanically Roland drew out some money and gave it to the messenger. He rightly believed that such an errand had been prompted by expectations of reward.

"Go on," he said.

"I don't know as I can tell you much. He applied at a factory near there for something to do, and they told him there was no chance. And soon after some one saw him lying in the snow and took him into a house. Then they got a doctor, and he says it's an even case."

Roland looked up, much startled.

"You don't mean that he thinks it dangerous !"

"Well, that's what he seemed to say," responded the messenger. "Perhaps it ain't so bad, but that's the way he talked."

Roland reflected a moment.

"Is there anything to prevent your going back with me, to show me the house ?" he asked. "That is, of course, if I pay you for your trouble."

"I don't know's there is."

"Harness up a double sleigh as quick as you can !" said Roland to Hanson, forgetting his announced intention of quitting the hotel. "Let William go with me. If that fellow is alive,—or if he's dead, for that matter,—we shall bring him back with us !"

## CHAPTER VII.

### OLD TOM HOBBS.

The most privileged character at Montvale, aside from its principal proprietor, was Tom Hobbs, father of Rufus, the cashier. He had long been a favorite with the senior Linnette, on account of a certain bluff quality in his nature, which assorted well with the latter's own disposition. On all occasions Hobbs was a welcome guest at his employer's mansion. The close friendship of the men dated from an occasion thirty years previous to the opening of this tale, when Hobbs—then in charge of one of the minor departments of the works—made so pronounced a stand against one of Mr. Linnette's projects that he was discharged in anger from his position. On the very next day the manufacturer repented of his act. He sent word to Hobbs that if he would apologize for the language he had used he could resume his place ; and as soon as the foreman could reach the office he was there.

"Did you send word that I could be reinstated if I would apologize to you?" he asked, as soon as he stepped foot in the counting room.

"Why, yes," was the pleasant reply. "I know you were excited and did not mean what you said."

"Do you think I am excited now?" inquired Hobbs, in his ordinary tone.

"No, Tom," responded his employer, with the utmost affability.

"Have you any doubt that I shall mean what I say this time?"

"No, Tom."

"Well, I shall *not* apologize, or anything of the sort? I came here to tell you to go to the devil!"

The employer looked at the speaker with consternation. He had never heard such words addressed to a man who was worth a hundred thousand dollars. What could the fellow mean?

"Do you imagine," continued Hobbs, "that you are any better than when you worked by my side over in Ashfield for a dollar and a quarter a day? Do you think you are going to run over me with your high talk of apologies? I am as good a man as you ever dared to be, and I will see you in hades," (only he used the old-fashioned word) "before I will ever cringe to you, when I am right and you are wrong."

He turned abruptly, and was about to leave the room, when Willard Linnette rose and stopped him with a word.

"Tom."

"Well?"

"You'd better go back to your work, Tom. And about that matter, perhaps it's as you say, after all."

"I *know* it's as I say! There's not the slightest doubt about it!"

"All right, Tom. And—Tom. You were speaking to me about your boy the other day. He's a smart little fellow, and when he gets old enough I want to give him a place in the office. Don't forget it, Tom."

"No," replied Hobbs, without so much as a "thank you." Then he asked, as if nothing had happened, "Do you want anything else, for I have got enough to do down to the works!"

"No. That's all, Tom. Good-day, Tom."

When the man had gone the employer sat for a long time in silence, pondering over the occurrence.

"It's a good thing this happened," he mused. "I've been piling up money pretty fast, and I'm afraid I've been getting into the habit of saying sharp things to the men, just because I'm a little better off than they are. Tom was right about the apology. He did a good thing to recall me to myself. I must cultivate Tom Hobbs. I must keep him near me, where he can act as a brake when I get to going too fast on this slippery road to prosperity. Getting a good deal of money in a hurry is apt to make a man domineering. If Tom finds me becoming too airy he will certainly take me down. Yes, I must find a new place for Tom where we shall meet oftener."

Tom Hobbs was promoted gradually until he became general superintendent of the entire establishment. Next to Linnette, or in any of his temporary absences, Hobbs' authority was complete. He never changed in the slightest degree the character shown in the incident narrated. He would always express his opinion of anything in the business—or out of it —as freely as if equal owner and partner. Nearly every evening he went to his employer's mansion and indulged in a smoke with him, a game of chess, or a talk on various matters, as the whim happened to seize the old cronies.

Nothing of importance came into Willard Linnette's life that Tom Hobbs did not know about, and in relation to everything he expressed his views at considerable length. He was consulted when the baby Roland was brought to Montvale, when he was sent away to school, and when he was given his freedom to travel around the world. Mr. Linnette did not necessarily adopt all of his friend's opinions, but he argued each matter over with him, in a quiet, companionable style, that enabled him to make a better decision after hearing all sides of the case presented.

Hobbs advanced the strongest opposition to the new housekeeper and her daughter, when he learned of their arrival. No good could come of it, he said. What Mr. Linnette needed was another old griffin like Martin, who would keep him in order. There was always danger of a man's falling in love with a woman of Mrs. Warren's youth and attractions.

"I am over sixty years old," smiled the other, "and I think I am quite safe."

"'There's no fool like an old fool,'" quoted Hobbs, wisely. "And there are no women so shrewd to get around a man as these young widows."

"Well, let us suppose the very worst should take place, and I should marry Mrs. Warren," said Linnette, jocosely, "what great harm would result? You are a married man yourself, Tom. It seems inconsistent for you tc argue against the state in which you are living."

Hobbs pulled at his long pipe, which he was smoking at the time, until his grizzled head was enveloped in a cloud that well nigh hid it from view.

"If a woman marries you now, Will Linnette," he said, "what will be her object ? Your money, and nothing else; and if you were not an old dunce you'd know it."

The optician glanced at his profile in a mirror that hung opposite to where he sat, and stroked his white beard complacently.

"I don't know about that, Tom ; I don't know about that," he answered. "There is a good deal to me yet, besides my pocketbook."

" Pshaw !" ejaculated his companion, contemptuously. "It's the queerest thing that you old men " —Hobbs was at least five years the elder of the twain —"always deceive yourselves in that way. You are forever thinking  it is you and not your cash that these designing creatures are after. Now, let us imagine this young widow—how old is she, should you say ?"

" Oh, thirty-five or six."

" Let us imagine her given the choice between you, with your fortune, and a fellow of something like her own age who hadn't a cent. Why, she'd marry you, of course. Let us imagine the case reversed, and say that the fellow of about her own age had the money. She'd marry him, then, as sure as you live. Let us imagine once more, and say that you and the other fellow had an equal amount. Which would she choose in that case?"

"Why, me, of course," laughed Linnette, who found in the whole matter nothing but a very entertaining joke.

"Not by a damned sight!" exclaimed Hobbs, with so much unction that the other roared aloud.

"But I don't want to marry, and I never shall marry, and that is all there is to it," said the capitalist, when he grew sober again. "I've got to have a housekeeper, if I live here, and I've had enough of your Martins. With Roland across the sea I'm glad to have this woman and her child to brighten up the house a little. You are getting to be a crank of the first water, Tom Hobbs, and you growl at everything."

Hobbs puffed away at his pipe.

"Perhaps I am," he replied. "Perhaps I'm always wrong, and perhaps you have had occasion to know that I'm pretty often right. Human nature is the same the world over, and I'm going to make a prediction right here. Either this woman will make trouble for you, or that little girl will make trouble for Roland."

"The little girl!" exclaimed Linnette, staring hard at his companion.

"Yes, sir!" said Hobbs. "He is about twenty years old. She is fifteen or sixteen. She and her mother will get a foothold here, and you won't be able to dislodge them. When he comes home they will make a dead-set at him. You'll see!"

Mr. Linnette pooh-poohed at this, calling it silly,

nonsensical, ridiculous, but Hobbs, with the dogma-
tism of his nature, persisted in reiterating his prediction.

The owner of Montvale could not connect such a
probability with the slender, golden-haired child he
had welcomed so willingly.  But, at that time, even
had he believed that Hobbs' worst fears would come
true, he would not have been alarmed at the prospect.  He had at heart only the most democratic
notions, and he did not see anything terrible in the
idea that his nephew might marry the daughter of
such a woman as his housekeeper.

Mrs. Warren went about her duties in a way that
pleased him much.  The dining table did not seem
at all like its old self when she sat at it with him,
the child between them.  The sunshine thus brought
into his life gradually reconciled him to the prolonged absence of his nephew, and finally made him
apprehensive of his return.  It was such a nice
family party at that board, and around the fireplace
of an evening !  He used to think of Roland as so
much older than when he went away, and agreed
with Tom Hobbs that there would be a vast difference between the school-boy and the young gentleman who would return from his travels.

" He is getting a great deal of experience," Hobbs
said, one evening, " and nothing alters a young man
like that.  He will learn all the good things—and
the bad ones—to be found over there."

" The bad ones !" echoed Linnette, with a start.

" To be sure !  Do you suppose he is going to
come home with the down still on his cheek ?  He's

seeing the men of many lands—ay, and the women, too! And it's a nice chase they'll lead him!"

Hobbs chuckled behind his pipe like some goblin of old, while his companion shivered from a sensation he could not repress.

"He is not a boy of bad mind," he said, with an effort to appear positive.

"Stuff!" growled Hobbs. "A young duck is bound to swim if it's allowed to get near the water."

"I'll write to him to start home to-morrow," said the uncle, anxiously.

"You'll do nothing of the kind. The best way is to let him alone. He'll get sick of it all the sooner, and settle down as steady as anyone, when you want him, years from now."

Somehow the time never seemed right for Mr. Linnette to cut short Roland's journeying. He developed such an interest in Eva that, before he was aware of it, his nephew's affairs became of secondary importance. He ascertained that the child had been very well taught for her age, and proposed of his own accord that she should be sent to a boarding-school, a short distance away. When Mrs. Warren expressed a guarded doubt whether she could afford the expense, he remarked that he intended to double her salary.

Though the widow knew that the increase in her compensation was made entirely on Eva's account, she appreciated the kindness of the proposition and felt herself justified in accepting it. Eva went to the boarding-school, but she did not remain long. Mr. Linnette missed her quite as much as her mother did, and when she came nome at the end of her first term he suggested that it would be better to engage a governess, and arrange with professors from the boarding-school to visit her at his house.

"It will cost more, very likely," he admitted, when this objection was raised by Mrs. Warren, "but never mind. I have noticed that the absence of the child wears on you, and I had rather pay the extra sum than to exchange you for another housekeeper."

Mrs. Warren had had a hard struggle to make both ends meet, before she obtained this position. She had lain awake many nights wondering what would be the ultimate result, and what would happen to her young daughter when she was no longer able to provide for her. The comfortable place into which she had drifted, the ease with which everything was now tided over, was very grateful after those years of doubt and anxiety. She did not look much into the future beyond the needs of the present hour, and was very far from being of the designing nature which Tom Hobbs imagined. Within a year she had come to have no further thought about Eva than that Mr. Linnette would see to everything.

"You are sowing a pretty crop of trouble to reap one of these days," said Tom Hobbs to his employer, when Eva had come home from the boarding-school and was receiving instructions from special masters.

"How is that?" inquired the other, laconically.

"Aren't you bringing up this housekeeper's daughter like a lady?"

"I am trying to," was the gentle answer.

"I mean, you're teaching her to regard herself as above her proper station?  That's not a kindness to the girl nor a piece of wisdom for yourself."

"What *is* her proper station?" inquired Linnette, dreamily.

"The station of a girl who ought, if she ever marries, to be a poor man's wife.  What comfort will she get in that position after you have filled her head with all the airs that the French master and the German master and the dancing-master will give her?"

"She won't be worse on account of her education, I hope."

Hobbs blew a cloud from his ever present pipe.

"When you get her fixed up she'll fascinate your nephew.  Wait and see if my words aren't true. When he comes home she'll wind him around her finger."

Mr. Linnette gazed abstractedly into the fireplace. What did he see there?  Perhaps a happy young husband and wife, and other little children that looked like Eva and spoke like Roland.

"Do you really think so?" he murmured.

"As sure as you live!" said Hobbs, impatiently. "What makes you so blind?  When he comes here this widow and her daughter will be ready for him. They've pulled the wool over your eyes nicely, and they'll do the same with your heir.  They've planted themselves here, and they'll own everything before they've done—yes, all the Linnettes and all Montvale!"

"Eva is only sixteen," said Linnette, absently.

And even as he spoke she came in to say good-night to him. And as no one saw her—Hobbs turning his face to the fire—she placed her fair arms around the neck of her foster-father and let him kiss her on the brow, as was his wont. Then, tripping out of the room like a fairy, she left him again to his gruff companion, the encircling clouds of tobacco smoke and another batch of dreary prognostications in regard to her future.

## CHAPTER VIII.

### "YOU MEAN THE YOUNG LADY."

I cannot help agreeing with the reader that it is hardly fair to leave young Guy Dalton any longer in his friendless condition, and we will proceed as fast as Mr. Hanson's best team can take us to the house where he is lying under the care of the country doctor. Roland found him conscious, but very weak, though able to take the sleigh-ride necessary to convey him to Montvale. Supported on extra pillows and covered with warm robes he rode as easily as if in the most perfect ambulance. The doctor came with the party and, before he left, gave minute directions in relation to care and medicines. He said the young fellow was merely suffering from exhaustion caused by lack of nourishment, and that he would come out of it all right, if given proper care.

"So you wouldn't come up and dine with me, eh?" said Roland, half jokingly, half seriously, when he had put his charge in bed. "But I've got you, and I shall keep you. You had your way this morning, now I'm going to have mine."

Guy was not long in recovering. The medicines ordered by the doctor, combined with the warm atmosphere of his new quarters, and the nourishing food that was given him, put him on his feet inside of three days.  Indeed, had his host permitted, he would have left his bed sooner.  He had a naturally strong constitution and this was his first serious illness.

Every time he spoke it was to express regret that he had put his new friend to so much expense and trouble.

"I must go to-morrow," he said, every morning.

"It will be time enough to see about that when to-morrow comes," was the smiling reply.

On the fifth day the lad declared that he was quite able to take his departure.  He was impatient to begin again his search for employment.

"I suppose I shall have to let you go, if you insist upon it," said Roland, when all arguments failed. "I will make out your bill at once."

Guy looked much troubled.

"I have nothing to pay you with," he said, "but as soon as I earn anything I will send it.  If you will trust me—"

"Oh, I can't do that," replied Roland, soberly. "With a stranger, you know, one must always have the cash—or reasonable security."

"Alas!  I can give you nothing but my word."

"It will not do," said the other, shaking his head with decision.  "When a debtor is unable to pay, the creditor has a right to hold his body.  That has been the custom in all ages.  You admit that you owe me some odd dollars and cents.  You say you have no money.  Very well.  I shall hold you for the amount. You will have to remain here until the debt is discharged."

The lad could not tell exactly how much seriousness and how much humor there was in these peculiar words.

"The debt would never grow smaller in that way,"
he answered.   "It would constantly be on the
increase.   The price of my board would be added to
what I already owe you."

Then Roland laughed.

"But if you are allowed to leave," he said, "there
will be various other items to charge you with.
Supposing you go away to-day.   This evening I
shall receive word that you have fallen ill at some
point on the road and have required the services of
another doctor.   I shall be obliged to hire a sleigh
to bring you back here, and go through all this nurs-
ing again.   Then there will be a second bill for
medicines and the *et ceteras*.   No, my boy, it would
really make you too expensive."

Dalton cast down his eyes, pained at the levity
with which his misfortunes were discussed.

"You think, because I did not get work before,
that I never shall," said he.   "The trouble was I was
nearly starved, and had no strength or courage.
When I was refused at the first place I fainted in
the road."

"Yes, and you would faint again," was the reply.
"There is no work for you in all this region.   The
only situation you can find in a year's search is right
here, at your disposal.   Refuse it as often as you
please, you will have to accept it at last."

Guy protested that it was no situation, but simply
charity, that was offered him.

"You are quite wrong," said Roland. "If you leave me when I want you so much I shall think you very ungrateful. Until within the past week I have been going insane. Now there are two people who may save me from that fate ; you—and Maud."

Guy had heard the latter name frequently during the past few days.

"You mean the young lady who brings up our meals," he said.

"There is but one Maud in the world," said Roland, rapturously. "Possibly there are thousands who bear that name, but there never was and never will be any other Maud for me. I believe," he continued, as if in a reverie, "you have never seen Maud."

Dalton replied that he had only heard her voice.

"Did you ever hear another so delicious ?"

Guy replied that he thought it very agreeable.

"It is the music of an angel !" cried Roland. "When I listen to it I forget that I am on this cold earth, and imagine that a bit of Heaven has been let down. And her face is sweeter even than her melodious tongue. I cannot describe it—you will soon see for yourself."

He said this so earnestly that his young companion was silent, for want of something suitable in the way of reply.

"How old are you ?" Roland asked, presently.

"Twenty-two years."

"Indeed ! As old as myself ! I shouldn't have thought it. Did it ever occur to you that this is a miserable, selfish world, to let such seraphs do its drudgery, reserving its luxury and favors for women not fit to tie her shoes? I am ashamed sometimes to live in it, and accept its bounty, for I am no better than the rest. Why was I made to want food and clothing—to desire delicacy and ease? If only I could bring myself to relinquish those things, there is in me the making of a hero. Willard Linnette, who owns this hotel, this village, that grand estate which you can see from the window, the factories yonder (where they had no place for you), even the bodies and souls of the workmen and their families who have helped him build up this gigantic possession, is my uncle. Of what use is it all to him? And when he is through with it, it will go to an ungrateful nephew."

Guy protested mildly against the arraignment which Roland made of himself. He was certain that his kind host had not so mean a quality in him as ingratitude.

"And your father?" he asked. "Have you been long an orphan?"

Roland's face grew bitter.

"My father," he replied, "has sense enough to know that there is more pleasure to be got from books than from children. To him I am only an unfortunate accident. It is my uncle to whom I owe all I have, and the only return I am likely to give is annoyance and disgrace."

Guy interrupted to say he was sure this was not so.

"And I am equally certain it is. What do you think he would say if I told him I thought of marrying Maud?"

Guy could not repress a start of astonishment.

"*And you do ?*" he exclaimed, breathlessly.

"Not at all. Being the heir of a great fortune makes it an impossibility. I only say, supposing I did intend it, and went to this man—who was once as poor as she, mind you—and told him. I can hear him now, in imagination : ' You young rascal, is this the way you requite my favors, throwing yourself away on a common working girl ? Never, sir, never, will I give my consent ! If you marry her you may cease to expect another penny from me !' "

Roland's imitation of his uncle's wrath was so striking that he could not help being moved to laughter by his own portrayal.

"Perhaps you misjudge him," said Guy, mildly.

"I know him well enough not to try it," was the reply. "And I am sure, consequently," he added, very slowly, "that the natural result will follow."

His guest looked up with astonishment in his dark eyes.

"What result ?" he articulated.

"As if you did not know !" responded Roland, with good-natured sarcasm. "How can it be otherwise? When she has learned to love me I shall go my way and leave her."

The younger man's lips opened slightly, and his attitude of strained attention relaxed a little at the answer. He looked more like a child, with his white face, than a man of twenty-two.

"Nothing more ?" he whispered.

"I hope not," was Roland's reply. "Our fates are with the gods. Come, you have talked enough for one day. If you are going to leave to-morrow you need rest. Can you spare me for an hour?"

Receiving an affirmative reply Roland went out for a stroll, desirous of breathing the cool air of the beautiful winter day. He wore leggings, in which his trousers were buttoned, and a slouch hat and fur-trimmed overcoat, giving him the appearance of a trooper. He walked up the road, taking his direction at random, and paused opposite the great Linnette residence, where he had passed so much of his boyhood.

The grounds were surrounded by a high wall. Thinking that he would step inside for a moment he went around to the massive gates, and found them securely locked. This surprised him much, as he had never known them in this condition except at night time. As he was revolving this matter in his mind he glanced up the road a little farther, and saw a man at work with pickaxe and shovel. Walking slowly toward the man he soon recognized him as Roger Butler, who had been in his uncle's employ much longer than he could remember.

"Hallo, Roger!" he said, affably.

The man paused in his work, and for an instant surveyed the newcomer with an expression of doubt.

"Don't you recognize me?" cried Roland.

"I do now, sir," answered the man, taking the hand that was offered him. "It's a good while since I saw you, Mr. Roland. I heard tell that you had come to Montvale, but I wasn't thinking of seeing you up here."

The young man paused to digest this statement.

"What are you doing?" he asked.

"Well, you see, sir," replied the man, "the drain is out of order, and we couldn't very well wait. I don't like to go to the expense of hiring a regular pipe layer, when your uncle's away, until I've made sure I can't do it myself."

The workman evidently expected something in the way of commendation, but Roland was silent for a moment.

"How long have you worked for my uncle?" he asked, presently.

"I began, sir, over forty years ago, when he first opened the works."

"You are not a young man."

"Nigh on to seventy, sir, but hale and hearty."

"You have worked pretty steadily?"

"Never missed a day, in all that time."

"You must be pretty well off, now, Roger."

The man looked in a puzzled way at his questioner.

"You must have a good deal of money laid away."

The workman shook his head decidedly.

"Not a blessed penny, sir. I have always thought I did pretty well to bring up the children—seven of them—and take care of the old woman."

Roland was not as much surprised as he pretended, but he was in the mood for this kind of talk, and he proceeded :

"I suppose you remember when my uncle was about as poor as you."

"Yes, sir. We worked side by side at Ashfield."

"*He* has something laid away, I believe?"

The old man leaned contemplatively on his shovel.

"You may well say that, sir."

"How much does he pay you a day?" pursued the questioner.

"A dollar and a half."

"And how much does *he* get?'

Roger shook his head, as if to imply that those figures were beyond the reach of his powers of computation.

"More than you, at least. Now, can you tell me why? Does he work any harder? Do you think he really earns a hundred times as much?"

Roger murmured that Mr. Linnette did a big business.

"That's true," assented Roland. "His business is large, but how long would it run without you and such as you. And you only get a dollar and a half a day!"

The man looked grateful at the interest taken in him.

"I would like it if I could get a dollar seventy-five," he said. "You might kindly speak to him when he comes home, not saying I asked you. He has treated me so well I wouldn't want him to think I was complaining."

Roland grew retrospective.

"Do you know what you were doing the first time I ever saw you, Roger? Just what you are doing now. You were working with a pick and shovel. I could not have been more than five or six years old, but I remember the very place in the grounds where you were digging. Here you are at the same kind of occupation. When will you quit it? When some one else has to use the same tools for you, over there in the cemetery. And he gives you a dollar and a half a day! Just the wages he would give a man whom he had never seen before, one with whom he had not eaten the black bread of poverty. Roger," the speaker raised his voice, "he ought to give you ten dollars a day, and tell you never to work again as long as you live!"

Butler, who had been surveying the young man with wonder, shook his head, as if to imply that this was not likely to occur.

"What are those gates locked for?" continued Roland, pointing to them. "Doesn't any one live there when he is away?"

"Only the housekeeper and her daughter, and the servants," was the response.

"Her daughter?" repeated Roland, surprised.

He glanced up at the windows that were nearest to him, and saw a fair face that disappeared almost instantly from view.

# CHAPTER IX.

## AROUND THE POST-OFFICE FIRE.

The next morning, when Guy Dalton spoke again of leaving, Roland answered him quite sharply. He declared that if he carried out his purpose he would have nothing more to do with him—no, not if the news came that he was dying on the road. Affected by this earnestness the young fellow yielded, and promised to remain for the present. It required a more prolonged struggle of mind before he would allow his friend to order him a suit of clothing from the village tailor, but finally he accepted that also.

The new garments made a striking change in his appearance. That he was not wholly oblivious to his good looks, a long stay in front of the mirror on the morning of their arrival, testified. Roland wished he knew more of his history, for he was certain that he had not always been in his present impecunious condition ; but he had too much politeness to annoy his guest with questions at a time when they could hardly help proving disagreeable.

The two young men took their meals together in Roland's sitting-room, now that Guy was able to be about. The first morning that they breakfasted together Roland asked his friend pointedly what he thought of their waitress.

"Is she not a beauty !" he exclaimed, the instant Miss Arline shut the door behind her.

"I did not observe her very closely," responded Dalton, evasively.

"Don't tell me that !" laughed the other. "I had my eye on you, and I feared by your expression that you considered her part of the *menu*."

"Has she not been in the habit of sitting at your table ?" asked Guy, to divert his companion's attention.

"For the last few days, yes. It was insufferable here, with no one to speak to, and you lying in the room yonder. She sat down with me and pretended to eat, but I know she didn't enjoy it. She is intensely sensitive and inclined to be easily frightened."

The young fellow looked up with a pained expression in his eyes.

"I can't see why you want her to do what was disagreeable ?"

Roland laughed lightly.

"Can't you ?" he asked, laconically.

"It does not seem like the other things you do."

"What other things ?"

"Your thoughtfulness on my account, for one," said Guy, in a shaking voice.

Roland studied his companion's face intently.

"But, you see, Maud is a woman," he replied, very slowly.

"I do not understand," was the quick reply, "why that should lessen your kindness to her."

"*Should ?*" repeated the other, with a rising

inflection. 'Should' is a great word, Guy. Probably Maud's sex should not lessen my consideration ; but it does, that is the thing at issue. It lessens the kindness of every man to every woman, the moment she becomes dependent upon his purse. I suppose I am as bad a man as ever lived, but in this respect I am no worse than the rest."

Dalton shook his head slowly, as though far from convinced. Still he did not like to enter upon an argument with his benefactor.

"Shall I prove it to you?" asked Roland, after a pause. "You are not a child, though sometimes you put on the look of one. I want you to come with me some evening to the village post-office, or one of the stores, and listen to the talk of the men who gather there. They may discuss politics or business while a dozen women come and go. But presently one will appear at whose advent all conversation languishes. While she remains little is done but staring her in the face, or nudging some newcomer to call his attention to her.

"What has happened? Why, gossip has begun to connect her name with scandal. Someone has hinted that she is not as good as she might be. Young Parkley has been driving with her, and everybody can guess what that means. She has been seen in another town, late in the evening, walking with a man not known in Montvale. The group in the store or post-office stare at her as long as she remains, and when she goes out they discuss her alleged faults with glistening eyes and lickerish mouths, leaning over each others' shoulders, fearful lest they should lose a word. Montvale is a town of more than average virtue, but I have seen this here, even in the brief time since my return. And what happens here occurs in increasing ratio in towns of larger size—all over the country—all over the so-called civilized earth."

An expression of the deepest horror spread over the face of the listener.

"These men who sit around the stores and participate in these discussions," continued Roland, apparently pleased to find that he was making an impression, "have, many of them, daughters of their own. If one of them saw a dog worrying a neighbor's sheep he would leave his work till he got the animal into its fold. If he heard that a wolf had been seen on the hillside he would mention it to every farmer he met, that they might bring in their young cattle. If his neighbor's daughter was going for a sail on the lake, and he knew that the boat was leaking, or noticed a storm coming up, he would run a mile to save her. But when he hears something that may wreck her life forever, how seldom will he warn either her or her parents!

"It is notorious that the father and mother of a girl who goes astray are the last persons to suspect that anything is the matter. Everybody else will tell you they have been suspicious for a long time, but to her own family her fall comes like a clap of thunder. The mother will say, ' I knew Mamie was fond of company and a good time, but I never dreamed that anything could go wrong with her.' Yet these men at the post-office knew! Some of them had talked with her in a way which showed they did not think very severely of her peccadilloes. Had there been opportunity they would have joined their guilt to hers, as freely as if they had not known her in her cradle, as if she had not played with their children in pinafores !"

The listener sat like one entranced.

"I have made a study of this thing, my boy, and I speak by the card," continued Roland. "I presume I have talked with hundreds of girls in all countries, for I have been a great traveller. Until a little while ago I had not seen my native land for three years. When I went abroad I was as innocent as you seem to be. I could hardly believe that I should find in the United States what had so astonished me on the other side of the world. Now I know there is no difference, or if there is, it is not to the credit of America. If I were to proclaim aloud what I have seen, there would arise a howl that could be heard from here to San Francisco."

The speaker rose and took a few steps up and down the room, and Guy found words to ask if Roland had any remedy to suggest for the state of affairs which he pictured.

"*I* suggest !" echoed young Linnette, suddenly dropping his sober manner and breaking into a laugh. "I would be a nice sort of individual to suggest things, wouldn't I ? My residence is made of crystal. I am not going into the stone-throwing business to any alarming extent."

"But something must be done," persisted Guy, earnestly.

"Some one has said," smiled Roland, "that the best way to reform the world is for each person to reform himself. It is easier for the child who never tasted wine to abstain from drunkenness than it is for the confirmed sot. It is rather late for *me*, but *you* can set the world a shining example."

He meant to bring a laugh to the countenance of. his guest, but Guy was as sober as ever.

"You began this," he said, hesitatingly, "by a reference to Miss Arline. Surely it has no rightful connection with her?"

"Indeed it has," was the reply. "Maud is poor as a church-mouse, pretty and friendless. Our wretch of a landlord assigns her to my especial use because he knows that my bills will be paid, no matter how large he makes them."

"And also, I hope, because he has confidence in you."

"Nothing of the kind. He knows that Maud is in danger."

Guy stared wildly at his companion.

"But she is *not* in danger—from *you* ?" he whispered, hoarsely.

Roland looked earnestly at the impetuous youth.

"Do—you—think—so ?" he replied.

"You cannot mean—"

"Don't get excited, my dear boy," said Linnette, with a trace of weariness in his tone. "I only know what results follow certain conditions."

Guy had risen and taken a step nearer his companion, where he stood with folded arms, defying him. He was as picturesque a figure, Roland thought, as he had ever seen.

"You *shall not!*" he cried. "*I* will prevent you!"

"I certainly give you leave," laughed Roland. "And, I assure you, you have my best wishes for success."

Guy looked into the amused face and heaved a sigh of relief.

"Forgive me," he said. "I forgot what I was doing. It is plain that you were jesting."

"Don't be too sure," replied Roland, putting on his overcoat. "But I am going out to take a walk. To-morrow, if it is pleasant, you ought to be able to stand a sleigh-ride with me."

It was to the counting room of the Montvale Optical Company that the young man took his way. Before he returned he had made Tom Hobbs promise to offer Guy a place in the manufactory, in such a manner that the young fellow would not suspect he had any hand in it.

Two hours later Miss Arline came to young Mr. Linnette's apartments to see if anything was required, and Guy found courage to say a few words to her.

"I fear I am making you double work while I stay," he ventured.

"That's nothing; I have very little to do," she said.

"I believe you have only these rooms to see to," said he.

"Only these," replied the girl, with a slight blush.

"Are you glad I came?" demanded Guy, earnestly, "or would you rather *he* were here—alone?"

The question startled her. It seemed almost impertinent, but as she regarded the eyes that looked into hers she could not take offence.

At this juncture Roland came unannounced into the room.

"What! Conspiring already!" he exclaimed, gaily, glancing from one to the other

# CHAPTER X.

## "I AM ROLAND," SAID HE.

The engagement of young Dalton as assistant in the Optical Works was hailed by him with the greatest delight. He had chafed severely at his enforced idleness, and at the indebtedness which he was piling up.

"Congratulate me !" he cried to Roland. "I am the happiest fellow in the world. Not only can I earn my bread and repay you what I have borrowed, but I shall still be where I can see you often."

"With all my heart, if you wish it," was the response. "And so, I am sure, will Maud."

Dalton blushed at this, which made Roland laugh heartily.

"You will share these rooms with me, just the same, I hope," he said. "If you go elsewhere there will be no one to keep an eye on me and the pretty waitress."

Guy answered, hesitatingly, that he feared he could hardly afford so expensive a home.

"That's an original idea !" said the other. "A man who is going to draw a salary can't afford as good quarters as he did when he was earning nothing ! Stay where you are, and I will see that Hanson makes it all right. He charges me enough for three or four, as it is. And, really, I need the restraint of your presence and example more than I can tell you."

So it was settled that Guy would stay at the Montvale House for the present.

Roland had been thinking a good deal of that face he had seen at the window of the Linnette mansion —the face, as Roger Butler had told him, of "the housekeeper's daughter." It was the kind to appeal to his love of the beautiful ; and there was another element which had its full effect on a mind so susceptible as his. There was a decided mystery connected with the affair.

Why had his uncle left orders that the great gates to his exetnsive grounds should be kept locked during his absence ? Roland could remember them from his earliest years, standing wide open all day. There could be nothing in the grounds which needed the special protection of their strong arms, unless it was this sylph-like creature.

" The housekeeper's daughter !"

She surely was not the daughter of the housekeeper that he remembered. Mrs. Martin must have gone away. What kind of housekeeper was it who could be the mother of such a creature? And what had Willard Linnette, the confirmed bachelor, the man who had always avoided feminine society, to do with either of them ?

Roland determined not to leave Montvale until he had found an answer to these questions. His heart, or what Miss Arline had left untouched of it, had gone out to the face he had seen at the window. For the fiftieth occasion in the course of his brief life he was entangled in what he believed a genuine case of unalterable affection.

The first time he found Butler alone he stopped for another talk with him.

"Do you know what became of Mrs. Martin, who was housekeeper here so long?" was his initial inquiry.

He had already heard from people at the hotel that she had left Montvale.

"I believe she went West to live with one of her sons," responded Roger.

"What a cross old lady she was!" exclaimed Roland, with a reminiscent laugh. "I used to think sometimes my uncle was really afraid of her. Not much like the one he has now," he added, at a venture.

"I think everybody likes Mrs. Warren," replied the unsuspecting old man, "though she keeps indoors so much. But, of course, Miss Eva's not being well makes a difference."

Roland replied, with a wise look, that it did, indeed.

"Miss Eva does not go out much, either?"

"Much?" repeated Roger. "Never. It is months since I saw her outside the grounds. She doesn't mix with the town people, you see. And since she left the boarding school her teachers always come on the train and go directly to the house. She has had all the eddication they can give her, but if she doesn't live to grow up it won't do her much good."

The young man felt a blow at the heart. Could it be that his idol was stricken with a fatal disease?

"What is it that ails her?" he found strength to inquire.

"They can't find out," replied Roger. "They've had every big doctor there is, and every one of 'em is puzzled. She looks well enough, all but the paleness, but she is failing every day. It's my opinion she'll go sudden."

Roland cried out, as if he had been struck.

"Don't say that, Roger!" Then, in return to the surprised look of the old man, he continued, "It seems dreadful that one so young should be destined to death! Not only for her, but for—"

He hesitated, being about to add "her mother," but Roger misunderstood him, and innocently revealed another secret.

"Yes, he does take it to heart pretty badly, Mr. Roland. Having never been married, and so having no children of his own, this little girl sort of filled a vacancy in the place."

He rambled on, with much more to the same effect, but the young man hardly heard him. He knew what vacancy this girl had filled. He saw, as if by the drawing away of a curtain, why his uncle had endured his absence so well; why he had shown such a mild joy at his return; why he had preferred to have him live at the hotel; why he had locked the big gates. But with all these reflections no feeling of selfishness came to the surface. His interest in the face he had seen at the window was too great for that.

When Roland went away it was with the determination to see Miss Eva, even at the risk of his uncle's displeasure. Though he haunted the neighborhood for a good part of each day, it was nearly a week before he had an opportunity such as he desired. He wanted a private interview with the girl, which he had no reason to believe he could obtain unless her mother was absent from the premises. At last his patience was rewarded by seeing a lady driven out by the coachman who had served the family ever since Roland could remember. She, he had no doubt, must be the new housekeeper.

The gates were closed and locked promptly after the passage of the carriage, and ten minutes later the watcher rang the bell at the lodge entrance.

A lame and aged servitor answered the ring, and stared with much surprise when he saw who had given the summons.

"Ah, it's you, is it, Mr. Roland?" he said, with an attempt at cordiality. "I heard you were in the village, but I did not expect to see you, and you have changed a great deal. You are looking finely, though. I suppose you thought your uncle had returned, but he has not come yet. We expect him, now, in a day or two."

There was nothing in this plausible address that implied a welcome to the prospective heir of the house. On the contrary, the porter seemed impatient to close the interview and the gate at the same time. Roland decided on a bold front.

"I want to get some books, Slocum," said he,

brushing by the man unceremoniously. " I know exactly where they are. There is no need for you to go with me."

The porter was in a quandary. Though Mr. Linnette had said nothing which absolutely directed him to exclude his nephew from the house, he had implied by innuendo that he was not expected there. Slocum had a grave fear of displeasing his employer, and, on the other hand, no one could tell how soon this young fellow might become master of Montvale. Roland did not give him long to debate these questions, for he started off at a good rate of speed toward the house.

" You cannot get into the library," called Slocum, hobbling after him, his lameness not permitting a faster gait. " The master locked up everything when he went away."

The young man did not slacken his pace in the least.

" Mrs. Warren must have the keys," he called back.

" Mrs. Warren has gone out, sir," protested the man, nervously.

" Well, she will probably soon return."

" No, sir, she will be gone several hours. She has gone to Steinberg, to consult the doctor."

This was exactly what Roland wanted to know. Feeling that undue haste was no longer necessary, he paused till the old servant could reach him.

" I hope Miss Eva is not worse," he said. And, in spite of all he could do, he looked anxious.

" No, sir, not specially," replied Slocum, thrown

off his guard by Roland's familiar manner. "She is no worse, but then again she is no better, and the doctor has to be consulted frequently. He comes here twice a week, but Mrs. Warren had not been out for some days, and I think she wanted the ride. It is confining for her, sir, just now."

Roland stood for a few moments in thought.

"Where does she keep the library keys?" he asked, finally.

"I—I think it will be better," stammered the man, "if you will wait till she returns. She does not like to have anyone go into the house when she is out."

Slocum had no sooner said this than he quailed before the glance that met his.

"When I want your advice," said Roland, severely, "I shall probably ask for it! You have a great deal of assurance to offer it unsolicited. You know where the keys are kept as well as you know where your tongue is."

Feeling that he had done all that could be required of him, and reflecting that, after all, Mr. Linnette had given no positive directions in the matter, Slocum began to make the most profuse apologies.

"Oh, drop that," replied Roland, shortly, "and tell me where those keys are!"

"I think Miss Eva has them, sir. Shall I go—"

"Yes, when you are asked to," interrupted the young man, stopping the servant as he was starting toward the mansion. "And let me tell you now, once for all, that I will not stand your impertinence. Show me where I can find Miss Eva, and then return to your duties."

The old man was plunged into new alarm. While it was true that no directions had ever been given upon the subject, he knew, by that unspoken and unwritten law on which tradition is based, that no person ought to make his way in such a manner into Miss Warren's presence. Teachers had always been piloted through the house, and not even her physicians had been permitted to meet her unchaperoned.

Slocum felt that his situation might depend on this unlucky dilemma, and yet he saw no way to escape from it. More sternly than before, Roland demanded in what part of the house he might expect to find Miss Eva.

The old man, in great perturbation, began to move slowly toward the dwelling.

"No, I will not trust you," said Roland. "You had as lief report some invention of your own as the truth. Go back to your lodge. I will ring the house-bell myself."

Glad to escape at any cost, Slocum limped away, and Roland proceeded up the walk toward the front door.

Before he reached the edifice, however, a young girl came forth unattended. It was the vision which for so long had haunted his waking and sleeping hours.

Seeing a stranger, the girl paused and seemed about to retreat; but he pressed eagerly forward.

"I am Roland Linnette," said he.

"Why, so you are," was the reply, delivered in a voice of wonderful sweetness.

Then, without more ado, she came to meet him, and as frankly as an old friend, put her hand in his.

# CHAPTER XI.

### A PARAGON OF INNOCENCE.

Miss Eva, though eighteen years of age, looked considerably younger, on account of the illness from which she suffered.  She appeared more like a child than a young lady, and her manner completely charmed the young man who had made such an effort to see her.

"You speak as if you had met me before," said he, as soon as the first greetings were over.

"I saw you—once," she replied.  "You were talking with old Mr. Butler, out there in the road. "One of the domestics· told me who you were; and besides, there is a large picture of you in your uncle's room, which I have often looked at."

In his uncle's room !  She was evidently on pretty familiar terms with her mother's employer.

"That picture was painted a very long while ago," he responded.  "It can't look much as I do now."

"Oh, yes, it does.  And I've heard a great deal about you."

He bent upon her his brightest glance.

"What have you heard about me ?" he queried.

"Why, I know that you have been a great traveller, and that you are staying at the hotel, and—but won't you come into the house ?  I can't remain out long on account of the dampness."

He accepted the invitation, though much surprised to receive it. This young girl had not been brought up so very strictly, or she would have declined to meet him thus alone.

"I have been in Montvale two months," he said, when they were seated. "I suppose you think it strange that I have not called here sooner."

She shook her head smilingly.

"No, I did not expect you at all."

"That requires an explanation. Didn't you know this was the home of my childhood, in fact the only place which could be called a home that I have ever known ?"

Miss Eva bowed thoughtfully.

"Yes, I knew. When I first came here your uncle was always talking of you. He read a great many of your letters to me. At that time he seemed so wrapped up in you that I thought he would soon send for you to return."

A contemplative sigh escaped from the listener.

"But he never did," said he. "I was gone more than three years, and he seemed to get along without me very well."

"Yes," assented the girl. "He got reconciled after a while. We can get used to anything in time, I think."

He could not help uttering the thought that was uppermost in his mind.

"And he had *you* to help him, you know."

"Yes," she said, with a bright smile. "He had me, then."

Was ever a girl of her age so childlike ! She had

stepped into his place in the uncle's regard, and talked as if he ought to be rather pleased to hear it.

"They tell me you are not well," he said, with a touch of anxiety in his tone. "What seems to be the matter?"

"I don't know. The doctors don't know, either, though I have had a dozen of them. But I'll tell you what I think. It is too dreary for me here, seeing the same things and doing the same things day after day. I need something to excite my mind, to stir my blood. Your uncle has tried to do everything for me. Before I had been here a month he bought me a pony to ride; but when I am on his back I have nowhere to go. They don't like to let me outside the grounds. It is very dull, cantering through the same roads and back again. Then I have my language teachers, and music masters, and I get so tired of them! If I was ever to put their teaching to any use it would be different, but every-one tells me I must do nothing, that I am to be a lady, and it all seems so selfish. I am not really sick. There is no pain in me anywhere, unless it is here, at my heart, like that of a prisoned bird that pines to escape from the gilded cage that is killing it."

She clasped her hands over her left side, emphasizing the expression.

"Does my uncle know how you feel?" he asked, breathlessly.

"Oh, no! I could not talk to him as I am talking to you. Indeed, I have never said as much before, not even to my mother. Something betrayed me into it, for which I cannot account. Perhaps it was because I have envied so much your opportunities to travel, to know what the world is by actual observation. I'm afraid my chief sin is that of envy. Why, I envy even the servants in this house, who have their regular afternoons when they can go out alone, without giving an account of every moment. I have actually dreamed of running away, to become a happy shop-girl, or to ask alms in the street, for the very beggars have more freedom than I."

What a wild idea to enter the brain of that child !

"If you are to be a lady," said Roland, thoughtfully, "you must take the trammels of your position along with its advantages."

The girl laughed softly.

"But I did not ask for any of these things. Though we were very poor when we came here, I was contented. We had only two gowns apiece, but that was quite enough. Mr. Linnette insists on all these extra expenses, and I wish so much that he wouldn't. I can't make mother understand the way I feel about it. She says it is very hard for a woman to earn a living who has only herself to rely upon. But I had rather live like a gipsy than the way we do."

Roland was getting information with a vengeance. It was evident that his uncle had practically adopted this girl and her mother. He began to wonder if a new will had been made, entitling them to a large share in the estate which was to have been his. Not a hateful sensation came with the thought, however ; only astonishment that the staid old bachelor could have had his heart so much affected by anything in the shape of womankind.

"My uncle did not intend I should know you were here," he said, exchanging confidence for confidence. "I only learned by accident that he had changed housekeepers. When he met me at New York, after my return from abroad, he suggested that I should go to the hotel when I came to Montvale. And as soon as I arrived in town he had his gates closed and locked, as if you were some criminal that I might assist to freedom."

"That is very odd," commented the girl, with her astonishing frankness. "Very odd, indeed, when people used to say that he intended you to marry me."

The statement nearly took the young man's breath away. There was no change in Eva's voice or manner as she uttered it. She spoke as if the idea was the most ordinary one imaginable.

"People used to say that, did they?" he managed to repeat.

"Yes. It seemed to be generally understood."

"But they don't say it any more?" he ventured, interrogatively.

"N-no," she replied, regretfully. "Not lately."

He noticed the tone in which she uttered this, and thought it about time to say something humorous.

"I suppose you are sorry," he remarked, smiling.

"Well, I knew I should like you. When I heard them talking in that way I used to go and look at your picture. 'If he marries me,' I thought, 'he will take me away, and I shall be glad of that.'  Of course, a married woman has more freedom than a young girl."

In all his travels he had never heard anything half so entertaining.

"It is rather a pity," he said, with a smile, "that the gossips who outlined your fortune should not have carried it to completion."

With her face as sober as ever, she seemed to entirely agree with him.  He resolved on a bold stroke.

"Eva, do you like me still?"

"Yes, Mr. Roland."

He leaned toward her, with his most bewitching expression.

"Prove it, then, by giving me a kiss."

She reddened a little for the first time.

"If you were going to marry me I would," she said.  "I should not like to have *two* men in the world who had kissed me."

He was so dumbfounded by her manner that for a moment he did not know what to do.  All that had been said was evidently of the utmost seriousness to her.

"It would hardly do for me to marry against the wishes of my uncle, upon whom I rely for everything," he remarked, tentatively.

The color faded from the fair cheek.

"We could not marry without his consent—could we?" he insisted.

She fixed her innocent eyes intently upon him.

"Not unless we ran away," she replied, slowly.

"Would you leave everything, your home, your mother, all—for me?" he cried, astounded.

Her femininity was asserting itself. Her eyes had left his face and were gazing at the carpet.

"Yes," she said, in a voice scarcely audible.

As he looked at her the full knowledge of his vacillating nature swept across his brain. He was "in love," of course. But he had been as much in love many, many times, and had awakened to find his passion at an end. He resolved to use a little more sense with this girl, for Willard Linnette might not be a good man to trifle with.

"There are many things to think of," he said, in a grave voice. "I like you very much, and I want to see you often, that we may talk this over. You are such a prisoner that we shall have to invent some method of communication. Have you no servant who can be bribed?"

Miss Eva looked pleased at the suggestion that he would meet her.

"There are none of them who would take your money, I am sure," she answered, "but Charlotte (she is my maid) would do anything I asked. There is a rear door in the high wall that is very seldom used, and to which I have a key. Would you mind coming at a very late hour, when everyone else is a-bed?"

The innocence of the face she turned toward him was a marvel. It surpassed anything he had ever seen or heard of. To meet such a Juliette in the manner she described was like a chapter from a story book.  Whatever the risks involved Roland Linnette was not the man to refuse this invitation.

"I will come at any hour you wish," he responded. "Only, be very careful.  There must be no doubt of your maid's fealty, nor of her thorough judgment."

The next half hour was spent on details, which were satisfactorily arranged.  Eva called Charlotte, who gave evidence of being wholly devoted to the service of her mistress.  A way in which notes could be exchanged—the first thing of importance—was provided for.  Then, remarking that risk enough had been run on the present occasion, Roland parted from the two girls and sought the library, in order to carry out the pretense with which he had entered the house.

As he expected, he found the room open, notwithstanding the fable that Slocum had invented.  The rows of volumes familiar to his boyish eyes began to interest him, and he was soon seated in one of the leather-covered chairs, engrossed in pages that he had read long years before—the "Adventures of Gil Blas of Santillane."  Delighted to con again that masterpiece of fiction, especially as he had since reading it visited many of the places described by Le Sage, he did not hear the opening of a door, nor see a man's form enter.  It gave him quite a shock when he looked up from the page he was reading, and saw his uncle standing within a yard of him.

"Why!  How long have you been here?" he exclaimed, rising, and speaking nervously.  "I did not hear a sound."

Willard Linnette did his best to conceal the anxiety he felt.　He had just left Slocum, who had told him of the young master's persistence in entering the house, in spite of all his efforts to dissuade him. He would have given a good deal to know whether Roland had seen Eva, but there was no way to find out except by asking one of them, which he was too . proud to think of doing.

"I have just arrived from New York," was the quiet answer.　"Business detained me longer than I expected."

Roland could see that his uncle was troubled, but he affected not to notice it.　As Mr. Linnette remained standing, he considered this a hint that he had best be going.

"Let me take a few of these books," he said, picking up several.　"I will send them back when I have finished them.　It almost renews my boyhood, to see these dear old authors again."

Mr. Linnette bowed.

"It is nearly time for supper," he said, constrainedly.　"Won't you remain and take the meal with me?"

"No, thank you, unless you are particular," replied the nephew, realizing that a refusal was the better part of judgment.　"Hanson expects me."

The manufacturer was growing relieved.　He began to feel certain that no meeting between the young people had taken place.

"As you like," said he.　"By-the-way, have you decided how much longer you will remain at Montvale?"

It was as plain as if the words had said it that

Willard Linnette would not regret the day when his nephew turned his back on the village. The young man felt a severe wound to his *amour propre*, but he was too much master of himself to show it.

"I would rather leave that to you, sir," he answered, dutifully. "I must admit there is more going on in the way of entertainment at New York than here. If it is quite the same to you I shall run on there within a few weeks ; though I can return at any time, should you desire."

A few weeks ! Mr. Linnette wondered what was the reason for this delay, but he could not lessen the time without exciting suspicion. There seemed nothing more to say, and the relations parted at the door.

When Roland reached the hotel he was met with the startling announcement that Miss Arline had left suddenly, giving no intimation as to where she would make her future home.

He made no comment upon this news, but young Dalton received it with consternation, when he returned from his work.

"I am afraid this means something disagreeable," Guy said to his friend, when he had deliberated for a long time upon the matter.

"D—n it, yes ! It means Giddings to wait on me !" was the only reply that Roland vouchsafed.

He did not intend to convey his suspicions to any-one else at present, but he was as certain as that he breathed that Willard Linnette's hand was in this thing.

# CHAPTER XII.

## PLAYING A GAME OF CHESS.

The second evening after the day when Mr. Linnette, Sr., came home, he was sitting in the library where he had met his nephew, and this time he had old Tom Hobbs as his companion. Hobbs was occupied in puffing clouds of smoke from his pipe, after his usual fashion, and a chess board that had served them for a quarter century stood between the two men.

"Do you suppose Roland came here for anything but to get those books?" asked Mr. Linnette, pausing between the moves.

"Shouldn't wonder," responded Hobbs, mechanically. "What if he did?"

The instrument maker made his next play with caution.

"I shouldn't like to have them meet," he replied.

"Why not?"

"That's a queer question, to come from you."

Hobbs looked up sharply from the chess board.

"You've done everything you could to prepare her for him," he said, vehemently. "Getting a little doubtful of your own work, are you?"

"I'm afraid Roland is not good enough for her," replied Linnette, deliberately.

Hobbs snorted in disgust.

"Good enough !" he echoed. " He's good enough
to be your brother's son, that's all you need to know.
I call him a very decent young fellow. What's the
matter with him ? It's no crime that he doesn't want
to buckle down to business. Every other generation
has a right to take a lay-off, if it can. And if it's
anyone's fault, it's more yours than his. You encouraged him to keep up his long journey. You
know why you did it, too."

There was something in this statement, and in the
manner of its delivery, that made Mr. Linnette forget the game he was playing.

"Why *did* I do it ?" he demanded, pettishly. "You
seem to ascribe reasons of your own to everything
lately."

Hobbs pointed out the fact that his opponent in
the game had not taken a pawn that fell to his
share, and then made his next move adroitly.

"I've a good mind to *tell* you why," he said, removing the pipe from his mouth. "By Godfrey,
Will Linnette, you'll need a guardian, if you keep
on ! Roland 'not good enough' for *her*, indeed.
Isn't a man's flesh and blood of as much account as
the children of his hired help ?"

Mr. Linnette controlled himself with an effort.

"Never mind, he's going away in a few days," he
said. "You didn't used to be so favorable to a
match between them," he added, pointedly.

"No, nor I don't favor it now !" snapped Hobbs.
"It's only when you talk as if the 'goodness' was all
on one side—as if that housekeeper's girl would have
to stoop to marry your nephew—that you stir me

up. I told you, when she and her mother came here, that they'd get around you till you wouldn't know whether your soul was your own. And now, look at it. Roland comes home and is sent to the hotel, while this child, no relation to you whatever, gets the cream of the mansion. I tell you, Will Linnette, you ought to be ashamed!"

The other player made a very ill-advised move that immediately resulted to his disadvantage.

"You say a good many things when you get to talking," he answered. "You never heard anything against Eva."

Hobbs laughed ironically.

"You've taken fine pains to keep her shut up," he replied. "She hasn't been allowed to go outside the gates without some one at her heels. Do you know what is certain to follow that kind of treatment? If she gets a husband who gives her the least freedom, she will be the prey of any man who wants her. Why—"

The proprietor of the house rose from the table and spoke in a stern voice.

"That will do, Tom Hobbs. You can't talk that way to me!"

The superintendent of the Montvale Optical Company did not seem in the least disturbed. He merely said, "Knight takes pawn 6," and waited for his antagonist to go on with the game.

"No, I will not play!" exclaimed Mr. Linnette. "There are bounds that you have no right to pass. You have hated my housekeeper and her child ever since they came here, for no better reason than the contrary spirit that's in you. Now, when it gets to making insinuations like the one you just uttered, it's got to stop. Do you hear me, Tom Hobbs?"

The superintendent affected to be engrossed in the condition of the chess-men, and his employer repeated the inquiry.

"Do you hear me, Tom Hobbs?"

"Oh, yes, I *hear* you," responded the other. "But whenever I think I have a duty to perform I shall speak out. You will talk till you're grayer than you are now before you put a chain on my tongue, when I see people bamboozling you as these Warrens are doing."

Mr. Linnette was in doubt what to say next. However unpleasant the words of his old friend, he knew the motive that prompted them was devotion to his interests, as Hobbs understood them.

"Tell me one thing," he said. "You spoke just now about my keeping Roland abroad, and said you had a good mind to tell me *why* I did it. I want you to explain what you meant by that."

"You don't want anything of the kind!" was the ungracious reply. "Come, sit down and make your moves. At this rate we shall be here all night."

"I tell you I *do* want it!" retorted Linnette, almost angry. "If you have anything to say to me, let it out. Anything is better than your everlasting hints."

Hobbs realized that it would create no ordinary commotion if he revealed what he had in mind when he made use of the terms referred to, but his doggedness was not proof against this demand. He pushed the table away from him, knowing there would be no more chess playing that evening, and after drawing two or three long puffs from his pipe, he took the article from his mouth.

"You're an old fool, Will Linnette," said he. "You'll tell me I'm wrong, but I know you better than you know yourself, and I've been watching this thing for a long time. Why didn't you want your nephew at home? Why did you keep him away from your house when he came to Montvale? The reason is not a very creditable one to a man who has seen almost seventy winters, and has a business reputation as a fellow of common sense, but it's the real one. You're in love with that little girl, yourself!"

For several seconds Willard Linnette looked as if he was going to strike the author of this bold declaration. He raised his arm and clenched his fist, while a terrible expression convulsed his countenance. Hobbs more than half expected that the blow would fall, but his sturdy character would neither have allowed him to retreat nor to make any effort to parry the stroke. Then a sudden change came across the face of the optician, and staggering to the chair he had vacated he dropped weakly into it.

"Perhaps you haven't gauged the extent of your own feelings," pursued Hobbs, as his employer gave no sign of replying in words to his accusation. "But it's as I tell you, as sure as you're alive. To put it plainly, you were afraid that young chap would excite sentiments in her heart that would lessen her affection for you, and you're seventy, and she's eighteen ! Her grandfather, if he were living, might be about your age. I know how it is— you've lived a solitary life, and she has twined herself around you, little by little, until you don't understand your own mind."

The seated figure made a clutch at the air, as if to save itself from falling.

"It's not true!" murmured Linnette, hoarsely. "I love her as a daughter—no more. It's not true, Tom ; no, I swear to you it's not !"

Hobbs had no idea of relenting in the least.

"Why don't you invite him here, then ?" he queried. "It's not my notion of the way to dispose of him, mind you, but you've shown in a hundred ways that it is yours. Why don't you have him up here, and let them get acquainted, and watch the result?"

Mr. Linnette roused himself slowly, like one who feels the first effects of a painful injury.

"There are reasons enough," he answered, faintly. "Eva is not well, to begin with. The doctors say she must avoid every species of excitement. But there are other things, which I have disliked to mention to you, because Roland is my near relation. He hasn't the kind of character I could wish. His experiences have given him a light opinion of women. I sent him to the hotel till I could ascertain if he was fit to associate with this white flower that I have watched so tenderly, and from what I learn I fear he is not."

These words came with difficulty, and there were many pauses between the sentences. Hobbs had a sneer in his voice and on his face as he replied:

"What the devil did you learn?"

"I'll tell you. I told Hanson to keep an eye on him and to report everything that he saw. It seems there was a very pretty servant there, upon whom my nephew cast his eyes. He immediately demanded that she should wait on no one but him, and has taken his meals in his own apartment, with her for his companion. His every act showed that he was quietly meditating her ruin. Then a Miss Giddings, who assists in the house, found an immense collection of female photographs in his bureau, some of them dressed in costumes which prove the depravity of his taste. Knowing these things, how could I introduce him to such a child as Eva?"

Tom Hobbs had risen and stood leaning against the mantel, with his hands in his trousers' pockets.

"Hanson is an ass of the first water!" was his snappish comment. "That Giddings is a scarecrow, who was probably driven to inventing lies on account of jealousy because Roland very properly preferred that the prettier girl should attend him. Goodness, Will Linnette, I never should have thought such things of you! Sending the boy to that confounded hole, and then putting such a set of spies on him! Well, what's the worst they found, believing all they tell you? A few pictures of youth and beauty that the lad would have to be blind not to like, and a conversation with a waitress over his chops and coffee!

That's all, isn't it? They don't accuse him of actually doing any harm to the girl?"

Mr. Linnette was very haggard. The discussion was wearing heavily upon him.

"She's been sent away," he said. "Hanson had a talk with her and gave her some money to take the journey."

The superintendent's lip curled in scorn.

"Where has she gone?" he asked.

"I don't know."

"So," cried Hobbs, with a rising inflection, "to save her from a *fancied* danger you've sent her where she'll be almost sure to run into a *real* one! You're a very moral man, *you* are! If any harm happens to that girl the blame will belong at your door. How do you know but he meant to *marry* her?"

Mr. Linnette looked incredulously at his questioner.

" She has neither property nor family."

" Has your housekeeper's daughter either of those qualifications?"

The maker of instruments paid no attention to the sarcasm in this remark.

" Roland has not evinced the least interest in her fate," he answered. " That disposes of your supposition in one word."

" It also disposes of yours," smiled Hobbs, ironically. " If he was so desperately set on her ruin, he would not let her escape him so easily."

There was something in this, certain'y, that Mr. Linnette had not thought of, but he replied that probably the nephew had found victims too plea-

tiful to feel the need of pursuing one in the manner indicated.

"Anything to fan your dislike," said Hobbs.
"Where that boy is concerned you have no leaning
toward the merciful. For the past three years,
through your neglect, he has had no tutor but himself. If he has found amusement in looking into the
eyes of a pretty woman, now and then, is it anything for which he should be hanged, drawn and
quartered ?"

Mr. Linnette was silent. He seemed too exhausted
to debate the subject any longer.

"You say the housekeeper's girl is not well," continued Hobbs. "I shouldn't think she would be.
You'd be an invalid yourself if you were fastened up
as she is. There's nothing in the world the matter
with her except a lack of something to interest her
mind. Bring your nephew up here, and you'll see a
difference from the start. Keep your eye on them,
if you think they need it—set the whole household
to spying, as you did Hanson's precious crowd.
But, for God's sake, don't steel your heart against
one of the best boys that ever wore shoes, a young
fellow you ought to be prouder of than anything
else you own !"

The lamp in the room—gas was not one of the
luxuries of Montvale at that period—had been
gradually flickering, and had at last gone out. The
moon was full, however, and its beams furnished
sufficient light. Mr. Linnette showed his caller
through the outer gate of the premises, and parted
from him there without another word.

## CHAPTER XIII.

### "THIS ONE I MET IN TRIESTE."

As it was apparent that Mr. Linnette, Jr., would probably be in New York before a great while, for either a longer or shorter period, he consulted with Rufus Hobbs, the cashier, as to the feasibility of getting young Dalton transferred from Montvale to the principal office of the concern at the metropolis. Rufus, who had never grown any fonder of the young fellow, and who would have sent him flying without hesitation had he had his way, was glad enough to make any arrangement which would relieve him from his presence. Correspondence with the main office soon resulted in the manner desired. Guy came to the hotel one evening positively radiant with joy and told his friend of his good fortune.

"It is better than anything I had dreamed of," he cried. "And as you are so soon to be there we shall not be entirely separated after all."

"You must have very uninteresting dreams," was the response, "if you see anything attractive in a seat on a high stool, with a pen in your hand, figuring up somebody else's profits out of your labor. What salary are they to pay you ?"

"Twelve dollars a week, to begin with, and more in a short time if I give satisfaction. Is it not generous ?"

"Noble," laughed Roland. "In fact, I should say magnificent! On that sum you'll be able to live like a prince. Over on Tenth Avenue there are places where you can get an attic bedroom and something they call food for seven dollars, which will leave you five to squander on clothing, amusements, and other unnecessary trifles."

Guy declined to be disconcerted by the tone his friend assumed.

"I shall do very well," he said, positively. "I know all about attic bedrooms and ordinary fare, for I have tried them before. I suppose those places you speak of—those on Tenth Avenue—are perfectly respectable?"

"Indeed they are!" was the humorous reply. "They don't throw in much sin at that price in New York. That comes extra, like coffee in Paris. *You* will find out. It takes the country boy, the one with high purposes and great ambitions, to sound the depths of a large city. If I should be a month behind you, you will be able to take me anywhere. Ah, Guy, what an awful bad lot you are!"

For a moment the younger man looked troubled, but the prospect before him was too bright for a cloud to remain long on his face.

"You will probably discover, before you have been long in the office," pursued Roland, encouragingly, "that you are receiving a few dollars less each week than other clerks who are doing the same kind of work. Of course you will not mind that. You may be giving more faithful service, may be more prompt at your desk in the morning, and less anxious to leave at night, and yet get half that they do.  A little matter like this would never breed discontent in such a head as yours.  No, I think it would rather please you than otherwise."

Dalton replied brightly that he should not consider it his affair what the others got.  He should do his own work as well as he could and let the rest take care of themselves.

"Just what I said," replied his irrepressible friend. "Do that, and according to all the story books they give boys to read you will succeed marvellously. You start without a single bad habit.  You do not drink anything intoxicating, I believe, not even a goblet of wine."  He lifted a decanter as he spoke, and filled a glass with sherry, which he put to his lips.  "That is an excellent thing. (I mean the principle, not this sherry.)  You do not use tobacco in any form "—he took up a cigar, and contemplatively bit off the end—"which is also to be commended.  I do not see how anyone—except myself, of course,—can be so foolish as to clog their brains with the vile fumes of that pernicious weed."  He lit the cigar.  "Tobacco (puff) is undoubtedly a curse (puff) which should be prohibited by statute. Our ancestors drank wine and smoked (puff) and we show the debasing results of their habit.  If we should quit both of these villainous things (puff, puff), our descendants might possibly look as beautiful as those of our modern temperance spouters."

He held the cigar contemplatively in his hand, as he finished the sentence.

"But the greatest reason why I have such complete

confidence in you," continued Roland, after blowing a vast quantity of smoke in rings to the ceiling, " is on account of your exceedingly correct views in relation to the sexes. You must know I was joking a few minutes ago, when I intimated that a residence in New York might undermine the most beautiful trait in your composition. It is my conviction that you will be absolutely impervious to temptation which endears you to me with such especial tenderness."

Rising from the chair in which he was sitting, the speaker proceeded to take a collection of photographs from his trunk.

" Here are some of the women that made my life endurable on my foreign journeys. How can I look on their countenances now but with melancholy ? From every one is reflected the accusing glance, the questioning eyelid, the trembling mouth. Be thankful, my dear boy, that you will never have on your heart the heavy load these pictures place on mine."

It was impossible to tell how much seriousness and how much irony there was in these expressions. Guy could not help a natural curiosity which led him to examine the collection.

" This one I met in Trieste," said Roland, taking one of the loveliest from the group. " You could not imagine a prettier creature. I was *in* the bloom of my youth then and she was hardly sixteen. You know the women ripen earlier there than here. How well I remember the last hours I passed with her ! We drove to a resort in the outskirts, where we had supper. She took rather more than I should have advised of the warm, rich wine of the country. As we rode back in the early morning hours she lay in a half stupor with her fair head in my lap. At the rear entrance to her father's house a faithful old duenna was awaiting us with some alarm, for Papa would have made it unpleasant for all concerned had he detected us. Just before we reached her home I aroused her from sleep, and twining those arms—those bare arms you see there—around my neck, she vowed that nothing should ever tear us apart. As I had planned to go away on the early morning train I could not very well coincide with this view. It required all my powers of persuasion to induce her to enter her abode—a temporary expedient—"

"Promising to return?" interpolated the anxious listener.

"I think likely, but—"

"Oh, how could you be so cruel!" cried Guy. "Or, having done it, how can you have the heart to tell me?"

Roland feigned surprise.

"I think I acted quite praiseworthily," he replied. "Would you prefer that I should continue taking a young girl on such excursions, with no chance whatever that good would result? I thought my sudden departure quite creditable, all things considered. But, as far as escaping temptation is concerned, I might as well have remained, for I had not been a week in Italy when I met this one."

He took the picture of a dark-eyed beauty from the pack, and held it up where he could study its exquisite outlines.

"I shall not tell you her story," he said, "because you are such an unappreciative listener. It was much more romantic than the other. Poor Alma—"

He was interrupted by an exclamation from Guy, who took another picture from the collection and held it up to his gaze.

" Here is one that should not be put in such company !" he said, with feeling.

It was a photograph of Maud Arline. Roland had placed it ingeniously with the others, in order to note its effect on his companion.

"I am glad you found that," said he, nonchalantly, "for I want you to take it with you. It is quite likely you will run across her in New York— such girls often gravitate toward the large cities— and you might need it to make the identification positive."

"Do you think I could forget her?" asked the other, incredulously.

"Such things have happened. However, if you don't care for the picture, you may leave it."

But Dalton had already placed the photograph in his pocket, ignoring the outstretched hand. Roland laughed roguishly, and turned the conversation into other channels.

" I shall not stay much longer at Montvale," he said. " You will find me in New York before many weeks."

" You must be anxious to see your father," suggested Guy.

" Oh, very !" was the satirical response. " Just about as anxious as he is to see me. If I were a book of poems, or an essay written by some famous man—himself, for example—I might interest him. Being only a son, however, makes it quite a different matter. He has only one redeeming quality in my eyes. He is picturesque."

Guy looked disappointed, not to say shocked, at this statement.

"It is the truth. He once sat as a model for a painting of Benevolence. Benignity shines from every muscle of his placid countenance. His very beard is a study of grace and generosity. And yet I know that no distress could be so deep and no agony so excruciating as to stir his calm eyes. He writes the most exquisite articles upon philanthropy, and if he had a million loaves of bread he would not give a crust to a blind beggar. But like yourself, my dear Guy, he is unquestionably picturesque, and to that extent worth calling upon occasionally."

As Roland paused, his companion said, reproachfully :

"Still, he is your father."

"Yes, unhappily. But I would rather own for my progenitor a half-clad tramp who did not know where to lay his head or to find his next meal, than such a well-kept, finely carved block of senseless marble."

There was moisture in Guy Dalton's eyes as the two friends waited at the railway station the next day. Roland was affected even while he laughed and said that tears were only for women.

"And that reminds me," he added, feeling the need of raising his spirits by a witticism, "I want you to be sure to avoid everything that wears petticoats, for therein lieth a snare. Of course, should you happen to run across Maud, you will try to ascertain why she left here so suddenly. Tell her I thought it very shabby, after all the pleasant hours we spent together. Tell her—"

But the train was starting. Guy wrung his companion's hand so sharply that he bruised it, and with a hasty "Good-by" left him alone.

# CHAPTER XIV.

## CAUGHT IN THE ACT.

For various reasons nearly a fortnight elapsed after the meeting which Roland Linnette had with Eva Warren in his uncle's library before he accepted her invitation to enter the grounds surreptitiously late at night. She had not been as well as usual, for one thing, and her mother had remained with her a good deal. The impatient lover was obliged to content himself with the daily missives that Charlotte contrived to smuggle to him, and he thought Montvale duller than ever, during the days after Dalton's departure. At last, however, a time was set for the long-delayed meeting. He was to wait near the wall door at the rear of the mansion until after Eva had seen Mr. Linnette's light extinguished and was sure Tom Hobbs had finished his game of chess and gone home.

The habits of the household, as the girl knew from experience, were very clock-like. Mr. Linnette seldom remained long out of bed after the departure of his regular visitor. Having allowed a half hour from the time she saw the light put out Eva sent Charlotte to find the anxious watcher.

All the innumerable adventures which the young man had experienced seemed to pale into insignificance in comparison with this one. He had climbed by a grapevine to the window of a wealthy beauty in Sicily; had been smuggled disguised into the seraglio of a great official of Constantinople; had barely escaped with his life from an avenging husband in Japan; but this escapade possessed a strangeness equalled by none of the others. To be prowling around the walls that had enclosed his head in boyhood—walls destined to be his own in the course of time; to creep like a burglar across these well-known walks and into this familiar house; to meet in this manner this paragon of innocence!

When Roland stepped into the room where Miss Eva was waiting, his heart knocked so loudly against his ribs that he could almost hear it.

"Well, I am here," he said, in a low voice, tuned to the most musical accents of which he was master.

Upon conducting him to her mistress the maid had retreated into the hallway, closing but not latching the door behind her. No sooner had she disappeared than Roland, overcome with joy, stretched out his arms to Eva.

"My darling," he cried, in tones of the deepest passion, "will you now refuse me that kiss which I have waited for so long?"

The young girl seemed quite composed, making a marked contrast to his impetuosity.

"You must have forgotten what I told you," she replied, gently.

He caught both her hands in his.

"That you would only kiss the man who is to be your husband? Behold him!"

She hesitated still, regarding him intently.

"Do you swear that?" she asked. "Do you swear that I shall be your wife?"

Only a minute before this, the young man had been firm in his resolution not to say anything to commit himself. The dependence that he had upon his uncle was so absolute that he had meant to be circumspect in his words, however careless his conduct might appear. But he was intoxicated with the sweetness of the creature before him, and to save his life he could not have made her a different reply.

"With all my soul!" he answered, earnestly.

Eva waited no longer, but permitted him to clasp her in his arms and press a kiss upon her lips.

"Have you thought how we are to arrange it?" she said, as soon as she could escape from his caresses.

To arrange it! Her thoughts were not to be turned even for a moment from the subject of marriage.

"That will be all right in time," he responded, after a slight pause. "For the present is it not wisest to take the happiness that comes to us and leave all difficult problems for the future? Such meetings as this ought to be devoted to the deliciousness of love, not passed in sober calculations how to escape the happiest period of life."

She looked slightly troubled.

"And does the 'deliciousness of love' end with matrimony?" she asked, in her ingenuous way.

"Why, no," he replied, confused for the moment. "But lovers usually like to prolong, as much as possible, that delightful time when they have become all in all to each other, and yet are unbound by legal ties. In our case there are a hundred barriers to marriage, which must all be broken down ; to our love there was but one, and that Charlotte and her keys has easily opened."

Eva showed the greatest interest in every word he said.

"Are there really so many barriers to our marriage ?" she asked. "Tell me what they are."

"Well, the two greatest, perhaps, are my uncle and your mother."

She brightened at this, for she had feared that his answer would reveal some terrible obstacle of whose existence she had been unaware.

"Those barriers are easily surmounted," she smiled. "My mother would not stand in the way of anything I insisted upon. And as for your uncle, he has no legal control over my actions."

Roland wished that she would not be so precise and positive. He blushed as he felt that he could not explain his own situation without laying himself open to the charge of selfishness.

"My uncle could refuse to do anything more for me in a pecuniary way, which, to say the least, would be embarrassing."

The girl knit her brows and relapsed into thought.

"You could earn a living, could you not, without his aid ? I supposed any man of education and talent could do that. We shall not need much, and I will gladly do all I can to help you."

She looked so infantile, as she uttered these

words, that Roland could not help embracing her again.

"I wish, with all my heart," he replied, and he had never spoken more earnestly, "that I had been brought up to do something useful. To tell the truth, Eva, I have no idea how I could turn my slight talents into bread. If all else fails, my dear, I will make a herculean effort to convince the world that I am a much-needed individual, for whom it has long felt a keen desire. It would be much better, though, if we could convince my respected relation that he ought to give us his blessing."

As Eva clasped her hands behind her head and leaned back in the arm-chair she made a very pretty picture.

"I am not so sure he *won't*," she said. "He seems to care very much for me. If I tell him I love you and wish to be your wife, I think he will want me to be happy."

She was so hopeful that Roland did not like to disturb her serenity, though he had little faith in her conclusions.

"I sincerely trust you are right," he answered. "For, if he does not, if he positively opposes us, we shall have to wait."

A pout altered the expression of her pretty mouth.

"To wait!" she repeated, dismally. "How long?"

Roland kissed her again, thinking her more bewitching than ever.

"We must be sensible," he said. "Is it not better

to let a little time go by, during which he may be induced to relent ?"

The girl did not take kindly to this suggestion.

"You don't know how tired I am of my humdrum existence," she said, wearily. "Oh, I want so much to get out, to go where I can see the world ! If they keep me shut up much longer I shall never live to be your wife."

The conversation progressed along the same lines for another hour, but nothing definite was reached. He could not make her understand why he was so cautious. Her ideas of love had been obtained entirely from certain old-fashioned novels that she had found in the big collection downstairs. In those romances the ardent swains dared everything to possess their sweethearts, and the recalcitrant parents and uncles invariably relented in time to make everything lovely at the close.

Before Charlotte came to let him out, it was understood that he would come again within a few days, and that in the meantime the lovers would exchange letters regularly.

With the most joyous feelings that he had known for many months, Roland set out to return to the Montvale House. He had only gone a short distance, however, when a most unexpected and unwelcome form confronted him in the highway.

For a few moments neither the uncle nor the nephew uttered a word. Roland saw that his evening's exploit was known, and from the set expression on Mr. Linnette's face realized that he had little cause to hope for mercy.

"I am a straightforward man," came at last in hard tones from the elder gentleman. "I know where you have been. I will listen to no explanations, for nothing can palliate your offence. To-morrow you must leave Montvale, and never return to it without my leave. Under no circumstances must you hold communication with any person dwelling in my house. You rely on me for your income. If you obey me you will continue to receive it as in the past. If you do not"—here Mr. Linnette made a significant pause—"you may expect nothing more from me."

A thousand thoughts rushed to Roland's brain during the delivery of this speech. All that he owed this man; the kindness shown him from his infancy; the sweet face and figure he had just left; the hardships experienced by those who are penniless, as shown in Guy Dalton's case. He did not dare begin an argument with his uncle, in that gentleman's present state of mind. It was a hard choice, but he must take the safer way. He could do as he was ordered, trusting to the future to right him.

"I will go, sir," he said, quietly.

Mr. Linnette had expected a different answer. He had prepared himself for harsh expressions and recriminations. When he heard his nephew's dutiful reply he could hardly refrain from embracing him and letting forth the torrent of tears that struggled to his eyes. But he restrained himself, and the two men parted without further parley.

Early the next morning Roland, with all his belongings, took a train for New York.

# CHAPTER XV.

### "NOW, DON'T SAY YOU'RE SORRY!"

Roland's feelings, as he rode toward the city, were far from enviable. Every revolution of the wheels under his car was taking him farther and farther from the one he loved best. He believed he cared a great deal for Eva Warren. She had made a most vivid impression upon his ordinarily fickle nature. He had really convinced himself that he was to find with her the true peace of mind and serenity of life that comes from an ideal marriage. She had led him to hope that his uncle would consent to remove the difficulties in their way, under the persuasive eloquence of her bright eyes and sweet voice. Now everything was changed. He had fallen under the displeasure of a man whose power over his income was as absolute as that of the Czar over his subjects. He had been sent away, with strict directions not to return under the direst penalty.

When he heard his sentence he accepted it, consoling himself with the belief that some fortunate circumstance would eventually intervene to save him. He had to admit, however, that there was very little clear sky on his horizon. The offence of which he had been guilty must seem upon the surface a heinous one. He had no reason to doubt that the very blackest suspicions were entertained in regard to his conduct. Should this be the case, how unpleasant Eva's situation must be! It was unlikely that Mr. Linnette would take any pains to explain matters to her. She would send her letters to the usual place, and when there were no answers, Charlotte would make an investigation, and report that the man who had professed the warmest affection for her so short a time before, had coolly left the place, without sending a word to explain the reason, or an address to which she could write.

Oh, it was scandalous! Even the fear of being disinherited, of losing the immense property which his uncle had accumulated, could hardly dissuade the young man from leaving the train at the first station, and returning, at any risk, to the girl he had deserted. But prudence conquered for the moment, and he decided to continue his journey to New York, where he might confide the whole story to Guy Dalton, and see if together they could find a way to untangle the knot.

It was on a holiday that he reached the city, and the office of the Montvale Optical Company was closed. As he did not know Guy's house address, he was obliged to wait until the next morning before he could see him. Strolling about at random during the afternoon, he happened to pass through East Ninth Street, where he encountered, as he had often done, an evidence of the fact that this world is a very contracted place. On the sidewalk a little ahead of him was a female figure, whose outlines seemed strangely familiar, and he was not long in deciding that it belonged to the late waitress of the Montvale House.

The pleasure of meeting anyone he knew, combined with curiosity as to the sort of life she was now leading, induced him to follow her. Fearing that if he made his presence known too soon she might decline to acquaint him with her place of residence, he lagged in the rear until he saw her enter a dwelling. Three minutes later he rang the bell, The girl who answered his summons directed him to a room up two flights of stairs, leaving him to make his own way to that locality.

"Now, don't say you're sorry to see me!" he exclaimed, the expression with which he was received giving rise to this suspicion. "Why, you don't even ask me to enter."

At this, Maud, who had stood stock still in her surprise, moved to one side and allowed rather than invited him to pass in.

"Let me quiet your fears at once, if you have any," he said, in a sprightly tone. "I found your abode by the purest accident, in fact by seeing you on the street just now, and it seemed only a neighborly act to call. I thought you and I were too good friends for such an abrupt leave as you took of me. At Montvale, which I left yesterday morning, no one seemed to have the slightest notion where you were. But now I shall learn all about it. What are you doing in New York; and what drove you away in such a hurry?"

He glanced hurriedly at the furniture as he spoke.

She had not found anything very luxurious, at all events.

A cloud that had gathered around the girl's eyes deepened at his question.

"I came away because—because I thought it best. And because I believed I could earn my living better here."

"I hope you have succeeded," he said, kindly.

"Not yet," she told him, with a sad frankness. "I find there are many others as much in need of work as I. Still, I am not discouraged. I shall keep trying."

It requires money to live in a city, even in the plainest manner, and Roland began to wonder where she had obtained enough for her wants. He had good reason to believe her purse was empty when she lived in Montvale.

"You must be well provided with funds to be able to wait so long," he said, boldly.

"I—I had a little," she stammered, much confused. "It does not cost much here."

"But the little it does cost," he said, with sudden conviction, "comes from my uncle. He sent you away for fear I should lower his great name by contracting a marriage with you! *His* name! He who has wheeled a barrow in his day, shovelled coal and handled a pickaxe. That's where the money comes from. You do not dare deny it!"

A tumult raged in the girl's breast as she heard him. A marriage with Roland! Could such a thing have been, for a moment, in the thoughts of the wealthy manufacturer? This was not the story that Hanson had told her, when he pressed the bank-notes into her hand and asked her to leave on the very next train.  He had represented that a scandal was imminent, that their close relations were causing talk, and that she would either have to go in this quiet way, with sufficient funds to relieve her present necessities, or be turned out ignominiously in the face of the village.

"You do not answer," said Roland.  "In this case I shall consider that silence is confession."

"You confuse me so much that I do not know what to say," she responded.  "I never dreamed of meeting you.  And—you must not call here any more, for—really—I cannot see you."

His mind was too full of Eva now to mind much this rather cool dismissal.  For, with the words, Miss Arline rose from the chair she had taken, as if to bid him farewell.

"I shall respect your wish," he replied, with a smile, "though I think you would be wiser to confide in me a little.  I am not half so great a villain as I have been represented.  If my uncle is supplying your purse, and if he, from any cause, ceases to do so, and you need anything, my city address is at his office on Third Street.  You will be very silly if you don't let me know.  And, let me tell you, though it may not seem encouraging, the chances are that you will.  I don't suppose you have a relation or acquaintance in town.  But," he walked slowly out into the hallway as he talked, "I am overstaying my welcome.  I wouldn't care so much if you hadn't got into this scrape on my account," he added.

The girl had a severe struggle with the conflicting emotions which these expressions brought forth.   It was true, as he surmised, that Mr. Linnette had made a bargain with her, through Hanson, by which he was to send her what money she needed until she could obtain a satisfactory position, in exchange for which she was never to see or speak to his nephew. She had been too overwhelmed at the landlord's accusations, when he made her the proposition, to attempt the least defence, but had followed his suggestions blindly, not knowing what else to do.   She was practically penniless, and, though Mr. Linnette's money almost burned her fingers, she dared not decline it.   Her main thought was to get away as quickly as possible,—away from Montvale, away from Roland, away from all those people to whom she had become, as was represented to her, an object of distrust.

By some mysterious fate the person she had promised to avoid had found her in this large city, on the very day of his arrival, and without effort on his part.   The short interview she had had with him could not be construed as a violation of her word to Mr. Hanson.   But, should she have given such a promise?

"I will keep your card," she said, while he wondered why it took her so long to answer.

"By-the-way," said Roland, as he was turning from her, "our friend, Guy Dalton, is here, in my uncle's office.   Is he in your bad books as well as I? If he isn't, and you happen to run across him, it will be a charity to give him a kind word. He always seemed to like you."

Then he went out upon the street and walked to his hotel. The next morning he went at an early hour to find Guy, and arrange a lunch together at one o'clock.

"How happens it that you are here without giving me the least warning?" asked Dalton as soon as he could control his delight.

"Oh, the devil is in it!" was the response. "I've had a set-to with my respected uncle."

"Not a falling out!" cried Guy, with distended eyes.

"Something mighty like it. I'll tell you everything at noon."

And at noon he did tell him everything. He related the whole Warren episode, from beginning to end, concealing nothing.

"Isn't it a fine kettle of fish?" he said, at the conclusion. "I'm in a condition of mind to kill somebody. And poor little Eva, she must by this time have voted me the cruelest and most inconstant man. If I wanted to mail her a letter, at the risk of my uncle's wrath, there is not one chance in a hundred it would ever reach her. Spies are undoubtedly on the watch, ready to intercept anything addressed to her name. Come, old man, tell me what to do. You ought to have an idea in that head of yours."

Guy was much affected by this recitation of his friend's misfortune. He counselled patience, expressing the belief that Mr. Linnette would not long hold himself in such an attitude toward his nephew.

To violate the quarantine regulations at present would be merely to invite ruin.   Nor was it wise, he added, timidly, to underrate the financial considerations.   As long as the uncle held the purse-strings, he could control Roland's conduct as readily as a pilot could handle a boat through the tiller.

"But you don't realize what a burning affection I have developed for that dear girl!" cried Roland, comically.   "I have been in love with a thousand women and never really had my heart on fire till now."

"I am afraid you never loved any of them," was the sober reply.   "It is not so very long ago that you seemed wholly wrapped up in another young lady."

A loud laugh greeted this statement.

"What, the pretty little Maud?" he replied.   "She did entertain me, in that frightfully dull Montvale, but I don't think I ever meant anything serious. Even if I had I could not but see how little chance there was for me after she caught sight of you. And that reminds me that you must run over and call on her.   She lives but a few minutes' walk from here and would welcome you warmly."

"Miss Arline!" cried Dalton, rising from his chair. "She is here, in New York!"

"Exactly," smiled Roland.   "I will cheerfully give you her address."

The younger man drew several long breaths, which he emitted slowly.   He was evidently much surprised by the news.

"I do not understand," he stammered.   "You say

you love Miss Warren. Then why have you se..
Miss Arline here?"

It was some seconds before Linnette could grasp
the full meaning of this question.

"You are wrong in your brilliant surmise," he
answered. "Miss Maud is the victim of another
ridiculous move on the part of my venerated kinsman. He had her sent away from the hotel on
account of a silly notion in relation to me. I learned
of her residence only yesterday afternoon, and then
quite accidentally. Oh, I give you my word! She
is of no use to me now, and I shall take great pleasure in passing over to you all my right, title and
interest."

Dalton shrank from these careless expressions as if
they were so many blows upon his shoulders.

"Don't speak like that!" he pleaded. "It hurts
me."

"Does it, really?" asked Roland, looking at his
companion in a puzzled way. "Then I am right,
and you are not entirely indifferent to the girl. You
see, I saw Maud in the street and followed her home
without letting her know she was watched. When I
called at her room she treated me with the coldest
civility, and even had the supreme impertinence to
remark, as I was going away, that she did not care to
see me again. Of course I lay all that to the lies—
or possibly to the truths—that Hanson had been
hired to tell her about me. Whatever the reason,
my mind is now too full of my newest inamorata to
let me shed many tears. As I am barred from
Maud's society, and as she is entirely alone in the

city, I know she would be delighted to see you often. And although I don't think I am much to blame for her present situation, I would like to hear from her occasionally, and even render her assistance if she ever needs it."

Guy made a number of inquiries in relation to Miss Arline which his friend could not answer positively. All he knew was that she meant to secure a position of some kind by which she could earn her living, and he had no doubt that Willard Linnette was supplying her temporary wants.

When the friends separated, Guy had in his possession the number of the house on Ninth Street, and that very evening he called there. Maud did not conceal her pleasure at the sight of his face, and gave him a very different reception from the one Roland found. Before an hour had passed the last vestige of nervousness had disappeared from both of them, and they chatted confidentially. Guy told how pleased he was with his place in the Optical Company's office, where he had been promised, without any solicitation on his part, a rise in salary at the end of six months' service. And Maud had that very day made an engagement with a milliner, which would give her almost enough to live on in the economical fashion she was practising.

Though intensely anxious to learn the exact connection of the elder Linnette with her affairs, Guy did not think of questioning her in relation to that matter. He was sure, whatever it was, that it reflected no discredit upon her. When they parted it was with an understanding that he would call frequently. The next evening they took a long walk together, and within a week had dined *ensemble* at a cheap French restaurant, where a dinner was served for forty cents. Several days later they had even viewed a play together from an upper gallery, at a cost of half a dollar.

As for Roland, he took rooms in a swell bachelor apartment hotel and set about drowning his regrets with the aid of several young gentlemen afflicted, like himself, with too much spare time and endowed with a sufficient quantity of greenbacks. He was not happy, but he could formulate no plan to get out of his difficulties. Theatres, rides in the park, and such light entertainment as was furnished by one or two clubs which he joined, helped to pass the time away. Dalton, whom he generally met at lunch time, still counselled him to have patience, and to do nothing rash.

"How much patience do you think *you'd* have, in my place?" Roland used to answer, exasperated at the long delay.

# CHAPTER XVI.

## UNCLE AND NEPHEW.

The disappointment felt by Eva Warren when she received no answers to the letters which her maid left for young Mr. Linnette was not over-estimated in the most vivid dreams of the absent one. All that Charlotte could learn, when she made a tour of investigation, was that he had left town on the very morning following their last meeting. The two girls talked it over for hours at a time, but they could not account for the circumstance. Eva felt intuitively that her mother's employer had had something to do with the matter, but she could not ascertain the truth of her suspicions except by direct inquiry, which she was naturally disinclined to make. It was incredible that the ardent lover, who had seemed hardly able to control his fond emotions, should have taken a wilful resolve to desert her. She believed that he would write, at least, explaining everything. But a fortnight elapsed and nothing was forthcoming.

Eva was a girl of naturally strong mind, notwithstanding the peculiar moods into which her strange and confined life had led her. She did not give vent to her feelings in tears, nor did she lose courage. When it was apparent that Roland did not intend to explain his conduct by letter, she determined to speak of him to his uncle, the first time she could find the latter alone. All at once, however, such opportunities seemed to have disappeared. The senior Linnette became visible only at meals, and as her mother was always present on those occasions, she did not like to refer to the subject. Evenings Mr. Linnette spent with old Tom Hobbs in the library as formerly. At last she could wait no longer, and one day, at dinner, she abruptly broke the ice.

"I hear that your nephew has left town," she said. "Isn't it rather strange that he should stay so long in Montvale, and never visit you here?"

Mrs. Warren looked up in a startled way. She knew that Roland had been to the house, and that he had talked with Eva there. Mr. Linnette had discovered the fact of their meeting, by a more thorough questioning of Slocum, and had thought it wise to convey the information to the girl's mother, in order to put her on her guard against a possible repetition. But he had not told the lady of the visit Roland made to her daughter's *rooms*, and he would not for anything have had her learn of it.

To Eva's remark he answered quietly, having schooled himself to expect something of the kind, that his nephew was master of his own movements, and in the habit of selecting his places of residence.

"Undoubtedly," responded Eva. "But it does seem odd to me, when I think how fond you used to be of him—"

"*Used* to be?" interrupted Mr. Linnette, without raising his eyes.

"*Used* to be," she repeated, with added emphasis. "When I remember that he is the only child of your only brother, that this was his home for many years, that he was gone abroad a very long time, and that on his return you have not had him here once, even to a dinner, and that now he has gone away, I cannot help being very much surprised. Pardon me if I speak too plainly."

Mr. Linnette's eyes were turned affectionately upon the speaker.

"I will pardon you almost anything," he said, gently.

"But, if this is your fault, I will not pardon *you*," replied the girl, with the freedom she was accustomed to use toward him. "Do you know what rumors are abroad? It is said that *I* have taken his place here, that I am crowding him out of his rightful position. Such gossip is not pleasant to me, I assure you."

The manufacturer was evidently much disturbed by this remarkable statement; while Mrs. Warren fidgeted uneasily on her side of the table, afraid to say anything, but wishing heartily that her daughter would select some other topic for conversation.

"I do not see how we can keep silly people from talking," replied Mr. Linnette, after a pause. He had been wondering who were the guilty parties, and thinking he would make the village too warm for them, if he could discover their identity. "The public has nothing to do with my private affairs,

and I heartily wish it would attend to its own business."

He said this in his ordinary tone, but Eva felt that
he was very much in earnest.

"I have only one thing to say," she remarked.
"If, it is true that I am creating a coldness on your
part toward any of your relations, I wish to go away
at once."

This was startling enough to make Mrs. Warren
drop a plate that she was filling with fruit, while
some tea that Mr. Linnette was about to convey to
his mouth splashed upon the table cloth.

"You will compel me," said Mr. Linnette, as soon
as he could command his voice, "to say things in
reference to my nephew that I had rather keep to
myself. If I have not invited him here it is on
account of matters I have learned which are not to
his credit."

Mrs. Warren, growing more and more apprehensive, touched the foot of her daughter under the
table, but the message, though thoroughly understood, had no effect. Eva had never been much
under her mother's control, and of late years
she had acted quite independently of her. She
answered the last speaker as boldly as if there were
not fifty years difference in their ages.

"Of course I do not know what you refer to," she
said, "but I should think it a poor way to improve
him, if he needs it, to send him forth again into the
world with no one to advise or direct his course.
Had you brought him here, he might have found
influences that would have benefited him."

Mr. Linnette could not refrain from looking at Eva with an expression that she could not mistake. She knew instantly that he was aware of the visit that Roland had paid to her room. With this knowledge came the certainty that he had sent his nephew away on account of it. She had learned more than she expected, and not caring to prolong the conversation in the presence of her mother, she made no further reference to the matter.

It being now morally certain that her lover had been forced into the action he had taken, she determined to write to him and assure him of her sympathy and continued devotion. The first thing was to ascertain his address. Charlotte, faithful to the utmost, discovered an opinion in the village that Roland was in New York. Eva knew that a letter addressed to the general delivery in that city would be very unlikely to reach its destination. When she was nearly in despair Charlotte learned another fact, which seemed of more account. She discovered that Roland's friend, Guy Dalton, was now employed at the New York office of the Montvale Optical Company. Eva believed he would be almost certain to know her lover's whereabouts.

Filled with new hope, Eva wrote Guy a letter without delay, telling him to direct his answer to an assumed name, in care of Charlotte's sister, Mrs. Merrill, who lived in the village of Montvale. Believing that she had entered upon what would prove a solution of the great enigma, Eva was in the highest spirits she had known for weeks. When she met Mr. Linnette at table that day she could hardly conceal her gaiety.

The wily maker of instruments was not, however, to be so easily outwitted as the young girl imagined. The postmaster, who was practically his own appointee, had agreed to let him see all of the mail that left the village. There were only two bags each day, one closing at two o'clock in the afternoon, and the other at nine in the evening. Aside from the letters of the Optical Company the correspondence that went through the office was trivial, and it required but a few moments for Mr. Linnette to examine it. He knew that Eva would do her best to learn Roland's address, and he had no intention that she should succeed in communicating with him.

"Here's a letter that may interest you," said Postmaster Hadlock, on the evening of the day when Eva had suddenly appeared so radiant.

Linnette took it eagerly in his hand. Yes, it was in Eva's handwriting. It was not addressed to his nephew, however, but to "Guy Dalton, Esq., care Montvale Optical Company, No — Third St., New York."

The name was wholly unfamiliar to him, and he turned in an inquiring manner to the postmaster.

"Do you know this gentleman?" he asked Mr. Hadlock.

"Why, yes," was the answer. "He is a young fellow whom your nephew befriended and kept at the hotel here for some time. He was hired finally at the works and at last was sent to the head office."

"That looks sufficiently suspicious," said Mr. Linnette, with a bright gleam in his eye, " to justify me in getting at the contents of this envelope at once."

He took up a paper cutter which lay on the desk, but the postmaster turned livid.

"Excuse me !" he exclaimed. " To open a letter after it has been deposited is punishable by a heavy penalty. You must find some other way, sir."

"I can at least take it to her mother," Mr. Linnette answered, his face darkening. "As her daughter is a minor, she certainly has a right to it."

The postmaster was in great distress. He disliked to offend this man, on whose goodwill his bread and butter depended, but he had a fear of the law that was even greater.

"I beg your pardon," he stammered, "but what is there to prove its authorship? Even experts are sometimes mistaken in relation to handwriting. It has been committed to the mail and I dare not do anything but forward it. If you wish to know what is inside, there is a much safer way. You can take the train to New York and get possession of it at your office. I am very sorry, but I am under oath."

Mr. Linnette uttered an impatient exclamation and strode into the street. In the morning he was a passenger on the earliest train. He had merely told his housekeeper that he was going away on business, something too common to attract any attention.

He arrived at his New York office in advance of the mail, and directed that all letters received be brought to his private office. When they arrived he found the one for which he specially waited. After deliberating a little he rang a bell and requested that Mr. Dalton be asked to step in.

When this message was given to Guy he was thrown into a state of agitation. He had seen Mr. Linnette at the office once before, and knew he seldom spoke to anyone except the head clerk or the messenger boy. He tried to think of something he had done to merit criticism, for he did not imagine his employer would send for him on any other account. When he presented himself in the inner office there was a bright red spot in each of his pale cheeks.

Mr. Linnette looked up at his entrance and told the young man to sit down.

"Is your name Guy Dalton?" he asked.

Guy responded with a faint affirmative. He had marked the serious look and his forebodings increased.

"How long have you been employed here?"

"About a month, sir. Though, before that, I was for some time at your Montvale Works."

"Yes, yes, I know," said Mr. Linnette. "Now, I have a little business to transact with you. It is in reference to this letter, which has just arrived in the mail."

Guy showed his astonishment, as he gazed at the envelope. He had no regular correspondent, and could not imagine who had sent it.

"Do you recognize that handwriting?"

"No, sir," responded the young man, after examining it with care.

"It was mailed at Montvale, you see,"

Guy nodded vaguely.

"Do you mean to tell me," asked Mr. Linnette, sharply, "that you were not expecting a letter from that place ?"

The young man's countenance grew still rosier. He felt like one charged with an unknown offence, like a man put on trial without being told of what he is accused.

"I beg your pardon, sir," he answered, "but won't you tell me the reason for this strange series of questions. That letter, judging by the superscription, appears to belong to me. I have no idea who wrote it, but if you will hand it to me I can easily ascertain. Then perhaps we shall get on better."

Mr. Linnette's brow darkened.

"Very likely," he said, satirically. "Very likely. But you will not read it until I have opened it. I mean to learn its contents before I give it to you."

As he took up a paper cutter from the desk, Dalton's attitude changed instantly.

"You have no right to open that letter !" he cried, hoarsely.

There was but one person that the instrument maker had ever permitted to speak to him in that way—old Tom Hobbs. For an instant he was disconcerted, but he had no idea of giving the missive to the one who claimed it with such a show of haughtiness.

"Be careful, young man !" he replied. "This letter is in the handwriting of a girl who is under my protection. I have reason to believe that it contains a message for an individual with whom I have forbidden her to hold any communication. I do not propose, Mr. Dalton, to have one of my employés use his position to frustrate me in the wise and proper management of my affairs."

Guy heard and understood. It was as plain to him now as the noonday. The letter was undoubtedly from Eva Warren, who had written to him because she could not write to Roland. Having come to this conclusion the young man determined that Mr. Linnette, whatever his financial or social position, should not possess himself of the sacred secret contained in that envelope. Had he been the president of the United States he would not have allowed him to open it.

"Give me that letter!" he said, imperatively.

The elder man was trembling under the strain. He had not closed his eyes all night.

"One minute," he answered, impressively. "I want you to understand what you are doing. I have told my nephew that if he ever attempts to communicate with this young lady I shall disinherit him—shall cease treating him as my relation from that day forth. I think you call him your friend. Consider, then, before you do an act that may ruin him."

"Give me that letter!"

The outstretched hand was still claiming the missive when an unexpected arrival complicated affairs still more. Roland Linnette had happened to call at the office for a word with Guy. On learning that his uncle was interviewing the young man in his private office, he immediately suspected that something of interest to himself was going on there. With this thought in mind he had no hesitation in walking boldly into the room.

"Give me that letter!" he heard Guy say, and his quick eye took in the address on the envelope that his uncle held up. He knew the handwriting, and the extraordinary tableau began to have a definite meaning for him.

Eva had written—to him, perhaps under cover of Dalton's name—but about him, at least. His uncle was evidently withholding the letter from its rightful owner, probably with the intention of violating its seal for his own purposes. The hottest anger he had ever known suffused his brain, completely turning his head for the moment; and before Willard Linnette dreamed of his intention he strode forward and grasped the missive in his hand.

The millionaire started to his feet, but, seeing the determined attitude of both the young men, he decided that it would be useless to attempt regaining the document by brute force. The group made a striking picture, the same expressions written on each face.

"You have done a fine day's work, you two!" sneered Mr. Linnette, between his shut teeth. "Mr. Dalton, you may go to the cashier for whatever sum is due you, and never show yourself in my office again. And you"—he addressed himself now to Roland—"may go where you please; to the devil, if you like! I shall cancel your letter of credit, and you will get nothing more from me. Let me tell you another thing. The poor girl you meant to

ruin, as you have a hundred others, will be kep.
from your clutches. To her will go the fortune I
had meant for you. When you are starving in some
garret, console yourself by remembering how easily
you threw a million good dollars away !"

During the delivery of this speech he choked frequently, overcome by the vehemence of his feelings.
As he paused, Dalton, appalled at the extent of the
calamity he had helped to bring upon his friend,
stepped forward.

"I have been wrong, entirely wrong !" he cried.
"Roland must not suffer on my account. No, the
letter is mine, but he shall give it to you. I with-
draw all objections. I accept my discharge, sir, but
I entreat you not to punish another for a fault that
was wholly my own. Give it to him, Roland," he
added, addressing himself to that young gentleman.
"I am sure he will then retract what he has said
about you and leave me to bear my punishment
alone."

Wrought up as he had been, Willard Linnette
would willingly have met even a halfway approach
on the part of his nephew. He felt a genuine alarm
at the extent to which his passionate nature had led
him. But, angrier even than he, Roland gave him no
opportunity.

"He shall not have it !" he retorted. "A letter
from such a girl shall not be touched by profane
hands. Do you think he is going to scare me by his
threats? What do they amount to, at the worst ?
Why, that he will give his miserable money—the
only thing there is to him, the only thing that makes

people doff their hats when he passes,—to the one I most love and honor! That *money* of his! He has spent too much of it for me already. It would have been a thousand times better had he sent me out years ago, with twenty dollars in my pocket, to fight my way. But let me tell you, sir" (he addressed himself to his uncle), "you will never steal Eva Warren's love from me. I am now free from obligation to you, and shall attempt no farther concealment. She has promised to marry me, and, if she will take me as I am, she shall be my wife."

Mr. Linnette's features seemed petrified as he answered. These words withered the olive branch he had been ready to stretch out.

"If that misguided young woman should link her life with yours—which she never will do, if I can prevent it—she will not receive a penny of my money. Don't imagine you are going to mock me and inherit my wealth through that channel. When you find that she is penniless we shall see how real your professions are!"

Roland gazed with a pitying look at the old man before him.

"Look at him, Guy," he said. "He is seventy years of age, and the only thing he can think of is money, *money*, MONEY! During his long life no woman's love has ever warmed his heart, no child of his own has ever played about his knees. He has not even felt the delights of passion. He has known nothing but *money*, and now that his hair is white he babbles of his possessions as children of their toys."

Putting his arm affectionately around his companion's shoulder Roland drew him out into the main office, where he found his hat and coat. Then the two young men, one of them white and dizzy, the other loftily serene, went out of the building together.

## CHAPTER XVII.

### "OH, I KNOW SOME THINGS."

As soon as he was left alone in his office Willard Linnette sank into his chair, and for more than an hour did not move from that position. He could hardly believe himself awake. The scene he had just witnessed was like an exceedingly unpleasant dream. It seemed impossible that his nephew could have dared him to his face, thrown away all his prospects like dross, and ended by those most insulting words. But he was obliged to admit that the crisis had actually occurred. The Rubicon had been passed. There was no longer any question of reconciliation. He must return to Montvale and carry out his threat.

Late that night he reached home, and all the next day he remained indoors, preparing himself for an interview with Tom Hobbs, which he had determined to have that evening. He knew that Hobbs would oppose him at every point, but he had no other person in whom he was willing to confide. In his present state of mind it would be a relief to unbosom himself even to him.

The collision with Roland made him desperate. For the past month he had tried with all his might to bring himself to the point where he could effect a full reconciliation with the young man. He preferred to believe he was not as bad as represented. He reflected that something must be allowed for his unguided youth. And he had even debated the possibility of surrendering to his nephew all hopes of possessing the sweet girl whose love filled the brightest spot in his lonely existence.

Now all this was over. Every time he thought of Roland he heard that mocking voice, "Money, *money*, MONEY·! All this old man thinks of is *money!*" Ah, well! The boy would learn what money was, when he had tried a few weeks to live without it, and would come creeping back, begging for ever so little of an allowance ; this fellow without a trade or profession. And he would give him nothing—no, not one cent. He was through with him, and forever !

In a short conversation which he had with Mrs. Warren, he gave her a dim impression that his nephew had met with a severe accident.

"Did you meet any of your relations in New York ?" she asked, anxiously.

"I did not," he replied, frowning darkly. "I have no relation there but my brother, and I was too busy to see him."

"Something serious has happened, then, to Mr. Roland ?"

"Something *very* serious, Mrs. Warren. It is a disagreeable subject, and I do not care to go into it. Let it suffice that I have discovered him to be wholly unworthy of my regard, and shall neither provide for him hereafter nor leave him anything in my will. This being the case, having already made full provisions for my brother, I shall have a handsome sum to bequeath to—to someone else. Within a few days I intend to have a lawyer here and re-arrange everything."

When Tom Hobbs came that evening, Mr. Linnette put on his very boldest front. Everything must now depend upon one cast of the die.

"You've often called me an old fool, Tom," he said, quietly. "You can't say anything much worse when I tell you what I am going to do next."

Tom was engaged at the moment in the important occupation of cutting tobacco for his pipe. He nodded his head, without looking up.

"I'm going to marry !"

Hobbs raised his eyes just enough to dart a look of contempt at his companion.

"You don't suppose that's any surprise to me," he said. "How many times have I said your housekeeper would pull the wool over your eyes and get to be mistress of this place, before she had done with you ?"

The error was a natural one, but Mr. Linnette bit his lip as he heard it.

"Well, for once, you were wrong," he replied.

"Wrong ?" echoed Hobbs, amazed.

"Wrong. It is not Mrs. Warren that I am to wed."

The superintendent was completely nonplussed. For a moment he felt a sensation resembling regret. If Linnette was bound to marry, Mrs. Warren would do as well as anyone else. She was at least used to his moods, his manner of living, and acquainted to a certain degree with his business. Hobbs did not like to contemplate a strange woman there, altering everything to suit her own tastes, and his employer had denied the suggestion of Eva so vehemently on a previous occasion that he never once thought of her.

"Not—your—housekeeper!"

Linnette laughed a little. He was becoming reckless. He meant to defy the entire universe, in the person of old Tom Hobbs. His superintendent undoubtedly represented popular opinion on this matter. All Montvale would have said the same. What business had Hobbs, or Montvale, to pick out Mrs. Warren for him? Could he not decide on his own wife, without their interference?

"No," he said, decidedly, and not without a tinge of malice. "It is not Mrs. Warren that I am thinking of marrying."

"Then you are a bigger fool than I took you to be," snarled Hobbs. "To marry her would prove you short of common sense, but to take another woman would show that you had become completely daft."

The man of wealth listened with no sign of disapproval. He was used to this blunt man and expected nothing less from him.

"Thanks," he responded, with polite irony. "And what would you call me if I were to tell you that the woman I mean to wed is her daughter?"

At this remark the slight control which Hobbs had retained of his temper gave way entirely.

"*A villain!*" he cried.

Linnette's manner changed like lightning at the appellation. He lost color and his voice grew stern.

"Take care!" he said, icily.

Hobbs was excited. He rose to his feet and took a dozen steps up and down the room. Then he turned to Mr. Linnette, and begged him, with the utmost earnestness, to admit that he did not mean what he said.

"Only tell me you were joking," he pleaded, "and I will—yes, I will even beg your pardon!"

Never had Mr. Linnette seen his superintendent in such a mood. He had not believed that an occasion could arise when Hobbs would admit, under any circumstances, that he had been in the wrong.

"I never meant anything more in my life," he said, coldly. "And let me add that if the announcement does not please you I cannot help it. I am old enough to manage my own business."

Hobbs was still struggling with his incredulity.

"*Old* enough!" he ejaculated. "God knows you are *old* enough! But this child—this school-girl—"

"She is eighteen," interrupted his companion.

"And she has *consented?*"

Linnette paused for some seconds before ne answered.

"I have not yet proposed to her; but, do you think she will refuse?"

No, Hobbs did not think so. He could see in

imagination the bauble dangling before her eyes—
the million dollars that would bait the hook.

"What does her mother say?" he asked, like one
who catches at a straw.

"Her mother is a sensible woman. She will not be
likely to stand in the way of her daughter's advancement."

Hobbs, in his wrath, shook his clenched fist at the
air.

"Advancement!" he cried. "God, Will Linnette! You drive me crazy!"

The man addressed vouchsafed no reply to this
exclamation. He was becoming angrier every minute
at the attitude taken—an attitude, he told himself,
that the world at large would be sure to copy.

"I've thought, a hundred times," continued Hobbs,
speaking as if the words choked him, "that the time
would come when you would marry the mother and
the girl would get your nephew. But—"

He stopped, appalled by the savage gleam in his
employer's eyes.

"Never speak to me of that boy again!" thundered
the latter. "He has interfered between me and one
of my clerks, insulted me, called me every name he
could lay his tongue to, abused and threatened me!
And that is not the greatest offence of which he has
been guilty. Before he left Montvale he entered
these grounds at night, in collusion with a servant,
and was admitted to Miss Eva's apartment!"

Hobbs stared at the speaker until it seemed as if
his eyes were frozen in their sockets.

"Who told you that last lie?" he demanded.

"Oh, I know *some* things!" was the retort. "I *saw* him enter the house, with her maid as his escort, and I saw him leave it an hour later. Then I stopped him in the road on his way back to the village, and charged him with it; and he had not a word to say for himself."

There was no questioning this direct evidence, and Hobbs decided to change the manner of his attack.

"And you tell me that you mean to marry a girl like that!" he exclaimed. "A girl who admits a young man to her chamber at night!"

Willard Linnette had not thought of the matter in this light. He had only considered the offense as his nephew's. It now occurred to him that he must have come by Eva's invitation. The color left his face and he was quite pale.

"You happened to discover *this* visit," said Hobbs, pushing his advantage, like a skillful general, at the point where his adversary's line was weakest. "By some accident you learned of that one call, but how can you tell there were not fifty others that escaped your observation?"

Linnette was plainly staggered by this suggestion.

"A man should select his wife of different material than this," pursued the other, relentlessly. "Your nephew was here at the hotel for three weeks while you were out of town. For all you know he may have gone to see her every night. If her maid could let him in once she could again. Don't let your infatuation blind your eyes completely."

Mr. Linnette drew a long breath that was full of pain.

" 'Love laughs at locksmiths,' " continued Hobbs, " and every post-office holds one of his representatives.  You have sent the boy away, but you can't keep them from corresponding."

Linnette shook as if he had the ague.  He knew the correspondence had begun, not by his nephew, either, but by Eva.  What terrible thing was this pressing upon his brain ?  Could it be that Hobbs had a basis for his insinuation ?  Was this girl, instead of the innocent creature she appeared, a scheming adventuress of depraved character ?  It was true he had seen Roland enter the house but once, but was it at all likely this was his only call there ?  No, he could not bear it ; anything was better than these horrible suspicions.  And he burst out that he would know the truth—that he would go that instant to seek the girl and force her to tell him the facts with her own lips.

But this was the last thing that Hobbs wanted him to do at that time.  As Mr. Linnette rose to leave the room he stopped him.

" Don't be foolish," he said, impressively.  " There is but one way in which you can preserve the honor of your establishment.  In the first place you must give up your senseless plan of marrying this child, and next you must compel your nephew to right the wrong he has done."

But Linnette lost his temper at this, and swore roundly that Roland's name must never again be mentioned in his presence.  If that boy had done anything criminal—anything reflecting on Miss Warren's good name—he would see that he was punished, not rewarded.  But he did not believe it, and he was going to see her at once and satisfy himself that it was untrue.

"You will probably make a mess of it," growled Hobbs.  "You had better let me go with you."

This offer was refused sharply.

"Then I will wait here," said the imperturbable man.

"You can do as you please."

Linnette went into the parlor and summoned a servant, whom he despatched for Charlotte.  When the maid arrived he inquired if her mistress was to be found in her apartment.

"Yes, sir," said the maid.  "But," she added, not liking the strange look on the master's face, "she is about to retire."

"I am going to see her," was the brief statement Mr. Linnette made.

"In her room?" exclaimed the maid, with vivid color.

Mr. Linnette bent toward her and spoke with a volume of meaning.

"It will not be the first time she has received a man there, as you know well.  She is not undressed, I suppose?"

"N-o, sir," replied Charlotte, frightened at his words.

"Then I shall go.  You need not accompany me. And, unless you wish to leave this house to-morrow, you will say nothing to anyone."

# CHAPTER XVIII.

### BEGINNING ALL OVER.

When Roland Linnette and Guy Dalton walked out of the office of the Montvale Optical Company, neither was in a very comfortable frame of mind.

Dalton was by far the most distressed. He could not help feeling that he had wrecked the prospects of his benefactor. It grieved him to the utmost that his proffered sacrifice had not been accepted as the best solution of the unhappy business. His own loss, that of his situation, seemed trivial beside his friend's misfortune. It was a terrible thing that such a rupture should have happened between Mr. Linnette and his nephew.

Roland, on the contrary, was too indignant to think consecutively. His uncle's conduct appeared to him entirely indefensible. Proposing to open a letter directed to another person was, in his opinion, the depth of meanness. As to Eva Warren, her mother's employer had no right to interfere with her actions in the way he had attempted to do. She was not his child, nor was he in a legal sense her guardian. The young man was stung again at the recollection of the ignominious manner in which he had been driven from Montvale. He had persuaded himself that his consent to obey his uncle's peremptory order was obtained quite as much from fear of injuring Eva as from care for his own interests. As

they walked along toward his rooms he lashed himself into a rage over his injuries.

"Confound the man, did he take me for a fool !"
he cried. "I should think by the way he talked he
considered me about five years old. The deuce take
him and his money ! I'm heartily glad to be rid of
both. I will get work and eat the bread of indepen-
dence. Yes, Guy, and when I can earn enough for
two, I will bring that charming girl from Montvale
and divide the loaf with her."

Guy, who had been through the experience of
looking for a situation, was not so confident. But
he did not mean to discourage his companion, whom
he believed much wiser and abler than himself.
Accordingly, he concealed his apprehensions, and said
they must sit down as soon as possible and form a
regular plan of action.

"We'll do it," said Roland, briskly. "Come into
the house with me and let us study out our problem
together."

Seated in the cosy parlor of the suite, they soon set
themselves to the task before them.

"To begin with," said Roland, "I shall have to
give notice that I'm going to move. They have the
assurance to charge me a hundred dollars a month
for this little box, which will certainly be beyond my
means now. I don't know exactly where I shall dispose of my time and talents, but it's very unlikely the
emoluments will justify this rate of expense at present. I shall have to pack these traps away somewhere, hire a furnished bedroom, and browse around
in boarding houses for my meals. Ugh ! it makes

me shiver! What do you suppose I'm fit for? Never mind. I've a lot of pluck, and they say the world owes every man a living. Wait a minute, now, till I send a letter to my landlord."

He went to a handsome desk and took out some elegant stationery, upon which he began to write.

"It must be awfully dreary in a furnished room," he said, pausing in the midst of his labor. "I shall never stay in it except when I'm a-bed or getting in or out. Is there anything to let over on Tenth Avenue? By George!" he exclaimed, springing gaily to his feet. "I have an idea!"

Dalton was the picture of interest. It is the nature of drowning men to catch at straws.

"Why not take a cheap flat?" said Roland, putting down his pen. "I have things enough to furnish all but the kitchen. Then, if we could get a house-keeper, we should at least have the satisfaction of knowing how our food was cooked. With two of us to divide the cost, it wouldn't be so recklessly expensive. Besides, if we got nervous, there would be several rooms to promenade in. And it would be a kind of home, which a mere lodging never is. What do you say?"

"It would be very nice, if the cost was low enough," responded Dalton, doubtfully.

Roland scratched the top of his head for a few minutes with the handle of a paper cutter. All at once he uttered a war-whoop.

"Tra-la-la-la-la! I have it! Don't say a word! Nothing could be finer. She is working for hardly enough to pay for her board and room, and she would certainly come. Yes, there is no question about it !"

Dalton shook his head in a puzzled way, wondering if his companion's troubles had unsettled his reason.

" Of whom are you talking ?" he asked.

" Why—how stupid you can be when you like !—Maud, of course. She's living a miserable life between that millinery shop and her poorly furnished chamber. She has been in a hotel and ought to make a famous housekeeper. We could hire the harder things done by those women who go around by the day, but as the presiding genius of our flat she would be adorable ! She'd come, wouldn't she ?"

Guy colored, as was his wont when women were the subject of discussion ; but he rallied presently, and replied that he believed Miss Arline might consider the matter.

" Consider it ?" laughed Roland. " She'll jump at it, if only for the chance of seeing you oftener. I believe you have quite fascinated her, by this time. Honor bright, between us, isn't she in love with you ?"

Guy did not give an answering smile to the one on the face of his friend, but he replied, very calmly, that he thought Maud liked him.

" Think !" cried Roland. " Hang it, don't you know ?"

" Yes," said the other, in his straightforward way. " I know."

Roland gazed at him with intense curiosity. He

wondered how far things had gone. He knew they were in the habit of meeting almost every evening. The pretty Maud! How shy she had been at Mont-vale, hardly daring to sit at the table with him, blushing when he addressed her, ready to faint when he hinted that he would like to touch her cheek with his lips. Sweet Maud! Innocent little Maud!

"Then that is settled," he said, rousing himself. "What a nice party we three will make. We shall have a common purse. There's not likely to be too much in it, but we'll share all there is. Do you consent to that? Shall we divide everything—all but the kisses of Miss Maud, which, it is understood, belong exclusively to you?"

Guy felt distressed as he heard these words. What would be Roland's attitude toward Maud, if they became one family? If he should make obnoxious advances, nothing could prevent a rupture, not even the recollection of old obligations.

"I'm afraid," he replied, ignoring the unpleasant part of his friend's remarks, "that I shall get the best of the bargain, if we have one pocketbook. You'll be sure to bring in much more than I. You have a number of acquaintances in the city, while I have absolutely none."

Linnette laughed lightly.

"We are equal on that score," said he. "I would starve to death before I would ask for help. No, we must depend on ourselves entirely. But my rent is going on at a fearful rate and I must send this letter to my landlord. After that we can take an account of stock."

Ringing a bell he placed the letter in the hands of a servant.

"A fortnight from to-day," he said, smiling, when the man had disappeared, "we shall have to do our own errands. These electric contrivances with a messenger on the end are really too luxurious and debilitating. Now, let us see what we have on which to begin our independent existence. We will empty our pockets and learn the worst."

In spite of the sober thoughts that afflicted him, Guy could not help being affected by his friend's gaiety. He found on investigation that he had the sum of $17.29, while Roland had $92.25. The latter counted the money in great glee, and remarked that is was much better than nothing.

"You are quite rich, compared with me," Guy remarked, regretfully.

"Ah, but my liabilities are greater. I shall have to pay fifty dollars on these rooms, before I can get out of them. Give up your chamber on the shortest possible notice and come here. That will save a little. I have a few rings, a gold watch and a diamond pin that will bring something. As we are to be so very economical Maud might come here also," he added, with a laugh, "if she could content herself with a sofa."

Guy rose, uneasy at this turn in the conversation.

"I will go home now and prepare to move," he said. "I will speak to Miss Arline about the house-keeping matter, when I meet her to-night for dinner. I am very, very sorry to have been the means of making trouble between you and your uncle," he continued, with a tremor in his voice. "Perhaps, when you have slept over it, you will feel like trying to make up with him."

"D—n him!" was the reply. "I am only too glad to be rid of him, to be able to do as I please.. But—what a crazy pair we are!—you have not read your letter yet, the one that made all the row."

It was true. The letter was still slumbering in Guy's pocket, where he had placed it when first handed to him. He took it out now and offered it to his companion, but Roland insisted that as it was directed to him he must read it. Persuaded by this logic, Guy opened the envelope and found its contents to be as follows:

"DEAR SIR:—Are you able to inform me of the present address of Mr. Roland Linnette? If so, you will confer a great favor. Please send your reply to 'W. E.,' Care of Mrs. Susan Merrill, Montvale.

"Yours Sincerely, EVA WARREN."

"Not very touching, is it?" laughed Roland, as he perused the letter. "Well, with your permission, I will answer it myself. She shall know the little scrape she has got me into. My uncle can't keep her from writing, as I see, if Charlotte continues true. I'll send a reply in time for the evening mail and she'll get it by noon to-morrow. Mrs. Merrill's name shows that she does not dare to have anything sent direct to the house. To avoid interference at this end of the road I will give her my new street and number. Don't forget to call to-morrow morning. *Au revoir, mon ami!*"

# CHAPTER XIX.

## IN EVA'S CHAMBER.

Roland's letter reached Eva, as he expected, on the noon of the day following the one on which it was written. It was composed in his best vein, and divided between a narration of what had happened in his uncle's office and a series of solemn declarations that he meant to make himself worthy of "the only girl he had ever cared for." Eva felt a great elation as she read it. How noble it was of him, to make such a sacrifice! He had given up fortune, comfort, ease—everything—for her dear sake. How different this from the picture his uncle had drawn!

"Now that you are able to communicate with me, through the assistance of your friend, Mrs. Merrill," he wrote, "we shall be able to nerve each other for every trial that enemies may put in our way. Have Mrs. M. write on your envelopes, and send your letters to the address and name which I enclose. That will make all perfectly safe both at Montvale and here. My uncle has evidently determined to keep you from me, if he can. He may try to fill your head with the most awful stories, but don't believe him. I have not always been a saint, which I lament sincerely; but I shall be true to you, whatever happens. Keep me informed of all that transpires. I shall await your replies with the utmost eagerness. As soon as fate smiles on my endeavors, rest assured I shall come for you."

Eva read this, first to herself and then to Charlotte. She could not resist the inclination to share her secret with some feminine breast, and she had the most perfect confidence in her maid.

"Oh, it is so sweet to be loved!" she cried, ecstatically. "This is what I wanted all the time instead of those dreadful powders and potions. See how much better my complexion is, how much more color I have. I hope he will not make me wait too long. I want very little—only a piece of bread and a roof to cover me, but in his arms I should forget even hunger and cold."

The next hour was taken up in discussing the matter, Charlotte looking on the bright side, like her mistress, and predicting that all would come out right in the end. Then Eva took her pen and poured out her soul to her lover. In the innocent freedom of her heart she kept back nothing. She did not hesitate to declare that she had never known happiness till now, to vow eternal fidelity, even to admit that she longed for the hour when he would be her own in deed and truth. Sneer not at her, my dear young lady reader. She had not acquired your power of concealing her feelings. She did not understand why she should be less frank than the man she had promised to wed.

When her letter was finished and crowded into its envelope she affixed two stamps, knowing that it must be over-weight. Charlotte took the missive to her relation, Mrs. Merrill, who wrote the address as requested and put it in the mail box.

The rest of the afternoon was passed by Eva in a delirium of bliss. She played for more than an hour on the piano, chanting a love-song that she found among her music. The words had meant nothing to her when the piece first came into the house. Now each fond expression referred distinctly to Roland, and she sang it over and over again.

At supper she noticed that Mr. Linnette said little, but for a long time he had not talked as much as he used at the table. Mrs. Warren was not equal to carrying the main burden of a conversation, and as Eva had nothing to say, the meal was passed in almost total silence. When it was ended Eva went back to her sitting-room, ensconced herself in a comfortable chair, and after reading Roland's letter through again, and kissing it many times, plunged into the pages of a love-story that Charlotte had found for her in the library.

The book was so suited to her frame of mind that she read a long time. She was accustomed to require the services of her maid at frequent intervals, for in that house she had grown accustomed to all the attentions usually given to a young lady of wealth. But this evening, falling into a reverie that she did not wish disturbed, she removed her clothing without assistance. Then, donning a white night-dress, and slipping over it a chamber gown, she put a pair of worsted slippers on her stocking-less feet, and curled up in the easy chair again.

Her hair floated about her shoulders like a clouu. She meant to have Charlotte braid it before she went to sleep, but for the present the novel filled all her thoughts. There was a young man in it that made her think of Roland, and—wonder of wonders! —a cruel uncle who threatened to disinherit him if he married against his will. But the young man— exactly like Roland again—declared on every third page that nothing should win him from the girl he loved.

There came a tap at the door. What a nuisance! Charlotte should know better than to appear when she was not rung for. Eva was at the most entertaining part of the story.

"Come in!" she called, without lifting her eyes from the page. As the door swung slowly open she added, "Sit down, and don't speak till I finish this chapter. I never read anything so interesting. It seems exactly like my own case."

It was not Charlotte, but Willard Linnette. He had come straight from his conference with Tom Hobbs, resolved to take this girl to task for her conduct in reference to his nephew, and to wring from her a confession as to its extent. He was not going to be made a fool of by this child any longer. She should not aid his graceless nephew to insult him. He would soon decide whether his fortune should go to her, or whether she was as unworthy as the one he had disinherited.

He had loved this girl. He had been mad over her. He had been very near to bringing on himself the derision of the world, as an old man who had succumbed to the charms of a child. For three years he had seen nothing but her beauty, he had cared for nothing so much as her smile. It was Tom Hobbs who had revealed to him the extent of his devotion— the fact that he loved her so dearly that he wanted to clasp her in his arms as his wedded wife! But there are limitations to what even love can endure.

If the last guess Hobbs had made was correct, if she had been more to his nephew than a virtuous girl should be, he would find it out. If she was determined to correspond with that young scoundrel, she had only to say so, and he would have done with her. Very likely he had been on the verge of idiocy over her charms, but that was ended. He would know, before he left her room, whether she was still worthy his affection and esteem, or whether he must cast her out of his heart.

These were the thoughts that traversed his mind as he came through the hallway and ascended the stairs. But, as he opened the door, in response to her voice, his resolutions weakened. He knew, when his glance rested upon her, that she had not intended to admit anyone but her mother or Charlotte. The floating hair, the negligé costume, the pose, all told him this. Still he did not retreat, nor did he inform her of her error. He was glad to have a minute in which to recover himself. They had been such intimate friends that he did not believe the condition of her dress would disturb her unduly, when she discovered her mistake. He must talk to her, *now;* he could not wait another hour. So he closed the door softly behind him and took his chair near it, awaiting her pleasure.

The first glance decided one great point. He could not look at that sweet face and think anything but innocence rested there. She had been guilty of no graver fault than indiscretion. Hobbs was a wretch to suggest such a possibility. Mr. Linnette's harsh thoughts began to fade away. He knew he could not say half he had meant to, nor could he assume the dictatorial tone he had intended to use. Before she raised her eyes from the book, he wished heartily that he had taken more time before rushing so heedlessly into her presence.

A low sigh escaped the girl's lips as she finished the chapter. Her hero had not yet had the happiness of pressing the pretty heroine to his breast. A hundred barriers rose before them at every turn, intensely aggravating to the fair young reader, who would have preferred to have them married in the first chapter and relegated to a life of bliss forever after.

"Well, Charlotte,"—she began.

When she saw who her visitor was, she rose from her chair with a look that was far from welcoming.

"Mr. Linnette," she said, "I am surprised that you should come into my room in this manner. If you wished to see me, you could have sent me word."

He was not pleased at the extreme haughtiness with which she spoke. She need not wholly forget, he thought, what she owed to his bounty. His temper had been severely tried during the past two days, and again it mastered him.

"Why this distinction?" he answered, coldly. "I knew you were in the habit of receiving gentlemen here—"

The attack was begun, almost before he knew it. He had entered on a campaign from which there was no retreat. With one great flash of flame he had burned his bridges behind him.

The girlish face lit up with indignation.

"Gentlemen!" she repeated.

He knew that she questioned the plural, but he seized his opportunity.

"I beg your pardon," he said. "The term was too complimentary."

The girl's bosom rose and fell rapidly.

"If a person ever came here," she replied, "it was not without an invitation, nor was I compelled to receive him in such attire as this. He may or may not be a 'gentleman,' according to the interpretation put upon that word. To-day, thanks to you, he is a penniless seeker after work with which to support himself. But it requires something more than money to make a true gentleman; and I feel justified in adding that your present conduct does not stamp you as one."

She had heard from Roland. Her words proved that. She was resolved to remain his friend. This was attested by her manner.

"Your words are meaningless," he replied, his heart growing harder. "It matters little whether you wear one dress or another, whether my coming is announced or not.  What I have to say to you is of the utmost moment, and must not be delayed an instant longer."

She shrugged her shoulders, as if to intimate that he might go on, if he was willing to do so after the protest she had made.  Wrapping her peignoir closer around her, and making sure that her feet were invisible, she turned a passionless face toward him.

"You have lived in my house," continued Mr. Linnette, "for three years.  You have had everything that I could give you.  There has been nothing—"

"Let us consider that understood," she interrupted.  "And let me remind you that it detracts greatly from the value of a gift when the recipient is reminded of it."

The old man's brows contracted.

"I have never alluded to it before," he retorted, "and I only do so now because it is a necessary prelude to what I intend to say."

"If the rest is not more agreeable than the prelude, I hope it will be brief," was her calm reply.

At that he broke forth hotly that he had a right to speak to her ; that he was in effect the guardian of her reputation ; that he should be remiss in his duty when he found her making a serious mistake if he did not inform her of it.  He then went on, not giving her time to interrupt him, to speak of Miss Arline, whom he said he had sent away from Montvale to save her from Roland.  He alluded to the collection of photographs which his nephew had brought home from Europe, of his hundred sweethearts in foreign lands, "white, black, yellow and brown." He declared that no good girl was safe in his company. Roland was capable of making love until her head was turned, and then deserting her without mercy. Lately he had conducted himself in such a manner that his uncle felt obliged to cast him off.

Then he referred to the visit his nephew had made her. He said Roland knew—acquainted with the world as he was—that he had committed a most flagrant breach of good morals ; and the speaker averred that no man could do less than denounce such an act, though the perpetrator were one of his nearest blood relations.

Eva listened to all this without changing her position, and with no evidence of special surprise. When Mr. Linnette paused for breath she kept perfect silence.

"What have you to say ?" he demanded.

"Nothing."

"You do not object to these things !"

"I do not believe them."

He had expected anything but this cool response. It was almost as if she had called him a liar in set terms.

"He has bewitched you !" he cried.

A smile came over her pretty mouth.

"I think you are right," she replied. "I love Roland too much to credit anything against him."

What a wall of adamant she was !

"Supposing I showed you proofs ?"

"I would not look at them."

"If I brought you witnesses ?"

"I would not listen."

These answers made him quite beside himself with rage.

"You shall never lower yourself by marrying that boy!" he exclaimed. "And I will tell you another thing: I have arranged to have my will re-drawn, so that you should inherit my wealth, which he has forfeited by his conduct. If you persist in this insane folly I will give you nothing!"

Eva laughed, actually laughed at him.

"When Roland is ready he will come for me," she said. "He will come for me, and I shall go with him. He is under no obligations to you now. You cannot frighten him any more. Yes, you may as well understand."

Mr. Linnette stared stupidly at the girl.

"Would you give up a million dollars for him?" he asked, gutturally.

"Indeed, yes! A hundred millions!"

It rose to his lips to tell her that she might go from under his roof at once; that he would harbor such an ungrateful thing no longer; but he restrained himself. Before proceeding to such an extremity he wanted to talk with Mrs. Warren.

He rose, hesitated a moment, tried to speak, and then left the chamber. He had accomplished nothing, and less than nothing.

And Tom Hobbs knew as much, before a word was spoken, when his employer re-entered the library and found him there, smoking his pipe in silence.

# CHAPTER XX.

### "CONFOUND HIS MONEY!"

When Guy met Maud Arline on the evening following the troubles in Mr. Linnette's office he gave her a rather full account of what had occurred there, besides narrating as much as was necessary of the circumstances which had led up to the final catastrophe. The girl listened silently as he told the story of Eva Warren, of Roland's wild infatuation for her, of his uncle's wrath, of the letter sent to his care, and of the complete rupture between the relations. She hardly tasted the food set before her, though her appetite for the palatable French dinner which they were now in the habit of taking together was generally good. Guy was flattered by the close attention she gave him, and rattled on for fully ten minutes, pausing only long enough to take an occasional mouthful of the soup or fish.

"I was so sorry that I didn't know what to do," he said, after describing the manner in which Roland and he had left the office. "He says I'm not the least bit to blame, but I can't help thinking I am."

He looked at Maud as if he wanted her opinion on the subject, and she replied, in a low voice, that she could not see how he could have acted differently.

"I am glad to hear you say so," said he, as if relieved. "He has done so much for me that I shall always feel indebted to him. But now I have something to tell you that will, it is possible, interest you even more than the recital I have already made. It concerns yourself."

Maud roused herself from the lethargy into which she had fallen and inquired what Dalton meant.

"When we found ourselves, both together, thrown out upon the world," he answered, "we went down to his rooms and held a council of war. The agreement that we reached was to share everything we had and all we could earn, for he is going to look for work as well as I. Our greatest watchword necessarily being economy, we began to consider what was the most frugal way of living, outside of a cheap boarding-house, which Roland would not think of for a moment. We finally decided to rent a low-priced flat, and to engage a housekeeper."

The girl's eyes opened wider as she heard this statement. Guy noticed their peculiar expression, and stopped to inquire whether she saw any objections to the plan.

"I am afraid a good housekeeper, such as you would require, is not the easiest thing to find," she said. "You need an experienced woman, to begin with ; one who would look out for your interests ; and you could not afford, I suppose, to pay very high wages."

Guy was obliged to laugh at her description.

"I think we know just where the right person can be found," he replied. " She certainly has had experience, for she was employed several months in a country hotel.   She would look out for our interests, because she knows us intimately and would share our home on equal terms.   As for compensation, she is not at the present time earning much more than her living.   She would be much better off managing a home of her own, for such it really would be, besides doing a genuine kindness to two stranded young men."

It was more than a minute before Maud spoke again.   She could not fail to understand that he referred to her, and at first she shrank from the proposition with a vague dread.   More than this, she did not know as she had a right to live under the same roof with Mr. Linnette's nephew.   It was hardly keeping faith with his uncle.   However, since their rupture, the latter would have little further interest in him so far as she was concerned.

She remembered also, very vividly, the nervous tension at which Roland had kept her when she officiated as his waitress at Montvale.   But if he was as deeply in love with Miss Warren as his actions implied, he would not be likely to trouble her much. To tell the truth, she was very tired of her milliner's shop, where the promised advance in wages had not materialized.   Her solitary room—when Guy was not there—was excessively lonely.   The only bright spot in her existence was the dinners they took together, and these would be lost if he adopted his housekeeping plan and she did not share it.   It would be delightful, after the discomforts she had suffered, to have a home, no matter how poor or humble.

"You mean me," she said, looking up at her companion.

"Yes," he replied, earnestly, "that is just what I mean. Roland was the one who first thought of you, but I saw in an instant what a fine thing it would be. Neither of us has anything to brag of in the way of expectations, but we shall do our best. If you say it is settled we will look for a flat immediately, and begin to pick out the pans and kettles for your new kitchen."

Maud wanted to think of the matter for another day, but Guy was so persistent, and represented the scheme in such bright colors, that before he left her that night she had given her full consent.

Within a week the flat was secured, a set of diminutive rooms up three flights of stairs on Sixth Street, overlooking some picturesque if not over-clean back yards of the neighborhood. When Roland's furniture was moved in, and the necessary purchases made, the place looked remarkably cosy. There was a striking incongruity between some of the expensive things he brought and some of the very cheap ones they had to purchase, but all three of the new tenants were in too good humor to find anything but amusement in this fact. A diamond pin had been sacrificed at the first start to replenish the exchequer, and it was announced with positive glee that a balance of $77 was in the treasury, with everything paid for, including an advance month's rent of the premises.

It was admitted on all sides that Maud developed wonderful capacity. Roland declared with enthusiasm that he had never dined better, even in the days when he made the grand tour. The coffee she prepared in the morning was decidedly superior, he solemnly averred, to that served by any *femme de chambre* in dear Paree. He liked to sit in the kitchen and watch her, with her sleeves rolled up, at the dish-pan or the bread-board, when Guy was out scouring the town in search of something to do. And his manners were so good, and his temper so equable, that he became as agreeable a companion as could be asked.

He had a shrewd way of seeming to admit Guy's proprietorship in Maud, though he never actually made any allusion to it. Believing that they enjoyed themselves better alone, he got into the habit, when the six o'clock dinner was over, of going out " to see a friend," and seldom returning before ten at the earliest. But if he heard that Guy intended to walk out with Maud, he would take a book or magazine and settle himself in their bijou of a parlor, announcing that he would spend the evening at home. The apprehensions that Dalton had felt were soon lulled into perfect repose by the admirable conduct of his friend.

Though Roland did not apply in person for any situation, he wrote a number of letters in response to newspaper advertisements. One of the reasons he gave for remaining at home so much during the day was that he wanted to be in when the mail arrived. If he were sent for in haste, he wished to be ready to respond. But the letters he deposited in the box over the way were much more numerous than those which the postman brought. The only one he was sure of came three times a week from Montvale and was answered as regularly.

In one of these letters he learned of the visit that Mr. Linnette made to Eva, though she did not give a full account of all that passed between them. " He assured me," she wrote, " that you were a very naughty fellow, but I refused to listen, though I fear he had some basis of truth for what he wanted to say. I told him to his face that I loved you ; that nothing would ever make me change ; and that as soon as you were ready for me I should marry you. Then he threatened, saying that he had intended to leave *me* all his money, but that now I shall get nothing. As if that would make any difference ! I fear he will be unpleasant to Mamma, and perhaps she will join forces with him. People used to say he meant to marry her. I wish he would, for she worries me very much. She is so afraid of poverty that she lies awake nights thinking of it. Keep up good courage, darling. All will come out right in time."

In a subsequent letter she made the interesting statement that Tom Hobbs had asked Charlotte for Roland's address, and that the girl, suspecting some trick of Mr. Linnette's, had given him an evasive reply, pretending that she did not know it. This set Roland to thinking. He had known Tom from babyhood. They had been unusually good friends, and he did not believe anything would persuade the old man to injure him. If Hobbs wanted his address it must be for some good reason. At dinner that evening he talked the matter over with Dalton.

"He is a shrewd old fellow," said he, "and there is a possibility that he has something of importance to tell me. He's a poor hand at letter writing, and the best way to get at the bottom of the matter would be to see him personally. But the trouble is he's not much of a traveller. He would consider a journey to New York as serious a matter as I should one to Australia. I don't think he's been ten miles from Montvale in thirty years. For me to go to him has its difficulties and dangers. So you see I really don't know what to do."

Dalton looked as if the problem was too deep for him, while Maud, on the other side of the table, expressed sympathy in her sober face.

"I say, Guy! Couldn't *you* run up there for a day or two?" exclaimed Roland, suddenly.

"I?" said Dalton.

"To be sure. You would not run the slightest risk. Hobbs may have something to say that we ought to hear. And then—I could even arrange an interview for you with Eva! They will not watch her so closely when they know I'm out of town."

Guy was much confused at these propositions. It was not at all clear that he could accomplish anything by the journey. But he wanted to please Roland, and he responded at once that he would go.

"I shall be only too happy," he said. "Tell me what you wish me to do."

Miss Arline moved her chair back a little from the table, and waited for the conversation to proceed. The young men had no secrets from her.

"Here is the case," said Roland, in a business-

like tone. "My uncle has threatened me with disin·
heritance. When I told him to go to the devil with
his money, and give it to whom he pleased, he replied that he meant to will it all to Miss Eva Warren. That did not sound so terribly, for in the
course of time I felt pretty certain to get it back
again. To prevent this possibility he has informed
the young lady that if she ever becomes my wife he
will cut her off also. Now," proceeded Roland,
placing both his elbows on the table, and looking
from one to the other of his auditors, " talk as we
may under the excitement of outraged pride, a million dollars is worth preserving if it can be done
without too great a sacrifice. It appears that Tom
Hobbs has some communication to make to me
Tom has an immense influence over Mr. Willard
Linnette. My uncle would do nothing so important
as the making of a new will without consulting Tom.
In my opinion that is exactly what the superintendent wants to see me about. I will send him a note
by you, asking him to unveil the whole affair. Then
if it turns out to be anything requiring my presence
I shall go at once."

Guy was rather surprised to see Roland's anxiety
about his uncle's fortune, remembering the haughty
way in which he had flung the gauntlet at his kinsman's feet. It was true, however, as he said, that
one might get over-excited and think better of
things, when time had cooled him off. The ill-luck
in finding a situation where he could earn something,
had, no doubt, affected his views.

“ Do you wish me to indicate in what way you would modify your position ?” asked Guy.

“ Modify my position !”

“ Yes, in order to save the money.”

Roland struck his fist heavily on the dining-table.

“ Confound his money ! I don’t want that old man to make a fool of himself, that’s all. When he threw me up I didn’t say a word. It’s a different thing when the loss is Eva’s. If I’m not to have the property I want her to get it.”

“ So that you can share it with her later,” said Dalton, insinuatingly.

Roland could not help laughing, like one detected in a sly game.

“ Well, that’s not so criminal, is it ?” he said. “ My uncle is growing aged. I don’t understand what has set him so severely against me. If he hadn’t acquired a prejudice from some unknown source he would never have been so violent. Hobbs knows him like a book and may have a key to the riddle.”

Guy indicated his belief that this might prove true, and the pair then proceeded to plan a way by which he could meet Miss Warren.

“ What shall I say to her if I’m able to get within speaking distance ?” Guy asked.

“ Oh, I leave that to you,” was the reply. “ You know the entire situation. She will ask you a hundred questions, which you must use your judgment in answering. Touch lightly on the fact that I am still a distinguished member of the Knights of Rest. If she don’t think that any too creditable of me, and believes it’s easy to fall into a salaried position in this town, let her come here and try. Now, the sooner you go, the better. I am impatient to hear what Hobbs has to say. Why can't you start to-morrow?"

"I can," replied Dalton.

"And will you?"

"I will."

# CHAPTER XXI.

### GUY TAKES A JOURNEY.

The proprietor of Montvale was ill at ease. Though the postmaster and himself were thrown completely off the true scent by the plan which had been adopted, he felt certain that Eva was sending letters to his nephew and receiving replies. The girl's cheerfulness at the table, the only place where he now saw her, convinced him that he was being outwitted. Since the night when he went to her chamber she had only spoken to him in the briefest manner, and the quietness in the dining-room at meal-time was oppressive. Mrs. Warren, though she did her best, could not add anything to her employer's stock of information. Eva was uniformly courteous to her mother, but managed to evade a direct answer to all questions.

"What an idea!" she would exclaim, when the matter of letter-writing was mentioned. "Doesn't all the mail for the house pass through your hands?"

Mr. Linnette could not help talking occasionally about his troubles with old Tom Hobbs. He did not receive much sympathy from that eccentric person, but it was better even to be abused than to be without any confidant whatever. Thanks to Tom, the threatened changes in the will had not yet

been made. Hobbs insisted that the present was no
time for alterations. Mr. Linnette, he said, should
at least wait until he had made up his mind whom
to sacrifice and whom to benefit before he set his
lawyers at work.

There was so much sense in this suggestion that
the manufacturer could not help acting upon it ;
though he remarked, with a grimace, that it would
not be agreeable if some complaint should carry
him off, leaving all his property to be handed over
to his scamp of a nephew. To which Hobbs replied
that he did not look like a man liable to sudden
death, and that he was quite as likely to outlive
both his former intended beneficiaries as to precede
them to the other world.

While laboring to secure the longest delay possible, in the interest of Roland, for whom he had
always entertained a warm liking, Hobbs grew uneasy over the present financial condition of the
young man. He thought it a great hardship to be
deprived of his income, after the way he had been
brought up, with no alternative but work, or some
disreputable method of getting a living. If Roland
found the former plan too difficult, it was not impossible that he would be driven to the latter. It was
with this in mind that Hobbs tried to get Roland's
address from Eva's maid. He had lived a thrifty
life and had a snug little sum laid by. He wanted
to offer assistance out of his own funds to enable
Roland to tide over the emergency, which he could
not help believing would be only temporary.

To effect this result it was necessary to move with

caution. Willard Linnette would not be likely to fancy a direct interference in his affairs. Hobbs did not like Eva well enough to confide too much in her, and when his attempt failed with Charlotte he was at a total loss which way to turn. But one very dark night, just as he was about to retire, the door-bell of his house was rung. On being called he found Guy Dalton awaiting him, with a letter from the " young master " in his hand.

"And so he sent you, clear from New York !" said Hobbs, when he had read the brief note of intro-duction. " Come in and sit down. It's almost nine o'clock and I was going to bed. How did you get here so late ?  I suppose you came on the six o'clock, and have been to supper at the hotel ?"

" No, sir," replied Dalton. " I did not wish any-one at Montvale to see me ; so I left the train at Ellsworth, where I got a lunch, and then walked over."

Hobbs eyed him intently. He looked a great deal better than he used, when he was employed in the Works. Life in the city evidently agreed with him. It was a long walk from Ellsworth.

"Walked over ?" repeated Hobbs. " Why, it's seven miles !"

"It didn't seem so long. The walking is good. I didn't mind it at all. I expect to go over the same road again to-night when I leave you."

Hobbs protested that a walk of fourteen miles was altogether too long for anyone, but Guy smiled confidently, saying that he was quite used to it, and, in fact, enjoyed the prospect. He then, in response to inquiries, told the whole story of Roland's life since he left the village, including, with particular detail, an account of the trouble in his uncle's office.

"And doesn't he show the least desire to make up?" demanded the superintendent.

"No. But you must remember Mr. Linnette has made no overtures, either."

"They are the biggest pair of fools ever born!" replied Hobbs. "The old man is the worst one, of course, but the boy is not far behind him. When he knew what a crank his uncle was, why couldn't he agree to anything, no matter what, until the wind took another direction? A million dollars doesn't grow on every bush! I've had all I could do to stop the destruction of the will by which Linnette left his property to his nephew, which would leave in force an old one bequeathing everything to some cannibal missionaries."

Guy remarked, as an explanation of his friend's conduct, that he was devotedly attached to Miss Warren, and could not bear to see anyone insult a communication that she had written.

"Stuff!" ejaculated Hobbs. "Nothing but stuff! There are a thousand better girls, if he would only look about him. He's exactly like his uncle—always wanting what he can't have, *because* he can't have it. I've a good notion to tell you something—for your own information, mind you! not his. Can you keep a secret?"

Dalton replied that he thought he could.

"Then keep this one. Will Linnette, seventy years old as he is, loves that little girl himself. He

would marry her to-morrow if she would accept
him."

The listener was plainly shocked.

" Are you sure ?" he gasped.

" Sure ?  Don't I know him, soul and body ?  Was
there ever anything in his head he could keep from
me if he tried?  Look at his pretenses.  He brings
up his nephew's immoralities, and makes a great
fuss about them.  But he knew all that long ago
and passed them off for what they are, the peccadilloes of a young man.  Roland might have gone on
in his own way as long as he lived if he hadn't come
between the old man and his sweetheart.  Now, this
must be a secret between us.  I don't know what
would happen if Roland found it out."

Guy promised again to say nothing about the
matter.

" Well," continued Hobbs, " all this is not to the
point.  What is the boy living on, and how does he
expect to meet his bills ?"

To this inquiry Guy responded with the utmost
frankness.  He told how they had got along thus
far, but admitted that their funds were steadily
running lower and that there were no means in sight
for replenishing them.

" Then he must take a loan from me," said Hobbs,
with decision.  " I don't ask him to accept a gift,
but he must borrow what he needs until something
better turns up.  Tell him to write me, whenever he
wants anything, and I will see that he gets it."

The two men went out to the front yard together,

as Dalton said he must be going.  The night was not a clear one and they were unobserved.

"You weren't brought up around these parts, I take it," remarked the elder man, with an inquisitive inflection.

"No," said Guy.  "I used to live in Vermont."

"Ah!  I was up that way once.  It was a long while ago.  What town did you come from, now?"

"Ryegate."

Hobbs loosened his hold of the gate, which he had pulled back, and the spring slammed it in its place noisily.

"Sho!  You don't say.  There's several of them Ryegates.  It wasn't East Ryegate, was it?"

"Yes," was the listless reply.  "It was East Ryegate."

The moon peeped out of the clouds just enough to light the faces of the two men.  Guy was looking at the ground, impatient to be off, as he had another call to make that evening, and it was getting late.  Hobbs observed him with renewed interest.

"And your name is Dalton?" he said, interrogatively.

"Y-e-s."

"Did you ever hear," began Hobbs, slowly, "of a family up that way by the name of Lincoln?"

Guy raised his eyes, with quick suspicion in their gaze, and slowly responded in the affirmative.

"There were two women of that name there once," soliloquized the superintendent.  "One of them died, a long time ago.  The other—"

"Died, too."

"Did she?" said Hobbs. "How long ago was that?"

"Eight years, I should think," replied Dalton. Then he took several steps that brought him outside the gate, and with a short "Good-by," started on the Ellsworth road.

A village clock was striking ten. Guy felt reasonably certain that he had not been seen by any person except Mr. Hobbs, since entering the precincts of Montvale, the residents being of that rural order who have a proverb that no honest person is out of doors after nine at night. But though he started on the road to Ellsworth he did not long continue in that direction. As soon as he dared he bent his steps by a circuitous route to the rear of Willard Linnette's estate.

A letter from her lover had informed Eva Warren that Guy would be in Montvale that evening, and had asked her to see that Charlotte kept watch at the familiar door in the wall that had played such an important part before in the meetings of the young couple. The girl was more than anxious to communicate with this messenger, and no place seemed safer for the purpose than her own rooms, now again free from the suspicion of those who had watched her. The maid was on the alert, and her ears detected the first sound that was made on the panel. The visitor was smuggled through the darkness, and reached Eva's chamber without attracting the attention of anyone else.

As Guy's eyes fell on his hostess, he thought he had never seen anything so lovely. She was arrayed

entirely in white, her favorite.　Her complexion, re-
minding him of a creamy rose tinged with pink, set
off the bright eyes that glowed with pleasure and
anticipation.

"So this is Mr. Dalton?"

Charlotte had left the room promptly, and they
were quite alone.　In a moment they were talking
together on the matters in relation to which he had
come.　The girl's perfect self-possession made it
easy for him to converse with her.　He felt before
he had been in the house ten minutes as if he had
known her for years.　She told him her story in the
frankest manner, and asked him a thousand questions about Roland and himself.

Everything was progressing nicely, when Guy pre-
cipitated an entirely new phase of the discussion by
a slip of the tongue, the simple mention of the word
"Maud," in referring to the new household that the
young men had set up.

"Maud?" echoed the girl, quickly.

"Yes," he answered, realizing instantly that a new
quality had come into her voice.　"Our housekeeper."

"And Arline?" asked Eva.　"Is her name
Arline?"

Guy stammered that it was.

"She was at the Montvale House formerly, I believe," mused Eva.

He indicated that she was right in her statement.
And he wished heartily that he had been more
careful.

"How did they come together?" she inquired, suspiciously.

Finding that he had put his foot in it, Guy did the best he could by claiming Maud as his own friend. He went on to describe her situation in the great city, hardly able to earn enough to keep her body and soul together. He wanted to work on Eva's sympathies for a sister in distress, but only the belief that her lover had no connection with the matter would have allayed her rising resentment.

"Then it was you and not Roland who suggested her," she said, apparently much relieved. "Mr. Linnette told me their names were coupled in a hateful way while here ; and though, of course, I did not believe there was warrant for it, I am naturally surprised to hear they were living under the same roof—as one might say, in one family. It is strange," she added, musingly, " that he never spoke of her in any of his letters."

It flashed across Guy's mind at this moment that it *was* Roland who suggested the engagement of Miss Arline, and a spasm of doubt took possession of his brain.

"He may not have thought it of enough consequence," he replied, trying to crush the unpleasant feeling. "I did not know there was any talk about them here, though. When I was at the hotel I am sure I heard nothing."

Eva was suffering under the lash of disappointment that such an interesting bit of news should have come to her in this roundabout way. Roland had referred to his housekeeper, without giving the least intimation that he had ever known her before.

" This is what his uncle said to me," she answered. " She was asked to leave Montvale because Roland's influence over her was not good."

Up to this instant Dalton had placed not the least credence in this allegation. He had regarded it, in the words of his friend, as a ridiculous surmise on Willard Linnette's part. But now a hundred little things occurred to him that pointed in an opposite direction. He knew that Roland was no saint. He remembered that he had remained at home most of the time since the housekeeping had begun, under one pretext or another, thus being thrown into the unrestricted company of the young woman in question. As for Maud, it was almost impossible to believe anything really wrong of her, but who could say what influences one so used to charming members of her sex might have brought to bear ? In the collection of photographs which Roland had shown him there were faces as sweet as hers ; and yet—

"We have happened to exchange information of mutual interest," said Eva, with a smile, for she saw the frown that covered his brow, and wished to dissipate it as soon as possible. " I do not believe, however, that it is of much account. While it is true Mr. Linnette urged Mr. Hanson to send her away, and furnished the money, and gave the reason I have repeated, that proves nothing. He has taken a dislike to his nephew that renders him blind to reason. As it is evident Miss Arline does not share his fear— else she would not be where she is—we may as well call it a baseless charge and let it pass. Probably she was not unwilling to exchange the dull life she led here for the brighter prospects of-the city, and cared little how the exchange was made."

Dalton was silent. He detested double dealing from the bottom of his soul. While he meant to defend Roland to this girl, he doubted him more and more. Why had he picked out Maud to be their housekeeper? And was there anything in this journey on which they had sent him, leaving them so many hours alone?

"I can quite sympathize with her," pursued the musical voice of his companion. "I often feel that I would accept almost any terms to get away from this place. Her position is far preferable to mine, for she is free, while I am under constant surveillance. If release does not come soon I shall take matters into my own hands, and actually run away."

Guy could hardly answer her. If his suspicions were in the least justified he never would speak to Roland again. He rose, with the remark that it was time he set out on his walk to Ellsworth, if he was to catch the early train.

"You were kind to come," said Eva, sweetly. "I shall never forget it. It seems almost like meeting Roland. Tell him the sight of you, and what you have said to me, has given me new strength and patience. But tell him also," and the pink ran riot over her fair complexion, "that he must not make me wait *too* long."

These ingenuous words impressed Guy with her perfect innocence more than the most modest expressions could have done. Her nature was evidently wholly unspoiled and simple. Pressing his hand warmly Eva gave him into Charlotte's charge, and he escaped without detection by the avenue through which he had entered the grounds.

"He's a splendid fellow!" was Eva's comment, when her maid returned. "And did you notice how handsome he is? His eyes are really poetic, and his voice is as gentle as a woman's. I hope Roland will send him here again."

Then she added, after a momentary pause—

"You used to see Maud Arline, who lived at the hotel. What kind of a girl should you say she was?"

# CHAPTER XXII.

## ONE KISS TOO MANY.

It was only twenty hours from the time that Guy Dalton left New York when he returned to it. Only twenty hours that Roland and Maud had been together. But a great deal can be accomplished in twenty hours.

Roland did not plan anything, either. Guy was quite wrong in his surmise that a deep plot had been laid and that he was its victim. Nevertheless, the result was not pleasant to any of them, and all on account of the strangest coincidence imaginable.

To tell the truth, Roland intended to behave in the most perfect manner. He could not have acted better that first day had Maud been his sister. Lunch was taken at a restaurant, and when he returned he suggested a very simple meal for the evening, as he had eaten late and Guy was away. Anything handy would answer, he said. Then, as the girl began her preparations, he sat down near her, talking in the good-natured, familiar way to which she had grown accustomed.

As he watched her a sense of her beauty grew upon him. How little she depended upon artificial adornment! That was the true beauty—the kind that dress does not accentuate unduly. He made her talk about herself, and execrated with her the heartless guardian who had compelled her to seek her own livelihood the moment her little fortune was exhausted. The story was a very pathetic one, and Roland was moved to compassion and indignation in about equal measure.

"And then," he said, "when you found a shelter, my uncle had to interfere and send you away on the ground that I might fall in love with you. How absurd!"

Maud blushed to her finger-tips.

"He's a queer old fellow!" continued Roland. "I'd like to know what he does want. He must intend me for a bachelor, like himself. He's just as set against my loving his ward, you know, as he was against you. But I ought to do him partial justice. I *was* getting to be a little too fond of you, Maud."

The girl, whose hands were in the flour, making biscuit, cast a reproachful glance at the speaker.

"It is unkind to say that," she remarked, in a low voice.

He rose and took a step toward her, with a very sober face.

"Unkind, Maud! I unkind to you! Do you think I would say a word you did not like, if I knew it? You think too hard of me for some of the things I said and did at Hanson's. The fact is, I liked you immensely—and—I do yet—"

He saw that her lip was beginning to quiver.

"Not quite in the way of a lover, you know," he went on, desperately. "Only as a friend—a very good friend. Hang it, Maud! I wish I could make you understand me! I'm afraid I never shall. We'd better drop it, before we get into deep water."

With this remark he left her abruptly, and walked into the next room, where he took up a book and busied himself with it until she called him to dinner. He was not hungry in the least, and only touched the daintiest bits, washing them down with a half bottle of ordinary claret. The girl's appetite was not much better, and soon he retreated to the parlor again and left her to "do" the dishes. When he fancied she must be through with her labors he went out into the dining-room, and found her sitting there, sewing. Her head was bent low over her work and tears had fallen upon it.

"Bring that into the parlor, won't you?" he asked, not noticing particularly what she was doing. "I'm awfully lonesome. If you don't come I shall have to go and hunt up a theatre, to kill the evening."

She came obediently, feeling that he was her employer, and had a right to command her. A ready handkerchief removed the traces of weeping from her eyes. Linnette sat silent for some minutes and then exclaimed—

"Do you hate me very, very much?"

She looked up in intense surprise.

"Why should I hate you?"

"Oh, there are reasons enough. If I had never insisted on your waiting on me at Hanson's you would be there yet."

"Do you think I was so entirely happy there?" she asked, smiling in spite of herself.

"No, but here you are utterly wretched. I am an unreasonable fellow, I know that very well. Nobody likes me, and nobody ought to. I wish I was like Guy. I don't wonder you're in love with him. When you're his wife you'll be a happy woman indeed."

She started at the statement, and then asked why he thought she would ever be Dalton's wife.

"That's a queer question," he replied. "Isn't it settled?"

She laid down the sewing in her lap and fixed her fearless eyes upon him.

"If it is, it has been without consulting me."

"But you can have no doubt—you certainly are lovers. Pshaw! You're only trying me, Maud. You wouldn't say he never mentioned marriage to you?"

She hesitated, wondering how far she was justified in answering such inquiries.

"No, he never did," she replied at last.

"That's strange," exclaimed Roland, showing his astonishment in his voice and look. "Why, you've been together about all his spare time for weeks and weeks. What could he find to talk about, if not love?"

The color began to mount to her temples.

"I did not say he had never spoken of *love*," she said.

What did she mean? He looked at the girl searchingly, but could make nothing of her expression.

"The man who speaks continually to a woman of

love, and never of marriage, is not one to be encouraged," he said, earnestly. "Yes, I would say the same if he were my brother."

The helplessness of the girl smote the libertine like a blow. In the heat of passion he had made light of such situations in his day, but now he felt as if he were the witness of the robbery of a house, the kidnapping of a child. He had no volition whatever, he was forced to the attitude he took by the overpowering pressure from within.

"Maud," he cried, drawing his chair nearer to her, "tell me, is it too late?"

Quite startled at his manner, she could not answer him, and he took her silence for a confession.

"I am so sorry!" he said, taking both her hands in his. "But you *shall* be his wife—I will *make* him marry you! Yes, as soon as he returns!"

She did not know the dark suspicion that was haunting him. But she could not leave his mind in the condition she found it. She begged him to promise that he would not speak to Guy about her.

"And you mean to tell me you are content?" he exclaimed. "You do not *wish* to marry him, is that it?"

"I do *not*," she replied, positively. "I do not wish to marry—anyone."

The riddle was too deep. He looked at her for a long time in silence. She took up her sewing again, to engross her mind a little with it, and he watched her as she plied the needle. How little one could tell about a woman by seeing her face !

He remembered a time, years ago, when he had

met at the entrance of the Jardin de Paris a beautiful girl, dressed in white, with the purest face he had
ever seen. And he had remarked to a friend that
someone should tell that innocent creature of the
infamous scenes which would soon dye her marble
cheeks with roses. And his friend had laughed and
told him that she was Mlle. D'Alencelle, of the
Cirque. Unable to believe it, he had returned to
the place where the shameless dancers were giving
their exhibitions, and watched mademoiselle view
the worst of it unmoved.

The more he thought of Maud the more unbearable
it became, and he excused himself, saying he had an
engagement and must go out for an hour or two.

The cool air of the night revived him. He walked
far up town and then slowly back again. As he
neared his apartments he found it harder and harder
to enter the door, and he went off for another long
walk, which lasted until he heard a clock striking
twelve. Then he went deliberately to the Morton
House, engaged a room and threw himself, fully
dressed, upon the bed.

He thought of a hundred things in those few hours.
He was very angry at Dalton. Such affairs were
the exclusive privilege of wealth. It was outrageous
for a pauper to imitate his betters in this fashion.
Roland stirred himself up to a genuine rage. He
would have it out with Guy. He would tell him
his opinion of his conduct !

But, with daylight, after some sleep that even his
ill-temper could not drive away, there came a
gentler feeling. Human nature was the same in rich

and poor, high and low. He was himself too impecunious now to criticise his equals. Maud was handsome. If she had been thrown too completely into Guy's company, who was more to blame than the man who criticised him? Roland rose, and after making his toilet, walked briskly to his home, determined to say no more about it.

The young housekeeper had also slept badly. She knew that something—she did not understand what—troubled Roland exceedingly, and realized that the entire night had passed without his return. Quite early she arose and went about her household affairs, making the coffee and taking in the French rolls that the baker's boy left at her door. When Roland came in he greeted her in the old way, which reassured her, and they sat down to take their coffee together.

"I met a friend and passed the night with him," he explained, briefly.

With the mercurial temperament which mastered him at all times, he soon went to the opposite extreme. There was nothing to do but make the best of it. Guy was a sly dog! Roland laughed and talked with Maud, coming into the kitchen every little while and making himself entertaining. When her work was done he sat with her in the sitting-room and grew more good-natured than ever. Why should he not be free with her, if he liked? A kiss from those red lips would not be wholly unpleasant, and it would be no robbery if he could secure one.

"I wonder what Guy has succeeded in finding

out," he said, to keep up the conversation. "That Tom Hobbs is a shrewd old fellow. And Eva ; I hope he got in and out of the mansion safely. He will be here, probably, this afternoon. I can't help thinking, Maud, of what you told me yesterday. I. surely thought he was engaged to you. He ought to be, that's all I've got to say. If I were in his place I'd make you so secure nobody else should ever put in a claim. And if it hadn't been for the interference of my uncle, I'm not certain I shouldn't have tried to win you myself."

Maud rose to get something from the mantel. As she passed the young man he caught her in his arms and drew her into his lap. The movement was so unexpected that she had no chance to avoid the embrace. His lips were on hers in a warm kiss, and she was as nearless helpless for the moment as one could well be. The time was badly chosen, however, and as Roland released her they were both startled to see Guy Dalton standing by the door.

Maud turned scarlet, but Roland summoned a loud laugh and cried out that they were caught that time.

"How did you find things at Montvale ?" he added, carelessly. "I am dying to hear your story."

He had no idea that Guy would make a serious matter of what he had unluckily chanced to witness. The obligation that the young fellow was under to him would, he reasoned, outweigh any little feeling he might have. He would tell him later that he had acted on the spur of the moment and that Maud was taken wholly by surprise. But he soon saw that

Dalton did not intend to take the event in a light manner. He stood there as if stunned, for a moment, and then, without speaking, passed into his bedroom.

Miss Arline went to a window that gave on the small courtyard, and pressed her face against the pane. She was trembling. Linnette called out "Guy!" twice, and receiving no answer, added in a low tone, "Oh, then, go to the devil, if you want to make such a fuss about it!"

Recovering herself, the girl withdrew to the kitchen, and Roland walked into the parlor and began reading the morning newspaper, though very ill at ease.

An uncomfortable quarter-hour passed, and then Dalton emerged from his room, dragging a trunk, which he put into the public hall. Returning, he brought out a satchel, and several other things, and started to leave the flat.

"Don't be a fool!" cried Roland, coming to the doorway. "If you'll give me half a chance, I can explain everything to your satisfaction."

Dalton straightened himself to his full height. A dangerous look came into his eyes, usually so soft and pleasant. Roland stepped aside and the door latched.

"*You'll* have to speak to him," he said to Maud, going to the kitchen. "He'll not listen to *me*. He's gone for a cab, I suppose, but you can stop him."

A look of intense suffering was on the girl's face, as she lifted her eyes to his.

"I could not," she said, simply.

"Nonsense!"

"Not after what he saw."

Roland was full of contrition.

"Lay all the blame on me. Tell him the truth. I'll endorse anything you say. He mustn't leave you like this. I don't care for myself, but he has no right to condemn you on such slight evidence."

The girl shook her head slowly and sadly. Finding that he could do nothing with her, Linnette went out into the hallway, to make one more trial on his own account. The baggage was not where he supposed it would be. On the lower floor he encountered the janitor, who said he had brought it down at Mr. Dalton's request, and had assisted in putting it on a carriage that was passing.

Was ever anything accomplished so quickly? Roland went out into the street, but no carriage was visible in any direction.

"Well, Maud, he's gone," said he to Miss Arline, when he reached his apartment again. "Gone like the wind, nobody knows where."

The girl paused in her work, looking on the floor.

"Then *I* must go, too," she said, quietly.

"You? Certainly not! He'll get over his fit in a day or so, and be back again."

Maud put her fingers in the neck of her dress as if it choked her.

"It will be better that I go. He will never be friends with you while I stay here."

"Friends with *me!*" exclaimed the other, excitedly. "That's of mighty small consequence. I must restore him to you!"

## CHAPTER XXIII.

### "HE WILL DO IT FOR ME."

The silent anger that rises to white heat is more dangerous than the kind that vents itself in outward show. Guy Dalton knew what it was to feel murder in his heart as he stood by the door of his apartment and saw that couple so close together.

Knowing he was not expected on the earliest train, he had gone softly up the stairs. He was hardly surprised at the sight that met his gaze, but he knew no course except to pack up and leave them.

To have uttered a word in reply to Roland's offer to "explain" would have been to release the torrent of rage that filled his being. Guy was afraid of himself at that moment. Only a thin veil separated his self-control from the revenge to which a loud voice called him.

He packed his things leisurely, like a man in a dream ; took his baggage into the public hall ; happened to meet the janitor on the landing, and secured his assistance in getting it downstairs ; saw a cab passing ; and, before Linnette could reach him, had gone out of sight, directing his driver to turn several corners for the purpose of throwing possible spies off his track.

He was nearly penniless, but at the time he did not think of that. He only wanted to get beyond the reach of those who had deceived him. He directed the cabman to go as far as Twenty-eighth Street and Seventh Avenue, and when that point was reached he stopped and bought a newspaper, scanning the columns in which rooms were advertised. A little distance from the corner he found a chamber, which he engaged, and as he appeared honest and respectable, the landlady did not require him to pay anything in advance.

He had eaten no breakfast, but he did not care for any. He took a chair and sat for hours, in a dazed sort of way, looking at the adjacent roofs. He was in a state that closely resembled coma. At last night came on. Long after dark he went to bed by the light of the stars. In the morning he awoke, cold and hungry.

Examining his purse he found less than a dollar in it. He sought a cheap restaurant in the vicinity and spent twenty cents for a breakfast. Having nothing else to do he returned to his room and relapsed into the listless attitude of the previous day. At night he went out again to a frugal supper. The next day he pursued the same course.

On the second morning he awoke with his thoughts on Eva Warren. In his sleep he had seen her sweet face, and she had asked him to come to her. Yes, it was his duty to make the journey. Roland had committed an irreparable wrong to that girl, and she ought to know it. Procuring writing materials at the desk of a restaurant where he went for a cup of coffee, he indited a note stating that he **would be at Montvale either that night or the one** following, and asking that Charlotte keep watch for him at the door in the wall. This letter he mailed, without stopping to think that it required money to purchase a railroad ticket, and that the price of the stamp was the last of his resources.

At noon, on starting for dinner, he recollected that he was penniless. Literally his last cent was gone. Discouraged, he tried to think what he could pawn best. There was his trunk and his satchel, and the thin overcoat that he wore on chilly evenings. He hated to part with any of them, and he passed the entire day without food. In the morning he lay quite late. No breakfast awaited him, and he was weak and tired. At eleven he dressed and descended to the street from sheer *ennui*.

Growing hungrier every minute he walked about, looking at the things in the shop windows. Bills of fare in front of eating-houses had a fascination for him. Dishes that he would have scorned ordinarily took on a positive deliciousness as he read over their names. "Baked beans!" How nice they would taste! "Stewed tripe!" A banquet fit for the gods could be made of that material. He eyed the joints of beef and mutton, and the fat turkeys displayed in the provision stores, until his hunger grew so acute that he had to move on. A whiff of air from a kitchen freighted with the odors of cooking made him dizzy.

At two o'clock he found himself in front of his old place of employment, the office of the Montvale Optical Company. He loitered as he passed, to see if any of his former acquaintances were in sight.

He did not mean to have them detect him, but the cashier looked up and beckoned to him with a smile. Dalton shook his head, and was moving on, when the man came to the door and called to him.

"I wish you would come in a minute," he said. "There is a balance due you, and I want to get it off the books."

The words rang in the hungry man's ear like the whirling of a buzz-saw.

"Balance—due me?" he repeated, vaguely.

"Yes, twelve dollars, for the last week you were here. It would be a convenience if you would take it now."

Though Guy wanted that money as bad as he had ever wanted anything, he held back. He hated to touch a dollar belonging to Willard Linnette. But, after all, he had earned it honestly. And he was starving.

"How can there be a whole week's pay?" he asked. "I left on a Friday."

"You were discharged rather suddenly, you remember," smiled the cashier, "and in such cases it is customary. I don't know but you could claim another week, as you were entitled to notice ; but twelve dollars is all I can give you in the absence of instructions."

Satisfied with the explanation, Guy entered the office and signed a receipt. The other clerks spoke to him, in a casual way, saying that he was not looking as well as when he left. The first thing he did after getting the money was to seek a restaurant and eat a hearty meal. Then he went to his room and paid his landlady a week's rent.  And after that he took a satchel with some necessary clothing and went to the depot, where he bought a ticket, and took a seat in the train.

Alighting as before, at Ellsworth, he walked briskly toward Montvale.  As he approached the village it was yet too early to think of gaining admittance to the Linnette mansion, and the young man turned into a by-road and paced up and down under the overhanging branches of the tall trees till the lights in the neighboring houses began to be extinguished. Then he emerged from his concealment sufficiently to gain a good view of the residence he sought, and found that it appeared to be shrouded in total darkness.  He crept quietly to the rear of the grounds and knocked gently on the door in the high brick wall.  Without an instant's delay it was opened to him, and Charlotte's well-known features were discernible in the dusky light.

No interference was found between this point and the rooms that Miss Warren occupied.

"I received your letter this noon," said Eva, greeting him in her sweetest manner.  "Now, let me hear what the latest trouble is.  As Mr. Willard Linnette has gone to the city, I presume it is something in relation to his visit there."

The excitement which he had undergone during the previous few days had worn very much on Guy. He shook his head slowly, to imply that her guess was incorrect.  Then she noticed that he was very pale, and commented upon that fact.

"You are ill, I fear," she said.  "Has something

so terrible occurred, then? Speak at once, and let me know the worst."

He struggled for a few minutes with the things that rushed into his mind. Now that he was with her, the importance of every move began to force itself upon his mind. She had shown a blind faith in her lover, on the previous occasion, when alluding to his uncle's accusations against him. How could he know that she would give a more willing ear to the statements he had come prepared to make?

"I have had troubles—serious ones—of my own," he replied, gravely.

He had counted well on the feminine trait of curiosity, for she warmly urged him to confide in her, saying she felt the strongest wish to know everything that affected his welfare. She said this so kindly, and with such a sympathy in her eyes, that his voice choked as he began his story.

"When I was last here I told you that we were living in an apartment together, and that a young lady was acting as our housekeeper. You must have gathered from what I said that she and I were on very friendly terms. I was absent from New York less than one complete day. When I returned—"

His feelings overcame him at this juncture, and he had to pause to recover himself.

"She was gone?" suggested Eva, leaning toward him, and speaking tremulously.

"No. There was a man, who professed the greatest regard for me, and who knew my feelings toward—toward Miss Arline. I entered our apartment unexpectedly to them, and the first sight that met my eyes was my supposed friend with that young woman in his arms, his lips pressed to hers."

Miss Warren had begun to tremble as if with a deadly chill. The thought of doubting him never entered her head. His tale was too evidently true.

"And the name of this man?" she asked, her teeth chattering.

"Was Roland Linnette."

She uttered a low cry and covered her eyes.

"What did he say?" she inquired, without looking up.

"He said he would explain everything, if I would listen to him," responded Dalton. "But I could not bear to hold a conversation then. I was too much afraid I might do him a mischief. I packed my belongings at once and had them taken away—and I have seen neither of them since."

The revolution that acts the quickest of all is that which takes place in the mind of a woman who discovers the infidelity of the man she has learned to love. Sometimes it takes the form of blind hate, and she searches for a physical weapon with which to strike the object of her wrath. Sometimes the effect is like the erasure of the page in their lives on which his image is imprinted. This was the effect in Eva's case.

If Roland had held another girl in his arms and touched her lips with his, he was no more to her, and never could be. It was painful to learn of it, her love and pride were equally injured; but the chief impression on her mind was one of a great vacancy. For months she had thought of little else than this man. All her plans were made with him as the central figure. Now the room in which she lived was suddenly stripped of its garnishings, and nothing but the bare walls confronted her.

"I am so sorry for you," she managed to say. "You must have been very fond of her, and her action is incomprehensible."

"It is not that," he replied. "I do not think, now that I look back on it, that I really cared for *her*. What crushed me was to think that *he*—who professed so much love for me—could betray me as soon as my back was turned. And I cannot tell how long his plan was maturing. It was he who suggested her as our housekeeper. Yes, you may as well know. It was he who asked me to come here on that errand. It makes me feel as if all the world was false, as if there was no one whom I could trust."

She assented with a thoughtful nod, and for some time both were silent. Then she asked what had brought him on to Montvale.

"I came to tell you," he answered. "I thought you ought to know. And I had nothing else to do, left as I am without work, without prospects, without a home, and without a friend."

The extreme sadness with which he uttered these words touched the girl deeply.

"Not without a friend, surely," she said, putting her hand in his, with a delightfully graceful motion, " though I fear there is little that I can do to aid you. Tell me your entire story, if you will be so kind, and see if there is anything I can suggest."

Charmed by her manner, Guy was led to talk about himself in a way he had never done to any other person. She drew out of him the tale of his life, from the earliest period he could remember up to the present day. When he related his meeting with Roland Linnette, and the care taken of him in his illness, the girl paid the tribute of a tear to the pathos of the narrative.

"I am glad to know Roland is not all bad," she said. "I shall always think of him hereafter as one who is dead, and I like to remember all the good things I can of him. What do you suppose he will do? His uncle is not likely to relent, and he does not seem able to find work."

Dalton reddened.

"That, at least, is no reflection on him," he responded. "I have tried as hard as he, if not harder, and there seems to be nothing. Is it not strange that in a world so vast there should be no one in want of a young man of fair talents, willing to labor faithfully?"

Eva agreed with him perfectly. Then she said, brightly, that she had an idea she could arrange the matter now. Mr. Willard Linnette had been very angry because she wished to become the wife of his nephew, and had treated her coldly of late. When she told him, as she intended to do forthwith, that her engagement was at an end, he would resume his fatherly attitude toward her, and she could get anything from him she chose to ask. The position in the New York office of the Optical Company would then be given back to Roland without question, or perhaps a much better one.

He did not answer, half pleased at the prospect she held out to him, and half inclined to reject it outright, because it seemed like charity, and from a woman, too.

"He will do it for me," she repeated, confidently. "When I go to him and call him 'Uncle' again there is nothing he can refuse. You cannot imagine how fond he used to be of me, and only this matter of Roland has ever made any trouble between us. Stay in Montvale a few days, till he returns, and I can almost guarantee to arrange it."

Stay in Montvale! More easily said than done, he thought. He had not enough money to pay his board at the hotel, aside from his disinclination to go there and be subjected to cross-questionings. As he was thinking this over, and wondering whether he might not as well return to New York and wait there for Eva's communication, in case she accomplished anything, the girl clapped her hands together in ecstacy, like the child she was.

"I have thought of the most romantic thing!" she exclaimed. "You can stay *here*, in this house, just as well as not!"

"In this house!" he repeated, surprised out of himself.

"Exactly. This wing is never visited except by Charlotte and me. You can take one of the chambers and remain as long as necessary. I will see that plenty of food is smuggled to you. In that way you will be handy at all times for consultation, and whenever you wish to leave, you have only to wait for darkness. I will even have my meals sent up, so that we can dine together! You have no idea how thoroughly I am my own mistress—that is, in everything except the thing I most crave, the right to leave the grounds and see the world. By-and-by, perhaps you can help me to that, too."

It was certainly an agreeable inducement that she held out to him. And after a reasonable time, during which he raised insignificant objections, Dalton agreed to remain for the night, at least, and to leave the matter of a longer stay to be discussed the next morning.

# CHAPTER XXIV.

### "POVERTY IS A WEARY THING !"

The poet who sang, "Oh, poverty is a weary thing !" made no mistake. Maud Arline had felt its sting many times since the day she was left, an orphan, to the tender mercies of her guardian. She had felt it when turned out the day her small fortune was exhausted, and when she had to take a menial's position in the hotel at Montvale. Then had come Roland, with his strange manners, so entirely different from anything she had ever experienced. And when she had been in his company less than a month, the inevitable happened. She fell violently in love with the young gentleman.

At first she would not admit this, even to herself, and, above all things, she did not wish him to guess it. It was preposterous ! He was heir to a fortune estimated at hundreds of thousands. She had literally nothing but the plain garments she wore. He had the legions of friends that wealth always carries in its train. She had no one on whom she could make the slightest claim. Since her reduction to a place in the "servant" class, she had become separated entirely from all she had formerly known. Only in story books would such a man stoop to lift such a girl to his side as an equal. And yet—she loved him.

She had supposed, from what Miss Giddings told her, that he would be a very disagreeable person to serve. She had made up her mind to endure a great deal of fault-finding. After her meeting with him in the road these fears were succeeded by still stronger ones. She dreaded the renewal of such attentions as he had begun. Had he made the slightest move at that time toward excessive familiarity, it would have put her on her guard. It was because of his unfailing courtesy that the revulsion took place in her feelings.

When Mr. Hanson came to her with his story, telling her what the powerful uncle of his guest demanded, she was momentarily stunned. The only thing she had of value, her reputation, was in danger of being taken from her, the landlord said, by the village gossips. More than this, Roland was represented as a most dangerous and insidious foe of honest womanhood. Penniless, she had no choice but to accept the offer to pay her expenses to New York, or whatever city she chose, and to see that she did not suffer for the necessaries of life while she was engaged in seeking a new situation.

It was a very dark hour for her when she landed, a perfect stranger, in the metropolis, and sought one of the cheapest lodgings she could find. Work, plenty apparently for the million people around her, did not seem so easy to obtain as she had been told. Insult was offered her more frequently than anything else, and her life grew lonelier as time went by. Then came the bright face of Roland, the face she had resolved not to look upon, the face she had been told menaced her peace in this world and the next. She had been given courage to tell him he must not call again, though it nearly tore out her heartstrings to do it. And then, when the night was darkest, Guy Dalton had come.

Maud liked Guy. More than this, she trusted him. He was as safe to admit to her confidence as a girl friend would have been. She walked with him in the summer evenings, took dinner opposite to him in the restaurants, paying her own share—something she insisted upon from the first. Guy's salary was small, and Maud hated to use a penny more than was necessary that came from Willard Linnette. Both lived, therefore, in the most economical way, but economy is no bar to happiness. Indeed, given a sufficiency of food and clothing to supply actual physical needs, I think more real contentment is found among the poor than among the rich. Maud liked Guy, but never did she dream of loving him. Removed by the hard hand of Fate from the man she still adored, her young heart was as true to its idol as if she had worn an engagement ring on her finger.

And what were Guy's sentiments toward Maud? At first they were those of sympathy merely, a desire to protect this innocent creature from the rude touch of the thoughtless, wicked world. As time passed he liked her better and better, and perhaps he imagined, just before he took that fateful journey, that he loved her. People get to liking each other so well that in the absence of proof to the contrary they imagine themselves afflicted with the *grande passion.* I have known of cases where marriages followed this state of mind, and it was only on awakening some weeks later that the unfortunate parties discovered their mutual error. Guy was almost as lonely without Maud as she without him. Roland was to both of them something not quite of their own station, not exactly a comrade, even when he seemed most like one. Their poverty and their friendlessness bound them together, but that was all.

When it became apparent that the elder Linnette had cast his nephew off, and would refuse to aid him in any way, Maud had a little flutter in her left breast. Were Roland to become in reality as poor as she, he would not look so far away. But there arose between them now the figure of Eva Warren, whose praises he never tired of singing to those ears that heard him so patiently, though with such pain.

Roland never dreamed what agonies Maud suffered when he chatted at the table, of this beautiful girl, and reiterated his determination to marry her, in spite of all the Linnettes ever born. And then Guy went to see Tom Hobbs, and to tell Eva that her lover would always be true to her, and that she must not let anything take her from him. And in his absence the deplorable event occurred that disrupted the little group of three, not too happy before, but now utterly miserable.

It was impossible for her to stay there with Roland, alone. Nothing remained but another struggle to support herself. She had used up all the money given her by Mr. Hanson, and had foreborne to ask for more since she had violated one of his principal injunctions,—that of keeping away from young Linnette. The life that opened before her was unillumined by a single ray of hope.

She was in such low spirits that she could not resist the friendly overtures that Roland made her on the morning after Guy's departure. He expressed such hearty sorrow for what he had done that she was quite overwhelmed.

"How did I ever do such a silly thing!" he exclaimed, twenty times, and with each exclamation his lips touched her fair cheek. "I resisted the temptation at Montvale till I thought I had been turned into adamant. Maud, my sweet girl, if you continue to cry I shall take a revolver, that I have in the other room, and spoil your best carpet."

Women are made for affection. In times of great mental distress they turn their faces toward the sunlight, no matter from which direction it comes. Roland continued to talk in a low monotone, vowing to set her right again with Guy, no matter how great an apology it required. He referred to that young man so often that she felt obliged to interpose a word.

"You are quite mistaken about Mr. Dalton," she said. "There never has been anything between us like—like what you seem to think. We were good friends, nothing more. But he has been very kind to me, and I wish he had not gone away with such suspicions in his mind. I have driven him from his home, and all I ask is to return it to him. He will

never come while I remain, and that is why I must
go as soon as I can."

Roland was much affected.

"Go, child !  Where can you go ?" he demanded.
" You have no relations in the city, as you have often
told me.  Your money from my uncle has been
stopped.  Let us talk sensibly.  Guy has run off in
a sudden fit of temper.  Soon he will come to his
senses and we shall have him back again.  It will
not do for you or me to desert the lighthouse.  We
must stay here and keep a candle in the window for
our wanderer, when he gets tired of his cruise and
turns his eyes toward home."

With that he kissed her again, and she did not try
to stop him, though she was by no means ready to
accept his plan.  She did not think it right to keep
house for him alone.  It had been bad enough when
three of them were together.  There were people,
she felt sure, who would look askance at such an
arrangement between young persons of opposite
sexes.

"I don't know what to do," she mused.  "I have
made trouble for you—with your uncle ; and now I
have made trouble for him—for Mr. Dalton.  You
have both befriended me and received a very poor
return."

Not less than three kisses contented Roland after
listening to that speech.  He put his arm around
her waist, declaring that both he and Guy owed her
the most abject apologies for what they had done,
and that it was a shame for her to accuse herself of
anything.

"You must do nothing precipitate," he added. · · I
shall never let you out into this town again, hunting
for work. That would be madness. I have a hundred dollars' worth of furniture that can be sold,
without seriously breaking up the *menage*, and when
that is gone, if all else fails, I have another string to
pull. I know, in spite of what you say, that I am
wholly to blame for all this row, and I shall do my
best to straighten it out."

Finally, an arrangement was made in this way.
Maud knew of a girl, one of the dressmakers where
she had worked, who lived down on Staten Island
and had to come and go every day, on very small
wages. She thought she could get this girl to come
and room with her in the flat, as a temporary expedient, for the looks of the thing. If this succeeded
she would remain for the present, while Roland
tried to make things right with Mr. Dalton. She
did not like the idea of putting on her hat and walking out into the New York streets, without money
enough to pay for carting her trunk to a room,
the rent of which she could not raise.

To all this Roland agreed with pleasure, though
he protested mildly that the feminine addition to
the household was a reflection on him that was un-
warranted. He also warned her solemnly that in
case her friend was handsome, she would be more
than likely to regret introducing her. He was so
bright, in spite of all his troubles, that the girl soon
resumed her old manner. She set out the lunch and
they partook of it together. Before it was finished
he had her actually laughing at his pleasantries.

During the afternoon Maud arranged the matter with her friend, the maker of dresses, who agreed to room at the flat and take her breakfast there, getting her other meals outside. This suited Roland very well, when Maud told him of it at dinner.

For the next three days Roland hunted for Guy. He went to the restaurants he had formerly patronized, inquired at the house where he had roomed on Tenth Avenue, dropped in at the office of the Montvale Optical Company, and walked the streets peering into every face that passed. In the intervals he tried to pick out the furniture he talked of selling, and once brought a buyer of secondhand goods to look at it. But when the man offered him twenty-three dollars for what had cost one hundred and seventy-five, he broke into blasphemy and frightened the dealer so that he ran away without looking behind him. "I won't give the stuff to these wolves till I have tried everything else," said Roland to Maud. "I am going to pull that other string I told you of. It's a thing I hate, but the landlord's agent will be on our necks in a week, and there's no help. Not only is the rent nearly due, but the ship is running short of provisions."

The girl put her hand instinctively on his arm.

"It is perfectly honest—of course—the way you are going to get this money," she said, with a deep blush.

"To be sure," he retorted, reddening also. "Do you think me a brigand, my child? I'm not half as bad, dear, as they've made me out to you."

He took her face between his hands and drew it to his own.

"If I had the fortune I have lost, Maudie," he murmured, "no other man should ever press his lips to yours."

The girl could not resist him. He kissed her without the least trace of passion and went out.

She stood where he had left her, pondering on those words of his. What did they mean? "If he were rich, no other man should ever touch her lips." But he was engaged to that young lady in Montvale! Ah, God! To be so poor, to hold so much love, and to hear such an intimation as that!

A flush of shame that she should have listened to him, that she should have permitted him to touch her, covered the girl's cheeks. And yet, he had not looked as if he meant to offer an affront. With the great riddle in her tired brain Maud turned to her household labors, tears coursing slowly down her cheeks.

An hour later she heard a knock at the door. Supposing it to be the grocer's boy, she went to open it.

"Mr. Linnette!" she gasped.

It was Mr. Willard Linnette, indeed. He was even more astonished, not to say grieved, than she, for he had no idea that he would find her in his nephew's apartments. But he silently entered and closed the door behind him.

# CHAPTER XXV.

## A BENIGNANT OLD GENTLEMAN.

As Roland walked along the street, after leaving Maud, he whistled a low tune. He had surprised himself by what he said to her. But he knew that he meant every word of it, and that, strange though it might be, he cared more for that girl than for any other who breathed.

Mecurial in temperament, changeful as a weather-vane, he was greatly influenced by the pathetic situation into which his actions had driven this young woman. It was clear to him that he had done her a wrong, and he wanted to offer reparation. If in doing so he proved false to another—that was an incidental that he had not yet had time to discuss.

The errand on which he had started was most disagreeable. He would not have believed, a month before, that he could do it. Now there was no choice. He was going to see his father and ask aid of him.

In front of a handsome residence on Thirty-eighth Street, not far from Lexington Avenue, he stopped. Mustering courage with an effort, he ascended the steps and pulled the bell. A man-servant in livery responded to the summons.

"Is Mr. Linnette at home?" asked Roland.

"Yes, sir; but he is very busy. Is it anything particular?"

" I wish to see him."

" If you'll give me your card, sir, I'll inquire."

Though he had not been asked to enter, either by word or look, Roland stepped into the hallway.

" I have not my card-case with me," he said, curtly. "Tell him a gentleman is waiting in the reception-room."

He turned away abruptly, but the servant did not seem satisfied.

" He's awful busy sir. Is it—have you anything to sell?"

The young man turned on his questioner savagely.

" He is my *father!* Tell him that his *son* is here!"

At that the servant bowed almost literally in the dust, or would have done so had the remarkably clean surroundings contained any of that material. He begged Mr. Roland's pardon, and explained that, " as there were so many agents about, and as Mr. Linnette had a horror of them, and never, under any circumstances, bought anything, and as he was so very busy to-day, and as—"

" Will you tell him I am here?" shouted the visitor.

This sufficed to cut short the apology that bade fair to be endless. Roland looked around the room, elegantly furnished, adorned with works of art on all sides. It was a very long time since he had been in that house—a time dating back to the last of his school-days. He had disliked his father ever since he could remember. Their few interviews had been very brief. Nothing like a war of words had ever arisen, but the coolness toward him of his nearest living relation, galled him terribly. And now, to have to come here like this !

The serving man returned.

"Mr. Linnette is very sorry, but he is editing an article for a magazine, and could you call Monday ?"

Roland looked so darkly at him that the man recoiled a step.

" Where is he ?" he demanded.

"In his chamber, sir."

Two steps at a time the son mounted the stairs. Throwing open the door without ceremony, he strode into the room where Payson Linnette was writing.

"Did you send word to *me* to ' call again ?'" he asked, bitterly. "And did you understand who wanted you ?"

The venerable gentleman looked up with a mild but slightly annoyed expression.

"You interrupt my work," he said, in a low tone.

His long gray hair swept the turned-down collar that was twice the ordinary width. He wore a velvet coat and a sailor-knot cravat.

"I will interrupt it but a minute," replied Roland. "I want some money ! It is the only time I have asked you for any since I was old enough to remember. Give me five hundred dollars and I promise it shall be the last."

The venerable brows were lifted slightly at the proposition.

"I must decline," said the elder man. "Your Uncle Willard assumed charge of you many years ago. There was a perfect understanding that you should look to him for everything. If you have lost his goodwill you must seek to regain it. As I have an important piece of work on hand, I hope you will not disturb me further."

The son's astonishment would hardly let him speak. He had known something of the nature of his father, but he had not anticipated a refusal.

"One word," he said, and again the benignant brows were lifted deprecatingly. "Whatever the cause, whose ever the fault, I and my uncle have quarrelled. I am at the end of my resources. Without money at once I shall be turned into the street. I have sought work in vain. Unless you assist me I shall become either a beggar or a thief."

The annoyed look deepened on the venerable face. Reaching slowly into his pocket, Payson Linnette fumbled among the bills there and finally drew out ten dollars.

"I ought not to do it—it will inconvenience me," he murmured, "but you may have that. If you are frugal it will last you till you can communicate with my brother and beg his pardon. Goodday."

The father turned to his writing, as if he considered the interview finished. For several seconds Roland stood there, unable to utter one of the indignant things with which his mind was filled.

"I am in doubt," he said at last, "whether to take that money and stuff it down your throat, or spend it in poison to end a life disgraced by being drawn from such a wretch! You have lived all these years—as I did—on the bounty of your successful relation, which, having no blood nor heart to cause you to rebel, you are able to retain. I care not what becomes of me now. No greater disgrace can fall to my lot than to have had you for my father!"

With the air of a sovereign ruler, Roland left the room and the house. A moment later Mr. Linnette summoned the man-servant who attended the street door and smiled upon him in his usual benevolent way.

"You know how much I hate to be disturbed, Kelly," he said. "Hereafter—if you wish to retain your position—be more careful."

"He told me he was your son, sir," stammered the man.

"Here-after," repeated his employer, "be more care-ful. No per-son must be al-lowed to dis-turb me, under any cir-cum-stances."

Kelly bowed humbly and was glad to escape to the floor below. He had served gentlemen, in his day, who were sometimes violent in their language; but never had he felt so uneasy as when in the presence of this pattern of propriety.

Roland, too angry almost to contain himself, returned to his home. He must tell Maud of the failure of that "string" which he had believed would save them, when worse came to worst. There was a half-formed idea in his mind of selling everything he had for what it would bring, giving her the sum, going to the wharves and shipping as a sailor.

The uncle, who heard his step, signalled to Miss Arline not to betray his presence for a few moments, and she, in great doubt how to act, stood, physically and metaphorically, between the two men.

"What do you think!" he cried, as soon as he entered the room. "I went to my father—my own father, mind you!—to ask him for a paltry five hundred dollars. I told him I had nothing left and that it was either this or starvation, or even robbery. Of course, I did not mean the last, dear, but I had to say something. And what did he do? He pushed me a ten dollar bill across the table, murmured that he was very busy, and said that was all he could give! I wanted to strangle him where he sat—I—"

Willard Linnette, who had been hidden by an open door leading to another room, stepped forward with distended eyes.

"Did my brother do that?" he exclaimed, in a trembling voice.

Roland looked from one to the other in amazement. Maud was gazing fixedly at the carpet, unable to speak or look at him. What did it mean?

"Yes, your brother did *just* that!" retorted the young man, when he could command himself. "Does it surprise you? Did he ever show the slightest interest in me? I was a fool to go to him, but it was either that or death. I can get nothing to do, and I am desperate."

Tears came into the old man's eyes—tears that changed the manner of his nephew toward him in an instant. The tender recollections of childhood returned and blotted out all that had happened since.

"*Uncle!*" he cried.

"*Roland!*"

In a moment their arms were about each other.

# CHAPTER XXVI.

### MR. LINNETTE'S STRANGE STORY.

"Would you mind leaving us together for a little while?" asked Mr. Linnette, of Maud, when he had again resumed his seat.

Then, when the door closed behind the girl, he had a long talk with his nephew. A very important talk it was, too.

"I want to say, to begin with," said he, "that I have questioned the young woman who just left the room and am satisfied that I have wronged her seriously. She is, if I am a judge, a pure, sweet girl, fit to be the companion of any man who lives. If I had not something to tell you, however, that completely fills my mind and heart, I should express a doubt whether it is for her lasting happiness to be thrown too much into your society. Do not misunderstand me," he added, as Roland's cheeks began to flush; "I mean nothing unkind. In the hour I have been here I have discovered, beyond question, that she cares too much for you."

Roland was not in a mood to comprehend the meaning of this statement, and he inquired what his relation meant.

"Why," stammered Mr. Linnette, "I believe she *loves* you, to put it plainly ; and you can see how unhappy that may make her, when she finds that your affections are enlisted elsewhere."

The young man breathed a deep sigh.

" Oh, uncle," he replied, " I must seem like a very strange fellow to you, but you should know the truth. Within the past few days it has grown clear to me that I have been mistaken all along ; that the sentiment which I have for Miss Arline is the true one, and that Miss Warren—"

Mr. Linnette sprang to his feet and held out his arms again, overcome with joy.

" You do not mean—" he began.

" Yes, I do," said Roland. " I regret deeply, for her sake, that things have gone so far. For I will not deny to you," he explained, " that we have corresponded, in spite of your prohibition. I began, I think, by pitying Eva, who complained of the closeness of her confinement, and before I knew it I had asked her to marry me and she had consented. I now mean to write again, telling my whole story and begging her to release me. It looks cowardly, but it is the only thing left under the circumstances."

The fact that his nephew was about to relinquish his aspirations to Eva's hand was all that Willard Linnette comprehended, or wished to know. He threw his arms around him once more, calling him his dear Roland, and assuring him that his affection had endured through everything.

" But now," he said, soberly, when he again became tranquil, " I have a story of my own to tell. Lask week I learned a secret that had been kept from me for many years, a secret of vital importance.

Roland, it is extremely probable that I have a living child somewhere in the world, who has no idea of its parentage."

The young man eyed his relation curiously. What kind of a statement was this, to be made by that venerable man, that stickler for forms, that detester of the very mildest dissipation !

" *You—have—a child!*" he repeated.

" Yes, Roland, unless death has taken it from me even before I have found and claimed it. I came here to tell you the story, and to ask you to enter with me at once upon the search that has been instituted."

Quite stunned by the revelation, Roland kept perfectly still.

" At the age of thirty-five," said Mr. Linnette, slowly, " I made a trip through New England, on a vacation, driving from place to place alone. Frequently I had to pass the night in villages so small that they did not boast a hotel. One night the family with which I stopped contained two daughters. One was about twenty-five years of age, the other sixteen. Their name was Lincoln."

And then he went on with a long story, which may as well be put into the words of the author. Something in the elder daughter interested the guest, who had been, up to that time, wholly oblivious to feminine attractions, engrossed as he was in his business enterprises. Although he had intended to remain but one day in the village, he stayed a fortnight. Before he went away a correspondence was arranged. For a number of years the manufacturer

made quarterly visits to his new friends. In the
meantime the parents of the two girls died, leaving
them to find their sole reliance on each other. Nothing definite had been spoken upon the subject of
marriage, but the elder girl, whose name was Bertha, considered this the unquestionable outcome of
the affair. She had fallen deeply in love, and waited
patiently for the day when she should be asked the
inevitable question.

In all this time, Mr. Linnette had never hinted to
the Lincolns that he was possessed of more than the
average fortune. His early life had been one of
great hardship, and when the thought of marriage
occurred to him, he wanted a wife who would wed
him for himself and not for his money.

On being asked once by a villager if he were
related to the Linnettes of Montvale, he replied
evasively that he believed he was connected with
that family. His letters were all dated at New
York, where, it was understood, he was clerk in an
office.

But Cupid plays strange pranks. After going
several times each year to visit Miss Bertha, after
writing her hundreds of letters, Mr. Linnette discovered that the younger sister, a child when he first
knew her, had blossomed into one of the prettiest of
women. His long delay had allowed Bertha to
reach an age when female charms begin to fade,
while Beatrice had just arrived at her full beauty.
The slow wooer turned almost unconsciously toward
the rising sun ; and the words he had never spoken

to the elder sister began to come upon his lips when he was alone with the younger one.

Not realizing the extent of the affection which Bertha had developed for him—none are so blind as those in love—he resolved to make Beatrice his wife if she would accept him. It was then that a hundred artisans were sent to Montvale, to create the most beautiful home in all that region for his future bride. But in the whispered confidences which he gave to Beatrice, nothing was intimated of the wealth he possessed. He meant to bring her, like the bride of the Lord of Burleigh, to

> . . . "a mansion more majestic
> Than all those she saw before,"

and to spend there with her the remainder of what bade fair to be a happy and contented life.

At last the day came when he proposed to the younger sister, and was accepted. The elder one had seen the drift of matters for some time, and though her heart was breaking, she bore the pain like a mediæval martyr, never uttering a word to lessen the happiness of Beatrice.

As the home which he intended for his wife was not yet completed, Mr. Linnette took her to New York, where he kept up the illusion of being in moderate circumstances, in order to enjoy her surprise the more when she should see the glories of Montvale. Prospects of an heir to his fortune and house came to gladden the husband and to make him feel that his cup of joy was soon to be filled to the brim. But, alas! The future is for no man to read!

As Beatrice seemed in excellent health, Mr. Linnette felt justified in leaving her for seven or eight weeks, when invited to join a party of scientific men who were going to one of the Pacific Islands to view an eclipse. The young wife urged him to go, saying she did not need the least care and that he would return long before the day of her especial trial. An unlooked-for delay occurred, however, and when he reached San Francisco, on his return, he received a letter from Bertha, containing the saddest imaginable news.

The young wife had been taken suddenly ill, so the letter said, and in spite of every effort, had expired with her unborn child. She had sent for her sister, who had done everything possible, but all in vain. The body had been taken to her former home and interred in her father's lot.

Mr. Linnette was so prostrated by this news that he felt unable even to visit his sister-in-law. He sent a generous check, asking her to accept it for the expense and trouble she had undergone, but the larger share was returned to him, with the statement that she would take only what she had actually expended. The manufacturer ordered all the work stopped on his elegant residence. He never saw Bertha again and soon ceased to hear from her. The little son of his brother Payson, left motherless some time before, then began to attract his attention. For this boy he had his mansion finished.

**And now comes the strangest part of the story.**

Beatrice, when she died, was the mother of a ten-hours-old babe, which, though born before its time, was healthy and likely to live. The mad idea seized Bertha to take this child away, and keep the knowledge of its existence from its father. She had lost both lover and sister, and her heart pined for some creature on which to lavish the affection that welled up in her maiden breast.

She supposed Mr. Linnette what he represented himself, a man in ordinary circumstances, who would find a motherless child a burden. There was plenty of opportunity to carry out her hastily formed plan. The death of her father had put her in possession of a little money, and she was in want of nothing in the simple way she desired to live.

Taken suddenly ill, years after, Miss Lincoln had been moved to confide her cherished secret to a clergyman of the town where she resided. She exacted a promise from him that he would try to find her adopted child's father. If he succeeded, the child was to be told of its parentage, but if not, it was to be kept in ignorance.

Miss Bertha only knew of Willard Linnette as a clerk in the employ of some house whose name she had never heard, and as a distant relation of the famous man whose name he bore. The minister did not mean to confide his secret to every person he met. It was his object to make inquiries, not to answer them. He went as far, on one occasion, as to penetrate the private office of the very man he sought, but left it no wiser than he came. The optical instrument maker told him that he had

never known of any Willard Linnette except himself. Discouraged at the obstacles he encountered
the minister returned to his home, feeling that his
duty was ended.

Roland listened to this tale with mixed feelings.
He was rather disappointed to find that his uncle's
life held no scandal, after all. He had expected,
from the introduction, to hear of an unchaste love,
and the thought of such a thing in connection with
that austere man had thrilled him to the utmost.
However, it was interesting enough.

"A short time ago," said Mr. Linnette, in conclusion, "the revelation was made in a most peculiar
way. At a dinner given in honor of a distinguished
foreign savant I was placed next to a prominent
physician, who long since abandoned the practice of
medicine for the more entrancing pursuit of astrono-
mical knowledge. In the course of our conversation
he remarked that the name of Willard Linnette always brought a sad recollection to his mind. 'The
first mother I ever lost in childbirth,' he said, 'was
the wife of a gentleman of that name.' Reminded
thus of the inquiries that had been made of me by
the clergyman, I inquired where the lady had resided. Judge of my surprise when he mentioned the
street and number where I had made my temporary
home with my young bride.

"Before he finished, this doctor had said enough
to convince me that my wife had given birth to a
living child. The next morning, as you may imagine, I was on the train that would take me nearest
to the town where Bertha Lincoln had resided.

There I learned that some months after the death of her sister she had 'adopted,' as she claimed, a child found in an asylum, but which I have proved she brought from New York. The clergyman has retired from the ministry, but by the description I gave of him he was easily identified and I have communicated with him."

Roland listened without interruption, and when his uncle finished he asked—

"Have you found your child yet?"

"No," was the sad reply, "but I shall move heaven and earth until it is accomplished!"

# CHAPTER XXVII.

## "YOU ARE A COOL ONE."

A more disagreeable situation could easily be conceived than that of Mr. Guy Dalton, during the next few days after he became the guest of Eva Warren. In the wing of the great mansion that had been practically given up to Eva, he was as secure from intrusions of an objectionable nature as if in a mountain fastness. Nobody dreamed of his presence there, else it is very certain he would not have been allowed to remain long. Mrs. Grundy would have viewed the affair with her severest frown, had it come to her attention. On general principles the usually meddlesome old lady would have been right, for this once. But with such a phenomenally good young man as Guy, such a paragon of innocence as Eva, and such a very wise young maiden as Charlotte, all was sure to go properly.

Eva was certain that, if she could only get an interview with Mr. Linnette, and tell him she would no longer oppose his wishes about Roland, she could enlist his kind interest in securing for Guy the position he had lost. What was to follow she did not exactly know, but she believed, when the manufacturer once got acquainted with Guy, he would see his good qualities and insure his subsequent rise in the business. As for herself, this plan left her at Montvale, it was true, but since her experience with Roland she felt more reconciled to her quiet home. She had dreamed of a happiness that could never have been hers, for a lover who would act as he had done would be sure to make a most unreliable husband. So thought this wise young woman, and more than likely she was not far out of the way in her conjectures.

But there was a certain satisfaction in the very presence of such a fine young fellow as Dalton. As she partook with him of the coffee and toast and eggs that Charlotte brought, she decided that it was, on the whole, the most romantic thing she had ever heard of. Roland's midnight visits were not to be compared with it. In the old novels that she borrowed from the library there were tales of mysterious underground passages, with pass-words and knocks known only to the initiated. But the caverns were always gloomy, and she was certain they must have been damp. It was much nicer to have your hero hidden in the upper story of a modern house, right over the heads of his natural enemies, where he could peep through the closed shutters at his baffled pursuers.

All day long these young people talked together, of life, and literature, and the things they knew and the things they thought. It was noon before they supposed it eleven o'clock, time for dinner long ere they felt hungry, the hour for retiring when the evening seemed only begun. Charlotte was their timepiece, and they obeyed her suggestions implicitly.

Weaned by that one blow from Roland, it is no wonder that Eva found the society of Guy more than delightful. A week may equal a month or a year when two people of their age are thrown into each others' exclusive company for almost every one of their waking hours.

One evening, when Guy had been at the Linnette mansion for nearly a week, he found himself unable to sleep, and after trying in vain to "woo the drowsy god," he dressed himself, took the key to the door in the rear wall by which Charlotte had admitted him to the estate, and went outside the grounds for a stroll. It was a most imprudent thing to do, but he thought it safe enough, from what he knew of the character of the villagers. In this case, however, he had made a mistake, for he had not been walking ten minutes when he came suddenly upon another stroller, and one of the last men he would have cared to meet.

It was Tom Hobbs. There was no escaping the keen eyes of the old man, which recognized him instantly, in spite of the semi-darkness, and Dalton stopped when he heard his name pronounced.

"Well, well! This *is* a surprise!" said Hobbs. "How came you here and where are you going at this time of night?"

Guy was, happily, on the road that led to Ellsworth, and apparently coming toward Montvale from that direction. He replied, with alacrity, that he had walked over again, to have a talk with Mr. Hobbs, and was just going to his residence.

"Pshaw!" said Hobbs. "You don't say! It's

lucky I happened to see you, for I got wakeful and was out trying to walk off the blues. That matter of Linnette and his nephew rests on my mind all the time. I'm afraid the boy is actually suffering for funds, and I can't make out why he doesn't write me a word. Did you give him the message I sent by you, that time you came up here?"

Somewhat confused, not only at the unexpected meeting, but at the question, Guy suggested that they had best go into the house as soon as possible, as his desire not to be seen in Montvale was still strong. In a few moments the two men were alone in the superintendent's parlor. Then Guy related his falling out with Roland on his return to the city, though without giving the cause of the rupture.

" I could not talk to him about anything," he said. " I did not speak a word. As soon as I could pack my things I took them away, and that is why I never was able to give him your message."

" The deuce !" said Hobbs. " And so, for all you know, he may be starving to death at this present moment."

" Yes," said Guy, coldly. " For all I know, or care !"

Hobbs stared at the young man for some seconds.

" There is but one cause that could so embitter two such friends as you were," he said, at last. " There was jealousy about some woman."

" No matter what it was," replied Dalton. " I will not discuss it. Our acquaintance is at an end."

" And why, then," asked Hobbs, " have you come to me ?"

Poorly prepared for contact with so shrewd a mind, Guy had a second of apprehension. But by good luck he hit upon an answer that looked reasonable.

"I am still out of work," said he, "and nearly penniless. You have great influence with Mr. Linnette. I want my old place in his office."

Mr. Hobbs laughed aloud.

"You are a cool one," he replied. "Don't you know that I love that boy Roland, as much as if he were my own flesh and blood? After abandoning him without even conveying my message offering assistance, you come to ask help for yourself! But I'm not going to be as cruel as you. Give me his address, and I'll give you "—he paused, noting the gleam in Dalton's eyes—"I should say *lend* you any sum you need."

Guy was struck by the position of the old man, and touched by the tenderness of his voice.

"I will gladly give you the address," he responded. "You will find him, unless he has moved away, at No. — East Sixth Street. As to your offer to lend me money, I shall have to subdue my pride enough to accept a little. If you can let me have ten dollars I promise to return it at the very earliest possible date. The truth is, I have not enough to get back to the city without walking."

Hobbs wrote the address carefully in a little memorandum book that he carried in his coat pocket.

"If it will ease your pride any," said he, "I have another proposition to make. I would like to employ you for a week or so on a very particular

and private affair.  If you succeed in what I wish to
accomplish you will be handsomely rewarded.  If
you fail, your expenses and a good salary for the
time employed will be paid."

The young man caught eagerly at the proposition.
While it was very agreeable to stay in the Linnette
mansion with Eva, he knew it was far from being a
sensible way to pass any more of his time.  He
wanted the pleasure of again earning something, the
sensation of having in his purse a few dollars that
would enable him to hold his head up among men.
He told Mr. Hobbs that he would willingly under-
take any honorable mission.

"I am going to impart a most profound secret,"
said the elder man, when this had been arranged.
"You will need to show the greatest judgment in
carrying out the investigations I intend to commit
to you."

Much impressed, Dalton inquired why he had
been selected for this work.

"For two reasons.  One is because you are available,—because you are able to begin at once.  The
other is because it will lead you to a location with
which you have told me you are familiar, that of
East Ryegate, Vermont."

Guy started perceptibly when he heard the con-
cluding statement ; but he recovered himself, and
begged his companion to proceed.

"You may remember telling me," said Hobbs,
" that you knew of a family by the name of Lincoln,
living in Ryegate."

Again there was the slight start, that did not escape the watchful eyes of the questioner.

"Yes," said Dalton, slowly, "I remember."

"There were two daughters in this family," pursued Hobbs. "One of them, the younger, was named Beatrice. She married and moved away a great many years ago. The elder's name was—"

He paused, and looked at Guy inquiringly.

"Bertha," said Guy.

"Exactly. She lived during the later years of her life in a village about twenty miles from Ryegate. The name of it escapes me at this moment—"

Dalton named it quietly.

"Precisely," said Hobbs. "And this Miss Lincoln—Miss Bertha Lincoln—did not live entirely alone, I believe. She had adopted a child, soon after her sister's death—and now comes the secret, that you must swear not to reveal without my permission."

Guy inclined his head in token of assent.

"I believe the child which Miss Bertha adopted and brought up was the offspring of her sister."

Guy looked intently at the speaker.

"Well?" he said, interrogatively.

Mr. Hobbs smiled, as he was wont to do when he cornered his adversary at a game of chess.

"Were you pretty well acquainted with things in Ryegate?" he asked.

"Quite well."

"Did you ever hear"—the old man bent forward anxiously—"the name of the man Miss Beatrice married?"

Dalton contracted his brows in thought. Yes, he

said, he had heard the name, but it had slipped his memory.

"Was it Linnette?" demanded Hobbs, triumphantly.

"I think it was," said Guy, with a nod.

"And Willard? Was it *Willard* Linnette?"

"I don't know. But—you don't mean—you wouldn't wish me to understand—"

Hobbs rose and rubbed his hands together with glee.

"Wouldn't I? Oh, yes, I would! Begins to grow entertaining, doesn't it?"

Then he told Guy, with all the flourishes of a romancist, about the long-past love and marriage of the master of Montvale, much as detailed by Mr. Linnette himself to Roland, and already explained to the reader. Hobbs had known all that his employer knew, even in those remote days, but upon the latter's return with the sad news of his young wife's death, it had been agreed that the matter should never again be mentioned between them.

Upon learning through the New York doctor that his child was born alive, the instrument manufacturer had confided all he learned to his faithful friend, by means of the mail. After himself visiting Ryegate, and setting a detective agency to work upon the trail of the lost child, Linnette had again written to Hobbs, telling him of the latest developments. It was then that the superintendent remembered that Dalton came from that town, and he was debating making a journey to the metropolis in the hope of finding him when the unexpected meeting took place.

If he could manage to find this child by his own efforts, directed in this way, what a crowning glory it would be for him !

"I want you," he said to Dalton, "to go to East Ryegate and learn what became of this adopted child. The clue does not seem an easy one, from what Linnette writes me, but perhaps a smart Yankee boy, who knows the neighborhood, may out-wit the New York detectives. You will see what an important matter this is. If you are successful, you may be sure not only of your old place in the count-ing room, but of almost anything else you want."

Guy had been growing very sober during the pro-gress of these arrangements. He rose like one who has slept on the bare ground and finds his bones aching.

"You are quite certain that Bertha's adopted child was Mr. Linnette's own ?" he asked.

"Quite. The coincidence is too remarkable to leave much doubt."

The young man listlessly took the money that Mr. Hobbs handed to him, not counting it. As long as it was no charity he did not care what the amount was.

"I will do my best," he said, simply.

He went back to the Linnette house and crept softly up the stairs. Writing a note explaining that urgent business called him away, and that he would communicate again as soon as possible by mail, he slipped it under Eva's door. Then, taking his satchel

In his hand, he went as he had come, carrying the key to the entrance with him.

Before starting on his way to Ellsworth, however, he stood a long time gazing at the roof that had sheltered him, and his fine eyes were dimmed with the tears he could not restrain.

## CHAPTER XXVIII.

### ROLAND AND MAUD.

The delight of Roland Linnette at being recon ciled with his uncle was fully shared by Miss Arline. The old gentleman remained to dinner with them, and became more and more impressed with the sweet and modest bearing of his nephew's young housekeeper. He refrained, by arrangement with Roland, from referring in any way to the startling information he had imparted to him, while in Maud's presence. But after he had departed (first assuring his nephew that his former income would be given him, and that he had only to present his letter of credit to the Barings' correspondent) the young man could not help telling Maud something of what he had learned.

"It is the greatest secret," he said, "and I ought not to say a word, but—"

"Then, don't," she interposed, mildly. "Two can keep a secret much better than three."

"I can't help it," said Roland. "I must at least give you an inkling. My uncle—you won't ever tell, will you?"

Maud shook her head, with a smile. She liked him very much, when he was in a mood like this.

"Well, years ago, you see, my uncle married. He kept it from almost every one, except his wife and a

sister of hers.   And when he was away on a journey,
Mrs. L. presented him with a child.   No, she didn't
either—that was just the trouble."

Maud's pretty face exhibited a puzzled look at
this statement.

"It was this way," said Roland, making another
start.   "She *had* a child, but she did not *present* it to
her husband.   She died, in fact, and a wicked fairy
—her sister—stole the innocent babe and carried it
off to her castle in the country, sending word to the
father that his wife died before the birth, you understand.   And through all these decades he never heard
of the truth till within a week or two."

The strangeness of this story was admitted by the
listener, who asked what object the sister had in
perpetrating the deception.

"The greatest in the world," replied Roland.
"She was in love with my esteemed relation herself,
and wanted something to console her for his loss.
Then she supposed him a poor man, who would be
rather pleased than otherwise to get rid of the care
of an infant, for he had never told her or his wife
that he was a nabob.   When a woman is in love my
dear, she will do anything."

He looked archly at Miss Arline as he said this,
and she cast down her eyes and reddened in a
charming way.

"*Won't* she?" he asked.   "When a woman is in
love, won't she do *anything?*"

Maud said she did not know, never having had
any experience.

"You are a story teller," replied Roland. "You certainly *have* been in love—with Guy."

The mention of this name made the girl put on a very serious look. She replied that she had never been in love with that young gentleman, and that Roland knew it well.

"All right, then," said he. "We will let the Dalton episode pass. But at the present moment you are very much in love with *Me*, and that you dare not dispute."

To this Maud made a still more vigorous protest, but her companion insisted that he was right, and greatly enjoyed her discomfiture when she could not, in response to his challenge, look him straight in the eyes and tell him the contrary.

"The fates have ordained it, Maud," he continued, when he had succeeded in making her laugh in spite of herself. "Bad as I am, wicked as I have been, there is mercy in store for me. I am to be made a better man by the power of your love."

She would not admit this, but she listened with a high-beating heart, while he told her that he should never be satisfied until a clergyman had bound her to him for life. And she looked still more pensive when he divulged the fact that his uncle had probed the depth of her feelings even in the short time he was at the house, and had spoken in the most complimentary terms of her.

. "We are nearer in worldly wealth than we used to be," he added, "if that could make any difference to him. What little chance I had of inheriting his property is disposed of by the discovery he has just related to me. If he finds his child I shall never tread the soil of Montvale as its owner. Confound him!" he exclaimed, comically. "He acted as if I ought to be excessively pleased at the news! Why, it knocks me out of a clear million!"

Then Maud talked with him quietly for a long time of the troubles that came with wealth, and the greater happiness that people in moderate means enjoyed. Before they parted that night he had urged her again and again, without result, to give him a definite promise to be his wife.

"You are so changeable," she said. "It seems but yesterday that you could only think and talk of Miss Warren."

"I know it," he admitted, ruefully. "I can't understand it in the least. It was nothing but pity —nothing whatever. I was drawn into it before I knew what I was doing."

"The same as you are in my case?" she suggested.

"Not at all. I loved you, dear, the day I first saw you, when that dunce of a Hanson sent you after me. I can see you now, standing there in the snow, with your pretty cheeks reddened by the exercise of walking, and the cold air, and the—"

She bade him "Hush!" and said it was time she retired.

"And won't you promise to be mine?" he pleaded.

"Not to-night."

"Well, then," he answered, pretending to misunderstand, "the first thing in the morning, at any rate. Not later than noon, I must insist. Really, Maud, if you hold me off till dinner time I shall die."

Her head was aching, as she went to her room, and found her dressmaker friend asleep before her. The happiness Roland held out to her was too great. She did not believe it could ever come.

---

Willard Linnette consulted daily with his detectives, growing impatient at the slowness of their movements. Happening to hear the name of Ryegate mentioned, Roland informed his relation that his late friend, Guy Dalton, had once lived in that place. This led to a consultation with the chief of the bureau that was managing the search, and it was decided that Guy ought to be found and an attempt made to put him upon the case at once.

But Guy was no easier to find than the long-lost child. As the reader knows, he was, during part of this time, in the Linnette mansion at Montvale, and later, on the errand suggested by Mr. Hobbs, of which Mr. Linnette had no knowledge.

"I have an idea," said the manufacturer, at last. "You remember, Roland, that Miss Warren wrote to him once—of course you do. Perhaps she has his present address. It is at least worth trying. I am going home to-morrow on business and I will try to find out."

When Eva learned that Mr. Linnette had returned she thought it wisest to appear at dinner. She had a curiosity to note whether there was anything unusual in his manner. She saw at once that all traces of anger seemed to have disappeared. He greeted her with great kindness, and when the meal was ended he inquired if she would favor him with her presence for a few minutes in the library.

Knowing no reason why she should refuse, though wondering greatly at the request, the girl complied without comment. Mr. Linnette followed her and closed the door behind them.

"Some weeks ago," he said, in an ordinary tone, after motioning her to a chair and taking another, "I spoke to you on a matter very distasteful to me, and my manner of alluding to it was hardly, I fear, less so to you. I now wish to say—"

She thought it best to set him right, before he had gone any farther in that direction.

"If you are referring to your nephew, sir, I can save you the necessity. I shall never speak or write to him again."

"So I supposed," he said, in the same voice. "I have had an interview with him—in fact, several of them. He tells me that for a time he was in the habit of hearing from you several times a week, and that it is quite a while since he received any reply to his communications. He believes that you must have heard from a certain source of an unpleasant occurrence that took place in his apartment, even before he wrote you, resigning all claim to your hand."

There were four unopened letters of Roland's in Charlotte's possession. She had been told never to bring another to her mistress with his superscription on the envelope, and she had put these away among her own things.

"I do not like to discuss this matter," said Eva,

with a sigh. "I felt justified in all that I did, even when it was against your wishes ; but now it is ended, and I hope we shall never have to allude to it again."

Mr. Linnette bowed profoundly. He had feared an outbreak of regret and passion, and was much relieved at the manner in which she referred to his nephew. It argued, he reasoned, that she had not been as deeply attached to him as he feared.

"I hope," he went on to say, "you are convinced that whatever I have done has been with an honest regard for your best welfare. I am quite glad to let this incident pass without further comment. What I now wish to ask you is if you can tell me the address of—of Mr. Guy Dalton."

The question was so unexpected that the girl's cheek flushed brightly. She thought at first that this was merely an ingenious way of showing that he knew the concealment of which she had been guilty. One glance at the calm face of the millionaire dissipated this impression, but still she was uncertain what answer to make him. She felt that she had no right to reveal Guy's whereabouts until she had consulted with the young man.

"Was there any indication of his residence in the letter he wrote you ?" asked Mr. Linnette.

"I have not said that he wrote me any letter, she answered, diplomatically.

Mr. Linnette looked troubled.

"I had hoped you could tell me where to find him," he said, gravely. "It is on a matter of much importance. I have hired the largest detective bureau in New York to hunt for him, so you can judge for yourself that it is no small affair."

Eva began to tremble again. What offence had Guy committed? Was there no man whose life was what it should be? There could be no prejudice on her account, as Mr. Linnette could not know of her relations with him. She had accused this man once in her thoughts of slandering his nephew, and had found that his charges were only too well founded.

"Eva," asked Mr. Linnette, after a pause, "are we good friends again?"

"Why, yes, sir, I hope so."

"You believe that all I have done has been actuated by a regard for your welfare?"

She assented cordially.

"And—do you—care as much for me as—as you did before any of these things occurred?"

He was bending toward her, and there was a depth of emotion in his voice for which she could not account. Again she answered in the affirmative.

"From the day you came to live here," he said, "you have been very dear to me. I love you as well—indeed, I think far more—than most men love their daughters. It would break my heart to find anything like a permanent estrangement growing up between us. Dear child, I want to say much more to you than I dare, and some day I hope to have the courage I need. You like me—you are sure you like me?"

Tears stood in his eyes. Quite innocent of what he had in mind, she felt a profound pity for the sentiments that had brought such visible sorrow to this old man, who had done so much for her. Rising, she put her arms around his neck as she had done a hundred times in younger years, and laid her fair cheek to his.

For a few moments he did not move. Then he arose and walked with her to the hallway.

"God bless you!" he said, in broken tones, as she said good-night to him, and went slowly up the staircase.

## CHAPTER XXIX.

### OFF TO GRETNA GREEN.

The second day after Guy Dalton's sudden disappearance from Montvale, Eva received a letter from him, through the agency of Mrs. Merrill. In it he told her nothing of the business upon which he had embarked, except that it was a secret which he had promised not to divulge. But there was something in this letter of more importance to its recipient than any other subject could be. Page after page was covered with protestations of the most ardent affection.

"I could not speak these words when in your presence," said the letter, "but now that I am able to call pen and paper to my assistance, I can no longer repress them. Within the past week I have learned that life without you would be unendurable. Even my unfortunate condition, penniless and without a permanent situation of any kind, cannot keep me from telling you the truth. It seems presumptuous to reveal the state of my feelings, when I have no home to offer, but I may not always be as poor as I am now. With the hope of winning you to inspire me, I shall yet surmount the obstacles in my path. Dear, dear Eva, if so I may call you, say I have not offended you, for if I have, I will never come into your presence or send you another line."

Clasping this letter to her heart, Eva felt for the first time the wonderful sensation of true reciprocal love. The sentiment she had conceived for Roland Linnette was quite different from that which had been growing up so rapidly in her bosom for Guy Dalton. Roland was the first young man with whom she had ever come in contact. Her secluded life left her ready to find perfection in any well-appearing person of the opposite sex, if sufficiently good-natured and attractive. But for Guy she had a much more powerful emotion. During the hours she had spent in his company she had longed earnestly for some spoken word to indicate that her feeling toward him was returned. The least expression, telling of his love, would have sufficed to let loose the full tide of her own affection. And now, when his sudden and unannounced departure had filled her with alarm and foreboding, came this sweet proof of all she could ask.

Her happiness was so great that for a few days she did not even communicate the news to Charlotte.

Three letters came in quick succession from Guy, the third one saying he should return on the following evening. The maid was told to be on the watch for him, and before he arrived Eva had told her all. Charlotte, happy at anything that pleased her young mistress, rejoiced also. As soon as Dalton appeared on the premises he was taken into Eva's presence and left alone with her.

There was a second of hesitation, and then the fair girl allowed her lover to take her in his arms.

"You do really forgive me, then?" murmured

Guy, who wore a haggard look, as of one who has passed sleepless nights.

For answer she gave him her lips to kiss; he needed no other.

"Have you been doing anything wrong?" asked Eva, as soon as she could speak.

"Wrong?" he repeated, with a dazed look.

"Yes. Mr. Linnette has been here inquiring for you. He says detectives are looking for you in all directions."

Then she told him the entire conversation she had had with Mr. Linnette in the library, as far as she could recall it.

"I give you my word," he answered, breathing more easily, "that I have done nothing of which you would not approve. Don't tell me, darling, that you lost faith in me!"

The girl, embracing him again, declared that such a supposition was the farthest possible thing from the truth. But even though he were a criminal, she protested, she could do no less than love him.

"I have thought so much of the dangers we run," she added, "that everything alarms me. Oh, I wish we could be married at once! Then, whatever happened, they could not tear us apart!"

The young man gazed at her with tenderness. What an innocent flower she was to open her full heart to him.

"I wish it as heartily as you, my love," he said. "If I had any money I could call my own, I would ask you to run away with me this very night. When we had found a minister and were made one, we could laugh at all their threats and insinuations."

The idea of an elopement completely fascinated the girl. To go away with him, to stand before a clergyman and hear the words that should make him her husband—that was charming indeed ! When she heard Dalton's suggestion, she burst into enthusiastic praise of it.

"Oh, that would be heavenly !" she cried. "And as for money, I have enough to last us several weeks. I will go with you immediately, if you think best."

Guy doubted the expediency of taking this child from her home, with the grave questions of future support that he knew would soon come upon him. But how could he resist the pleading eyes and the flushed cheeks with which she offered to throw herself into his arms ? He found, on examining the money she hastened to bring him, that there was nearly a hundred and fifty dollars of it. It is easier to look on the bright side than on the dark one when a luscious young maiden offers to lead the way. Within an hour the plans for flight began to be matured.

"It is hardly twelve o'clock," he said, looking at the timepiece on the mantel. "I can go to Ellsworth, rouse the stable keeper, and get here with a carriage by half-past three. You can have the things that are absolutely necessary to take packed in valises by that time, and Charlotte can bring them out to the door in the wall where I entered. Luckily," he added, going to a window, "there is no moon

and the night is dark as pitch.  You cannot take a
great many things, and you must select carefully
those you will need most.  You are certain you can
rely on Charlotte ?"

Eva laughed merrily.

"She is as sure as my own hand," she answered·
"Go at once, and get your carriage.  You will have
to walk so far !  I am very sorry for you, but—I'm
worth it, am I not ?"

Before the hour announced Dalton returned with
his vehicle, but he did not permit it to come nearer
than a hundred yards of the place he had agreed
upon.  He found Eva all ready—as, indeed, she had
been for a long time—and Charlotte wearing her
outer wraps and an air of mystery.

"Is *she* going with us ?" he whispered in a rather
blank tone.

"Now, my dear Guy," laughed Eva, "isn't that a
peculiar question ?  Did you imagine I was going to
travel alone with a man before I was married to
him ?  And what do you think would become of
poor Charlotte if I left her here to bear the blame of
my escape ?"

He saw the force of both reasons, but he felt compelled, lest she should think him worse than he was,
to pretend he had alluded to the extra expense that
a third person would entail.

"That's true," mused Eva, thoughtfully.  "Perhaps, if we continue to be very poor, I shall have to
find a new place for her by-and-by.  But now, really,
I couldn't go a step without her ; you must see that.

Let me show you the letters I have written to leave behind me."

He had no more objections to offer, and he read the letters with interest. The first one was as follows :

" MY DEAREST MAMMA :—You could not be my mother and not know what love is. A few hours, at the latest, after you read this, I shall be Mrs. Guy Dalton! Does not that sound strange for little Eva ?

" And who is Guy ? you may inquire. He is the handsomest, sweetest, dearest man in the world, and I love him. That's all.

"I should have confided in you ; yes, that is true. But you might have thrown a hundred obstacles in our way, and that would not have been agreeable to us.

"Charlotte is going, too. As soon as we are settled enough to have a permanent address I shall let you know of it.

"In the meantime, dear mother, believe me,

"Your dutiful daughter,

"EVA."

And the second one read like this :

"MR. WILLARD LINNETTE.

"DEAR FRIEND :—Do not think me ungrateful for all your kindness. Indeed, I am not. I have left your house with him who is to be my husband, because love is the strongest feeling in the breast of woman.

"You told me last night that you had detectives searching for Mr. Dalton. They need search no longer. As soon as we are married and in a home, he will tell you where to find him. He knows of no crime that should cause him to evade you.

"Think of me as gently as you can. Forgive me as soon as you can. And, if it is possible, come to us and be the same dear 'Uncle Willard' you have been to me so long.

"Your 'little treasure,'

"EVA WARREN."

Willard Linnette rose at his usual early hour that morning, ate his breakfast and went mechanically to his office. When Tom Hobbs came in they talked of the ill success of the detectives.

"There's one good thing ought to come out of this matter, at any rate," said Hobbs. "Now that you know you've a grown-up child you won't think any more of making a fool of yourself."

An expression of pain flitted across Mr. Linnette's features.

"That is your delicate way of referring to my regard for Miss Warren, I presume," he said.

"Exactly."

The manufacturer suppressed an inclination to reply in an impatient manner, for he knew the good intentions of this old friend so well.

"Ah, Tom!" he cried, "the coming on of years does not deaden the heart in a healthy man, nor does the springing up of love in his bosom indicate decay of the mental faculties. She has promised me to have nothing more to do with Roland. I see no reason to change my mind. No child will regret to learn that a father's last days are to be brightened by the companionship of a beautiful and loving woman."

The door opened at this moment and one of the clerks entered.

"Mrs. Warren has come down, sir, and says she must see you immediately."

"Show her in," said Mr. Linnette. "Don't go, Hobbs," he added. "There need be no secrets between us three."

But when Mrs. Warren came into the room it was seen that she was laboring under great excitement. The traces of tears were on her cheeks, and she repressed another outburst with the greatest difficulty. Both gentlemen rose to proffer her their chairs, but she would accept neither.

"Oh, Mr. Linnette!" was all she could say, and this she repeated not less than a dozen times in rapid succession, clasping her hands together in distress.

"What is it?" asked her employer, taking alarm. "Is Eva ill?"

She wrung her hands in pain.

"Oh, Mr. Linnette! How can I tell you? Read these letters!"

Each sentence came with a gasp, and then Mrs. Warren, handing him the missives, sank into one of the chairs offered her and began to sob violently.

The manufacturer took the letters and began to read first the one addressed to himself. He had only reached the words "with him who is to be my husband," when a mist came over his eyes. He thought at the moment that Roland had lied to him after all—that his pretence of love for Maud Arline was a mere blind to conceal his real intention, and that it was with him that Eva had gone away.  He staggered against the desk at which he had been sitting, and handed the notes to Hobbs.

"Read them, Tom ; I can't," he ejaculated, in a smothered voice.  "Read them distinctly that I may know the worst."

Hobbs did as he was bidden.  Linnette listened as one listens to a voice at the distant end of a telephone. He did not understand the situation perfectly until the second letter was read.  He believed at first that Dalton had only been a co-conspirator with his nephew.  But when the plain declaration was made, "I shall be Mrs. Guy Dalton," he uttered a stifled cry, threw up his arms and fell fainting to the office fioor.

# CHAPTER XXX.

## "YOU HAVE MARRIED HER!"

Maud Arline was too much in love with Roland Linnette to hold out long in the face of his ardent wooing. Their situation was somewhat to blame for the denouement that speedily took place. As he told her, with a happy laugh, they were already housekeeping and knew each other as well as an unwedded couple was ever likely to. He had determined to ask his uncle for a place in some department of his business, where he could honestly earn the living he received. The difference in worldly wealth between him and his hoped-for bride had been shown to be a very thin and flimsy one. It would not be a "marriage in high life," in any sense, now that he was no longer the prospective heir of Montvale.

"We are just two ordinary human beings, Maud," he said, "in whom the world at large has not the slightest interest. Don't put me off any longer. Let me take you to the nearest minister and have it over."

And this is what was done, a few days later. The ceremony took place in the clerical parlor, with as little fuss as possible.*

---

* The author of this novel is conscious at this point of departing from the rule which he long ago adopted, never to

The first visitor the newly wedded couple received was old Tom Hobbs. The superintendent, who had only once or twice in his life made a journey of this magnitude, had come to New York with a most noisy bee in his bonnet. He brought the astonishing news of Eva's flight with Guy, and of the effect it had had upon the senior Linnette.

"He's a very sick man," said Hobbs, in conclusion. "The doctors don't know yet whether they can save him. Everything is confusion at the house, or they would have sent you word sooner."

Roland looked at Maud, who sat silently listening.

"I shall go at once, of course," said he.

Hobbs nodded his approval of this plan.

"You ought to understand, though," he went on to say, "just what the situation is. Your uncle is violently in love with that girl. He confided to me weeks ago his intention to marry her. Knowing how much you thought of her, I—"

The younger man stopped the speaker by a gesture.

"You surprised me so by your unexpected appearance," said he, "that I forgot a very important matter. Mr. Hobbs, let me present to you *my wife*."

---

write anything in the remotest degree immoral. He must agree with the conscientious reader that Roland Linnette, after his life of dissipation, deserved no such happy fate as to wed a pure, virtuous maiden like Miss Arline. It looks like rewarding vice, instead of punishing it, which should be the object of all truly moral literature. But in this case, to do otherwise than as I have would clearly spoil my story, and I must choose the lesser of two evils.          A. R.

The superintendent rose with old-fashioned formality, and took the hand that the blushing Maud extended. He was so confused, however, that he could not utter a syllable.

"You don't understand it," smiled Roland, "and there is no need that you should. My uncle has been here and fully approves my choice. I *liked* Miss Warren very well, but Maud is the only woman I ever really *loved*. Now, you can proceed to finish your story, which is not so much of a surprise to me as you might imagine. It was probably the knowledge of this feeling on my uncle's part that drove Eva to such a desperate step."

There was a pause of several minutes, during which Mr. Hobbs was allowed to recover himself. Mr. and Mrs. Linnette, Jr., went into the next room and talked over Roland's projected trip to Montvale, which it did not seem best for her to take with him. It was their first parting, and Maud was doing her best to appear brave.

"Well, that's about the whole of your story, isn't it?" said Roland, cheerily, when he returned to his guest's presence.

"Heavens and earth, no!" exclaimed Hobbs. "You say you were not astonished at what I've already told you, but I'll guarantee you will be before I get through with the rest of it."

Roland and Maud surveyed the speaker with new interest.

"You have heard," said Hobbs, "that Mr. Guy Dalton formerly lived at Ryegate, Vermont?"

"Yes," assented Roland.

"And that your uncle had detectives looking for him, in the hope that he would be of valuable service in the recovery of his lost child ?"

"Yes."

"And you knew, I suppose, that the name of the child's adopted mother was Lincoln ?"

Roland bowed again.

"Well, what would you think," asked Hobbs, impressively, "if you heard that this same Mr. Dalton's real name is Lincoln, too ?"

The wedded pair looked at each other in wonderment.

"How do you know this ?" asked Roland.

"I'll tell you. I came to the conclusion some days ago that if anything was to be accomplished in finding that child, someone besides the city detectives would have to take a hand. Without saying a word to your uncle I sent Dalton to Vermont to hunt up a son that had been raised by Miss Bertha Lincoln, now deceased, and whose present whereabouts is a matter of pressing interest. I—"

Roland burst into a loud laugh.

"And you think he went off to hunt for himself !" he cried.

"It looks like it," said Hobbs, gravely. "I happened to ask him once before if he knew the Lincolns of Ryegate, and he admitted that he did. He knew the date of Miss Bertha's death, too. When I found him the last time and asked him to go on this errand, he had the strangest look in his eyes you ever saw. And you know how proud he always was about money. Well, he took over a hundred dollars that I handed him, without even counting it. He must have known that he would soon be able to pay it back."

Roland shook his head as if to say it was mysterious, truly.

"Where was it you found him?" he asked.

"Right in the middle of the Ellsworth road at Montvale, after ten o'clock at night," answered Hobbs. "Look at the smartness of the fellow. He was undoubtedly hanging around there and communicating with Miss Warren. And, when he learned through my story to him that he was the lost heir, he arranged this runaway match for fear he would encounter his father's opposition, if he waited until his identity was established. Oh, he's deep enough, I tell you!"

It looked like a sure case, but another question came to Roland's lips.

"You haven't told me," he said, "how you discovered his true name."

"It was this way," replied Hobbs. "As I said before, I got tired waiting for these slow detectives. I went to Ellsworth and found a conductor who remembered taking Miss Eva and her maid, whom he knew, to the city on his train. The young fellow shrewdly kept out of the way, and the conductor supposed the girls were travelling alone for some good reason. Inquiring among the depot hackmen, I discovered the driver who took the entire party to the Bartholdi Hotel. There I learned the name of the minister who was called to perform the marriage, and when I went to him he said he had not married any person by the name of Dalton."

The listeners looked with admiration upon the amateur Vidoq.

" Goodness !" exclaimed Roland. " You should apply for the position of Chief Inspector at once."

" The minister told me,  pursued the now unruffled Hobbs, " that he had married a ' Mr. Clarence Lincoln ' to a Miss Eva Warren, at the Bartholdi, day before yesterday.  The description of the party tallied with that of our acquaintances."

As this seemed the end of the superintendent's tale, Mrs. Linnette inquired why Mr. Hobbs had not looked on the hotel register.

"I did," was the reply.  "And I found that the young fellow had written there, ' Joseph Gibbs and party.'  He did not mean to be tracked so easily."

Roland smiled softly to himself.

" Just tell us where this Mr. Lincoln is now," said he, " and your remarkable history will do for the foundation of a romance."

"I wish I could," said Hobbs.  " The morning after their marriage they left the Bartholdi, and no one remembers anything indicating the direction they took.  The hotel folks supposed it an ordinary wedding trip, and paid no attention to the carriage in which they left."

The upshot of the conversation that now followed was a decision that the most vigorous search must be instituted for Mr. and Mrs. Clarence Lincoln—as it seemed most absurd to call them.  Mr. Lincoln must be apprised as soon as possible of the precarious condition of his father's health. If all else failed a newspaper personal must be used.

Mr. Hobbs confessing to being nearly exhausted from lack of sleep, a bedroom was assigned him in which to recuperate, and Roland went out upon the street to begin his search alone. By one of those strange happenings for which no one can account, he had not gone a dozen blocks when he met the object of his hunt, on the Broadway sidewalk.

Flushing rosy red, Dalton, or Lincoln, as he may now be called, made a stiff bow and attempted to pass without further recognition. But Roland planted himself directly in front of him and spoke with determination.

"You are the very man I want," he said, with earnestness. "Come, don't be the first to reject advances. Whatever harm I may have done to you was unpremeditated, and should be forgotten now that you have married another woman. I have a most important message to give you. My uncle has been taken very ill, and your presence is consequently wanted at Montvale."

Lincoln's face bore no sign of relenting.

"Excuse me," he said. "I have no desire or intention of returning to that village. If you know of my marriage you understand why."

"I do not understand at all," retorted the other. "After taking the liberty of inheriting the estate that was to have been mine, you can afford to treat me with politeness. If I committed any fault toward Maud Arline, you can hardly reproach me with it, now that she is my wife."

Lincoln's manner changed with lightning speed.

" You have *married* her !" he cried.

" More than a week ago."

The extended hand was grasped and shaken heartily, and the two young men were again friends.

" Well," asked Roland, as they walked along, " how do you like the prospects of becoming a millionaire ?"

" I do not know what you mean," answered Clarence.

" Do you tell me," asked Roland, stupidly, " that you have learned nothing—about your parentage ? You are unaware that your father is living and very rich ?"

" Some one has deceived you," was the reply. " My father died twenty years ago."

Roland shook his head with decision.

" You are the one who is mistaken," he said. " Your father is certainly living—unless he has died within a few hours. In short, you are the son of Willard Linnette, the owner of Montvale. Why, you must know that what I say is true !"

Then Lincoln smiled for the first time.

" I know it is not," said he, " and for the best of reasons. I was sent by Mr. Hobbs to ferret out the whereabouts of that child, and I have done so. Before many days I will prove to you what I say."

Overcome with astonishment Roland invited Clarence home with him, and the invitation was accepted.

# CHAPTER XXXI.

## EVERYTHING EXPLAINED.

Some days later nearly all the characters in our story were gathered at the mansion of the optical instrument maker of Montvale. Seated in the large parlors were Roland Linnette with his wife, Clarence Lincoln with his, Tom Hobbs, Mrs. Warren and a Mr. Lewis, the latter representing the detective agency that had undertaken to restore the missing child of the millionaire. Between all of these people there appeared to be the greatest cordiality, in marked contrast with the divisions that had separated some of them so long. Indeed, there was on each face a good-natured smile, as if the present had a happiness that completely atoned for the troubles of the past.

It was evident that Mrs. Warren had entirely forgiven the escapade of her daughter, for she sat with that young lady's hands in hers, while the proud young husband, not far away, listened with brightening eyes to the conversation between them. And well might he be pleased, for the burden of Eva's remarks, delivered in a tone just loud enough for him to hear, was that no other girl had ever possessed such a wonderful treasure in the form of a marital mate. The mother's critical eye had no fault to find with her daughter's choice, and she was a witness to the old adage that "all's well that ends well."

Mrs. Roland Linnette, if possible, seemed happier even than her newly-made friend, Eva. Her husband was talking in a low key with the detective, Mr. Lewis, and her sweet face was completely wreathed in smiles at the remarks he was making. Occasionally Roland interposed some word that sent the rosy blood to her fair cheek, making her still more beautiful. She had to touch his arm surreptitiously very often to keep him within proper bounds, lest the attention of the detective should be called to the stolen pressures given to her hand that lay nearest the contented fellow. The experiences of the bride had not caused her to lose, but rather had accentuated, the modesty so charming in her as a maiden.

Old Tom Hobbs, of all that group, sat alone. But his face was not a sad one, either. He was pretending to look over a book, that lay on a table at his elbow, and glancing about three times a minute at the tall clock in the corner, as if impatient at some delay.

Finally a door opened, and a tall figure was seen at the threshold. Every one present rose, with the greatest politeness, to welcome Willard Linnette. Tom Hobbs, crossing the room, took the arm of his employer, who was evidently still weak from his sudden illness. In response to a whispered direction, Mr. Linnette was piloted to a seat by his nephew and Maud. The old gentleman walked slowly, but otherwise he looked remarkably well, considering everything. Eva whispered to her husband, "Isn't he handsome!" as he passed her, and the tired face of her foster-father lit up as the faint sound reached his ear. When Mr. Linnette and the others were seated, Mr. Lewis rose and asked if he should proceed, to which an answer was given in the affirmative.

"Ladies and gentlemen," began the detective.

"Not so formal," protested the weak voice of Mr. Linnette, Sr.

"Talk it right out," put in Tom Hobbs. "You can't tell many of us much that we don't know."

This remark raised a laugh, just the thing that was needed. Mr. Lewis was as glad as the others to have the icy air of the room melted.

"You all know this, at least," he proceeded. "I am the head of the detective bureau of Lewis & Co., New York. Some weeks since, Mr. Willard Linnette came to me and said he had found evidence that a child of his, in relation to whose birth he had been deceived, had been brought up by a certain Bertha Lincoln, its aunt, residing near the town of Ryegate, Vt. The woman had died some time previous, and the child had disappeared. He wanted us to find it and restore it to him."

"Which you never would have done if it had not been for me," interposed Hobbs, at which sally everybody laughed again.

The detective could not resist the general contagion, though he felt injured in his professional feelings by the observation.

"I would not say too much if I were you," he

responded. "You made about the worst mistake in the entire business, as I shall show."

Then the laugh turned upon Hobbs, who was restrained with difficulty from defending himself, then and there. Only the protesting hand of Mr. Linnette, with its warning finger raised, prevented him.

"I undertook the job myself," continued Mr. Lewis, when quiet was restored. "I went to Ryegate with Mr. Linnette, and found that all the points he had been able to give me were correctly made. I found also that Miss Bertha had left her small fortune to her adopted child, committing its interests to a guardian who lived some distance away, in another State. And I discovered that this guardian had proved quite unworthy of his trust, if not actually dishonest, as I believe I shall yet demonstrate."

Tom Hobbs had fidgeted uneasily in his chair for several seconds, and at this stage in the proceedings he could contain himself no longer.

"I must protest," he ejaculated, "against this continual speaking of Miss Bertha's adopted child as '*it*.' When we all understand the matter, it is simply exasperating. That confounded pronoun has bothered me enough, and I don't want to hear it again."

Another laugh, this time a very hearty one, passed around the circle.

"You will have to humor him," spoke up the voice of Mr. Linnette. "Tom is a privileged character in Montvale, Mr. Lewis."

"What *shall* I call the child ?" asked the detective, mischievously. "Shall I say ' *he* ?' "

"No, that would be worse yet !" blurted the superintendent.

All eyes were now turned on Maud, whose face was suffused with blushes. Her husband's uncle had motioned her to his side, and his shaking arm was clasped about her form. Strangely enough, Roland did not seem to object in the least to the proceeding.

"Very well," said Mr. Lewis. "We will use the right pronoun this time and call the child ' *she.*' The girl, then, that Miss Bertha Lincoln brought up, and which I have absolutely proved to be the daughter of Willard Linnette, was left in the care of a man named Redding, with the sum of seven thousand dollars. He was believed to be a most honorable man, who would educate her well and give her whatever balance was left when she reached the age of twenty-one. On her deathbed Miss Lincoln's conscience overcame her, and she asked her religious adviser to make an effort to find the child's—I should say the girl's—father, which we all know he failed to do. If he could not make this discovery, according to Miss Lincoln's desire, the girl was not to be told of her origin, as it would only add to her distress of mind. In that case she was to continue to bear through life the name by which she had been known."

But here Roland interposed.

"Not ' through life,' Mr. Lewis !" he protested.

"Until her marriage, then," corrected the detective. "Miss Lincoln had pretended that the girl was taken from an asylum and that her right name was Arline. The man Redding kept this girl till she was of age, and then coolly informed her that the amount left with him for her care was exhausted and that she would have to shift for herself. I have learned—and I hope the lady in question will not prevent my repeating it—that his course was influenced by her refusal of his offer of marriage, he being at that time a widower and much fascinated by his ward's beauty. It is also said—"

Maud's distress was so evident at this point that the detective desisted of his own accord ; while Roland, with a dark look, declared that he would go that very day to find this Redding, and punch his head.

"At any rate," resumed Mr. Lewis, when the pretty object of his remarks had succeeded in partially quieting her beligerent spouse, " this guardian turned Miss Arline out without a penny. She obtained work at the hotel here in Montvale, and from that time her story need not be repeated. She is now acknowledged as the daughter of the father she lost so long, and, as the story books say, they ought to live happily ever after."

Congratulations to Mrs. Roland followed, lasting several minutes. Eva and Mrs. Warren kissed her several times, and so did her husband, and Mr. Linnette, while Tom Hobbs and Mr. Lewis looked as if they had as lief follow suit.

"And now I wish Mr. Lincoln would explain pre-

cisely the hand he had in this matter," said the elder
Linnette, with his feeble voice.

Clarence blushed like a school-girl.

"I had very little part in it, I assure you," he
replied. "I knew Miss Arline quite well, and she had
told me considerable of her early history. It interested me when I learned where she came from, for I
recognized her adopted mother's name as that of a
distant relation of my own, whom I had never happened to meet. After this search was begun, Mr.
Hobbs, who had heard me speak of Ryegate, engaged
me to go there to pick up evidence. In the course
of what he told me I learned enough to make me feel
sure that Miss Arline would prove to be the lost
child. I traced her to the town where she had lived
with her guardian and satisfied myself beyond doubt.
Then I returned to Montvale—"

He paused, reddening more than ever ; but Mr.
Linnette smilingly encouraged him to proceed.

"And then I went to New York—on my—on my
wedding trip," stammered Lincoln. "I was so full
of my own happiness that I could think of nothing
else for a few days. I meant to write the full text
of my discoveries to Mr. Hobbs, but before I reached
that point I met Roland in the street. He told me
of his marriage and I saw that everything would be
clear."

A glance of gratification was exchanged between
Mrs. Linnette and her father.

"One thing more," said Roland. "How did it
happen that you took the name of ' Guy Dalton ?' "

"I will tell you. When I left my home in Ryegate I believed I should succeed in making a fortune for myself and return crowned with success. My experience was far otherwise. Bad luck seemed to follow me everywhere, and at the time I came into the counting room here I was so reduced as to be ashamed to own my true name. When you asked it I gave the first one that came to my lips."

Mr. Linnette called all present to witness that the speaker should never have a like tale to tell after that day. He would give him one of the most important positions at his New York office. At this Eva rose impulsively and went over to press a warm kiss on her foster-father's cheek.

"The only thing wanting now," said Mr. Lewis, with a smile, "is to have Mr. Hobbs tell us how near he came to convincing Mr. Linnette that our friend Lincoln was his long-lost daughter !"

The merriment that followed was terrific. Out of it all Tom Hobbs came, resolute and defiant.

"If some of you had known enough to describe a female child as '*she*' instead of '*it*,' there would have been no trouble," he retorted. "Oh, you needn't join in the laugh at my expense!" he cried, to his employer. "It's the first time I've been wrong in over thirty years, as you'll have to admit."

Dinner was announced at this juncture, and all proceeded to the dining-room. Willard Linnette walked with a much stronger step than when he entered the parlor, for the contagion of good cheer had had its effect on him as well as the others. He was placed at the head of the board, with Maud on his right and Eva on his left, their husbands next to them, of course.

When the champagne was brought, he rose and in a steady voice asked all present to drink the health of "My darling daughter, the heiress of Montvale."

# CHAPTER XXXII.

## A PEEP AT THE STARS

Although our story can now be said to be fairly finished, the reader may, if he desires, witness a scene or two that took place in Montvale six months after the events narrated in the last chapter.

The Linnettes and their most intimate friends and relations were gathered in the mansion, for a re-union. It was evening; and while Willard Linnette and old Tom Hobbs were playing their game of chess in the library, Mr. and Mrs. Clarence Lincoln and Mr. and Mrs. Roland Linnette were engaged in a merry talk over old times.

"I never shall forget," said Roland, "how pictur-esque Eva's husband looked that day he came into the counting room. If I had been an artist 1 would have given him a hundred dollars to sit for his por-trait. And Rufus—what a fuss he did make because the door had let in a little cold air! I expected his stay at the works would be cut short when the new order of things went into effect."

"Oh, no," responded Lincoln, who had reddened a little under his friend's compliment. "Rufus is too valuable a man to turn off. He came to me and offered his resignation, and I told him to tear it up. It won't do to remember old grudges when the time for them has passed."

The ladies applauded this statement, though Eva declared that she could not see how anyone could have had the heart to speak crossly to a poor fellow looking for work on a winter's day ; especially such a nice fellow as Clarence.

"There were some terribly narrow escapes besides that one," smiled Roland. "It really looked for some time as if I were destined to occupy the eligible position of being your husband. There must be a kind fate that watches over imprudent girls, or you never would have escaped. And we would have made a very poor match, wouldn't we, Eva ?"

Mrs. Lincoln shook her head, as if she had not the least doubt of it.

"I was shut up here, you remember," she said, "with nothing to get my ideas from but a lot of ancient novels. So I naturally fell in love with the first man I saw. And then, he was such a persistent one, and so used to affairs of the heart, a more experienced girl might have been beguiled."

All laughed at the manner of the speaker, which was grimly sarcastic, but Roland replied that if there was anything fickle in this world it was a woman.

"Why, Clarence," he said, "I had letters by the dozen from your wife, vowing eternal fidelity to me ! What can one expect of a girl like that ?"

"You need not say too much, or I will expose some of *your* frailties," retorted Lincoln. "I have not forgotten when you told me Maud was in New York, and advised me to call on her, saying I could have 'all your right, title and interest.'"

Maud looked her husband quizzically in the eyes.

"Did you say that?" she asked, sweetly.

"I am afraid I did," he replied, with mock sorrow. "But if he was dunce enough not to accept the offer, he needn't bring it up at this late day."

This satisfied everybody, and the conversation turned upon the question of Mrs. Lincoln's health.

"I have been well enough ever since I got out of that everlasting routine of my early life," she said. "I believe half the illness in the world is caused by stagnation of the mind. It begins often in some slight affection and the patient is confined so closely that it grows chronic. You don't think me much of an invalid now, *do* you?" she asked her husband.

His answer was eminently satisfactory on this point. Had it not been, Eva's rich color and the bright gleam in her eyes would have proved her far from the state of an invalid.

"*I* ought to be the happiest one of you all," put in Maud, when there was a pause. " Not only have I found a husband, but a father. And you cannot imagine how dear he has grown to me! I never dreamed that anything could be so tender. His only desire seems to be to ascertain my wishes and comply with them in every respect. How quickly he has recovered, too! The doctors never come to see him now, and his step is as light as a young man's. He tells me that I ought not to 'sacrifice myself' for him, as he calls living here in this beautiful house, but nothing would induce me to leave him. Since Roland went into the firm it is the best place for us both."

Her husband admitted this, but said he could not understand why he had found Montvale so dull when he first returned from Europe. It was now, he actually believed, the most delightful place in Christendom. Three or four times a month he and Maud would take runs down to the city, to enjoy the theatre or opera, and stay a night or two ; but for the rest of the time there was something wonderfully attractive in that little village in the hills.

"Do you hear anything lately from Charlotte ?" asked Maud of Eva.

"Yes, and she is perfectly contented. It is odd to think that all the time I was confiding to her my own heart troubles she was having an 'affair' of her own. I was thunderstruck when she told me she was engaged, and that the day was set for her wedding. He is a nice fellow, I judge, from his appearance and all she says of him. They were overwhelmed with the check you sent them, and are going to put the amount into a cottage. I have promised to go and see them when they get settled."

The party of talkers then broke up, each couple going to their own apartments, the young brides kissing each other affectionately as they parted.

In the library, Mr. Linnette, Sr., played his game of chess with Tom Hobbs. Between the moves they talked of various things, as was their habit.

"I'm going to give Lincoln an interest in the business next month," said Mr. Linnette. "He's showing great capacity, and he might as well be under cover."

"Can't get over the old feeling about his wife, can you?" smiled Hobbs.

The manufacturer drew a long breath.

"Not over the *old* feeling, no," he responded. "She will always seem like another daughter to me. But, as true as I sit here, I'm glad she has a husband fitter for her—nearer her years—than I would have been."

Hobbs growled that it was a good thing for a man to have common sense, even if it did come late in life.

"The biggest joke of the century, though," he added, "is the way Roland outwitted you. When it looked as if he hadn't a single chance to inherit a cent of yours, he stepped into the whole pile by accident. I always was fond of the scamp, and I'm glad he's turning out so well."

Mr. Linnette nodded, reminiscently.

"I have heard all about his kindness to Clarence," said he, "and it shows he was never as bad as I imagined. It looked, at one time, as if the saving of that boy's life had deprived him of his inheritance, but he never said a word, even after their quarrel. Do you know, Tom, what it was that completely revolutionized my feelings toward Roland?"

Hobbs indicated a negative.

"It was the horrible heartlessness of my brother. I have not been to see him since the day he refused his son the paltry amount he asked to save him from starvation. If it were not for Maud's protest I would have cut him off without another sou. He had no excuse but that of miserliness. There was no trouble between him and Roland, as there was in my case. The young fellow had said pretty hard things to me, I can tell you, but when I heard what Payson did I forgot them all."

The game was finished. Hobbs rose and put on his hat.

"Well," he said, as he turned to go, "those young folks seem pretty happy, don't they?"

"Yes," was the serene reply. "We are *all* happy over the outcome of things, I am sure."

The night was clear. Above his head the astronomer could see a thousand stars whose names he knew and whose diameters he had measured. One was all alone in its part of the heavens, as if the others, who clustered in groups, shunned its company. But the lone star gave its full share to the splendor of the night!

Up the stairs to his chamber walked the old man with a slow step. Passing the rooms where slumbered the wedded couples, rich in their youth and marital felicity, he found his vacant pillow and stretched himself to a sleep that was untroubled. And the moon's rays touched his features with a soft and mellow light, typical of the infinite repose which comes to one who has met his Enemy and vanquished him utterly!


**THE END.**

# NEW BOOKS
## AND NEW EDITIONS

**JOHN MARSH'S MILLIONS**

A novel by CHARLES KLEIN and ARTHUR HORNBLOW.
12mo, Cloth. Illustrated. $1.50.

**NEW FACES**

A volume of eight stories by MYRA KELLY. These stories first published in the *Saturday Evening Post, Woman's Home Companion* and *Appleton's Magazine*, now in book form. 12mo, Cloth. Illustrated. $1.50.

**THE HOUSE ON STILTS**

A novel by R. H. HAZARD. 12mo, Cloth. Illustrated. $1.50.

**BUCKY O'CONNOR**

A novel by WM. M. RAINE, author of "Wyoming," etc. 12mo, Cloth. Illustrated. $1.50.

**CHILDREN OF DESTINY**

A play in four acts by SYDNEY ROSENFELD. 12mo, Cloth. Illustrated. $1.00. Paper covers, 50 cents.

**THE PEACOCK OF JEWELS**

A detective story by FERGUS HUME. 12mo, Cloth. $1.25.

**THE SILVER KING**

Novelized from the great play by ALFRED WILSON BARRETT. 12mo, Cloth. Illustrated. $1.50.

**TINSEL AND GOLD**

A new novel by DION CLAYTON CALTHROP, author of "Everybody's Secret." 12mo, Cloth. Illustrated. $1.50.

**THE RED FLAG**

By GEORGES OHNET, author of "The Ironmaster." A powerfully dramatic story of the conflict between master and men. 12mo, Cloth. $1.50.

**THE EDDY**

A novel by CLARENCE L. CULLEN. Illustrated by Ch. Weber Ditzler. 12mo, Cloth. $1.50.

**IN OLD KENTUCKY**

A novel founded on the famous play. By EDWARD MARSHALL. 12mo, Cloth. Illustrated. $1.50.

## REDCLOUD OF THE LAKES

By FREDERICK R. BURTON, author of " Strongheart." 16mo, Cloth. Illustrated. $1.50.

## BY RIGHT OF CONQUEST

A powerful romantic novel. By ARTHUR HORNBLOW, author of Novel " The Lion and the Mouse," " The End of the Game," " The Profligate," etc. 12mo, Cloth bound. Illustrated. $1.50.

## WHEN I AM RICH

By ROY MASON. 12mo, Cloth. Illustrated. $1.50.

## THE CITY OF SPLENDID NIGHT

A novel. By JOHN W. HARDING, author of " Paid in Full," etc. 12mo, Cloth bound. Illustrated. $1.50.

## THE THOROUGHBRED

A novel. By EDITH MACVANE. 12mo, Cloth bound. Illustrated. $1.50.

## BELLES, BEAUX AND BRAINS OF THE 60'S

By T. C. DE LEON. 8vo, Cloth bound, with one hundred and fifty half-tone portraits. Net, $3.00.

## THE WARRENS OF VIRGINIA

By GEORGE CARY EGGLESTON. 12mo, Cloth bound. Illustrated. $1.50.

## TRUE DETECTIVE STORIES

By A. L. DRUMMOND. 12mo, cloth. Illustrated. $1.50.

## ARTEMUS WARD

Complete Comic Writings. 12mo, Cloth. $2.00.

## JOSH BILLINGS

Complete Comic Writings. 12mo, Cloth. Illustrated. $2.00.

## STRONGHEART

Novelized from WM. C. DE MILLE'S Popular Play, by F. R. BURTON. 12mo, Cloth. Illustrated. $1.50.

## GERTRUDE ELLIOT'S CRUCIBLE

By MRS. GEORGE SHELDON DOWNS, author of " Katherine's Sheaves." 12mo, Cloth bound. Illustrated. $1.50.

## STEP BY STEP

By MRS. GEORGE SHELDON DOWNS. 12mo Cloth bound. Illustrated. $1.50.

## KATHERINE'S SHEAVES

By MRS. GEORGE SHELDON DOWNS. Illustrated. Popular Edition, 50 cents.

## THE LAND OF FROZEN SUNS

A novel by B. W. SINCLAIR, author of "Raw Gold," etc. 12mo, Cloth. Illustrated. $1.50.

## JOHN HOLDEN, UNIONIST

A Romance of the Days of Destruction and Reconstruction. By T. C. DE LEON. 12mo, Cloth. Illustrated. $1.50.

## CRAG-NEST

A Romance of Sheridan's Ride. By T. C. DE LEON. 12mo, Cloth. Illustrated. $1.25.

## THE LOSING GAME

A novel by WILL PAYNE. Expanded from the serial recently issued in the *Saturday Evening Post.* Illustrations by F. R. Gruger. 12mo, Cloth. $1.50.

## THE SINS OF SOCIETY

A novel founded on the successful Drury Lane drama by CECIL RALEIGH. 12mo, Cloth. $1.50.

## THE THIRD DEGREE

By CHARLES KLEIN and ARTHUR HORNBLOW, authors of "The Lion and the Mouse." 12mo, Cloth. Illustrated. $1.50.

## SAMANTHA ON CHILDREN'S RIGHTS

By MARIETTA HOLLEY. 8vo, Cloth. Illustrations by Chas. Grunwald. $1.50.

## THE WRITING ON THE WALL

A novel founded on Olga Nethersole's play by EDWARD MARSHALL. 12mo, Cloth. Illustrations by Clarence Rowe. $1.50.

## DEVOTA

By AUGUSTA EVANS WILSON. Illustrated. (Third large printing.) $1.50.

## THE LION AND THE MOUSE

By CHARLES KLEIN and ARTHUR HORNBLOW. Illustrated. (180th thousand.) $1.50

**THE FORTUNATE PRISONER**

A novel by MAX PEMBERTON. ██████ Cloth. With four colored illustrations. $1.50.

**THE CALL OF THE HEART**

A novel by L. N. WAY. 12mo, Cloth. With beautiful frontispiece illustration in four colors. $1.50.

**EVERYBODY'S SECRET**

A novel by DION CLAYTON CALTHROP. 12mo, Cloth. $1.50.

**THE DISAPPEARING EYE**

A detective story by FERGUS HUME. 12mo, Cloth. $1.25.

**RIDGWAY OF MONTANA**

By WM. MacLEOD RAINE, author of "Wyoming." 12mo, Cloth. Illustrated. $1.50.

**A QUARTER TO FOUR**

A Thrilling Story of Adventure. By WILLIAM WALLACE COOK. 12mo, Cloth. Illustrated. $1.50.

**THE HAPPY FAMILY**

By B. M. BOWER, author of "Chip of the Flying U," etc. 12mo, Cloth. Illustrated. $1.25.

**THE LONG SHADOW**

By B. M. BOWER. 12mo, Cloth. Colored illustrations. $1.25.

**THE LONESOME TRAIL**

By B. M. BOWER. 12mo, Cloth. Colored illustrations. $1.25.

**THE LURE OF THE DIM TRAILS**

By B. M. BOWER. Illustrations in four colors. $1.50.

**HER PRAIRIE KNIGHT**

By B. M. BOWER. Illustrations in four colors. $1.25.

**THE RANGE DWELLERS**

By B. M. BOWER. Illustrations in four colors. $1.25.

**CHIP OF THE FLYING U**

By B. M. BOWER. Three illustrations. Popular edition, 50 cts.

**THE MAKING OF A SUCCESSFUL WIFE**

By CASPER S. YOST. $1.00.

**THE MAKING OF A SUCCESSFUL HUSBAND**

By CASPER S. YOST. $1.00.

www.ingramcontent.com/pod-product-compliance
Lightning Source LLC
Chambersburg PA
CBHW031031120726
47905CB00007B/2138